QUEEN OF TWILIGHT

A DAUUR MATE NOVEL

OCTAVIA KORE

DESCRIPTION:

Abducted from Earth and dropped on an alien planet, Inoxia finds herself the accidental guardian of a six-year-old girl. As a single woman in her thirties whose only worries are the plants in her greenhouse, this is a monumental challenge. The two of them aren't alone for long when two hulking neon aliens with quills on their heads and color-changing eyes happen upon them.

As a Darkborn Dauur, Aquilian has spent his life being seen as a curse by his people. The fact that he is also a twin doesn't help matters at all. With the deck stacked against him, he spends most of his time in the forest where there are no judgmental eyes. While on the hunt for a rare medicinal bloom, Aquilian finds himself trapped within a dome with some of the ugliest creatures he has ever met. Even worse is the fact that one of them happens to be his mate.

Although Ettrian is a Lightborn Dauur, he hasn't always lived an easy life. Growing up as a twin in a society that believes them to be unlucky, the male has had his share of stares and gossip. When he is abducted from the forest and taken to an alien lab to be tested on, Ettrian is told to do something unthinkable. After being reunited with his twin, the male is shocked to find that Aquilian has located their mate. The only problem? She is the most hideous creature he has ever laid eyes on.

With everything around them coming undone, can this unconventional family pull together to create their own happily ever after?

FOREWORD

For those of you familiar with our Venium Mates series, the Dauur Mates series is set within the same world, but some time after the war. The Earth is dying due to the effects of the conflict.

In this time, the war with the Grutex is over, and the Venium have "saved" humanity. While some may find this to be a spoiler, if you read the original short story for Ecstasy from the Deep then you know these events had already happened by the end of the book.

This book is a standalone and you do not need to read any of the Venium Mates novels to understand and enjoy it. One thing to keep in mind is that this is not our heroine's first contact with aliens. Humans have lived with the Venium for some time now and have had both positive and negative experiences.

We will attempt to keep most spoilers from the other series at a minimum.

CHAPTER 1

*I*noxia

This is the worst May Day celebration I've been to, and it only just started. I snatch up another wildflower from the baskets in front of me, weaving its stem into the crown made from twisted branches we tied together earlier in the day. Anything to try not to notice the man walking around the field the town held the festival in like he owned it.

Trent. He's my ex and achieved that status for very good reasons.

"Is that who I think it is?" My mother leans into me, whispering like we're two schoolgirls gossiping behind the bleachers. I watch as Trent grabs the ass of a woman passing him, and my lip curls in disgust. "What a jerk," she comments.

"Glad I got away when I could."

"Dodged a bullet with that one, for sure."

We were together for two years before I worked up the courage to end it. I swore an oath to myself and any gods that were listening that I would never allow him back into my life. His sweet-laced lies had ruined me for so long, and seeing him after all this time apart did nothing but make me wonder what I had ever seen in him. Lucky for me, Trent seems to be avoiding our little area. It's the same one I work every year with my mother, the make-your-own-flower-crown station.

"Now twist this one right here," I tell the boy in front of me as I point to the stem he has in his hand.

"Like this?" he asks, holding it out to me with pride beaming on his face. It could be better, sure, but considering he's only about five years old, I nod enthusiastically and continue on to help the next child.

Flowers and plants in general are my specialty. I've spent my whole life underfoot while my parents were running their own greenhouse, starting the seedlings, repotting, watching them mature into beautiful plants that eventually left to new homes. Plants make me feel at home and they simply seem to respond to me, reacting to my moods and giving comfort when I need it most. I've grown every single wildflower the children sitting across from me were weaving into their own crowns. Looking out into the crowd of milling locals and curious tourists, I'm thrilled to see the fruits of my labors adorning their heads or pinned to their clothing in celebration of the town's May Day festival.

"Thank you, Miss Xia!" the boy says gleefully before running after his parents. "Look, Mom!"

"That looks great, sweetie!" she tells him, patting his head.

Seeing the kids excited to create crowns is half the fun. It's one of my favorite times of the year. Tradition says May Day was meant to divide the year in two, separating the light half and dark half. It ushers in the spring and summer months and brings new life into the world. While I can't say that the festival we have here is completely traditional, it drew a lot of people into the area, and more people means more sales for the greenhouse.

After the war with the Grutex when they invaded Earth, and then the battle between the Grutex and the Venium, sales weren't the easiest thing to come by. People weren't worried about religious celebrations or festivals much anymore. Most were just trying to get over loved ones that had been lost or rebuilding lives that had been torn apart. There are a few radical religious groups, but those are few and far between. But as time went on and the skirmishes died down, our business rebounded, and I'm grateful that my parents have passed down their green thumbs to me.

Warm sunlight spills over my skin, and I reposition myself so I'm under the shade of the small portable canopy I set up early this morning. With skin as pale as mine, I'm not going to risk being exposed longer than I needed to be. I have my Scottish grandparents to thank for that and all the rest of my features. Long, curly red hair, eyes as green as the grass I'm sitting on, and freckles dusting my nose, cheeks, and forehead. Yep, I am the poster child for Scottish ancestry.

"Miss Xia! Look at my crown!"

I look up from my work to see one of the little girls I'm teaching, Kareen, holding up a mass of wildflowers that have been haphazardly tucked into the woven headdress. Kareen is one of the children from the local orphanage who's taken an interest in everything to do with plants. She's the first one into the greenhouse anytime they take a day trip, and the last one into the vehicle when it comes time to leave.

I admit that when it comes to the little girl, I have a massive soft spot. Before stuff went bad with Trent, I was considering adopting her and had even begun the long process, but then he had to go and ruin all of that. Adopting as a single woman or man is basically impossible at this point. The moment I told the agency about our split, they politely rejected my paperwork and said I was welcome to try again once I "found a nice man to settle down with."

I guess I could have spoken with other agencies, but Kareen stole my heart and I couldn't imagine trying for any other child. The rejection hasn't stopped us from spending time together, and

I soak up any moment with her that I'm given. She owns my heart completely. The second she spotted me today, she ran over and threw herself into my legs, wrapping her little arms around my body and staring up at me with big, adoring blue eyes. *Cuteness overload!*

"It looks great, Kareen! You did an amazing job, baby!" The girl grins and plops the crown atop her mop of curly blonde hair. It tilts down the left side of her head, and my heart squeezes at how sweet this moment is.

Whoa, there ovaries. Calm down.

As the hours pass, I work through my supplies, showing kids and adults of all ages the magic of creating something one of a kind with their own hands. Each person leaves me with a big smile and a treasure to show off. It's already midday by the time I start loading up my empty baskets, piling them into the little wagon I hauled my goods here in earlier.

"Hey, Xia!"

My childhood friend Mina weaves her way through people, hand held high in the air to catch my attention. She smiles brightly as she breaks free of the crowd, coming around my folding tables to get a look at what I'm doing. Although I'm not exactly the tallest woman in town, Mina makes me feel like a giant. She's a solid five feet of pure joy and positive energy, and I don't know what I'd do without her in my life.

"Good! You're almost packed. I was worried I'd have to drag you away from your floral headgear demonstrations."

A laugh bubbles up from my chest as I watch her rifle through a selection of ribbon still on the table. "Crowns, Mina. Flower crowns." She waves away my words before tossing the basket into the wagon.

"Same difference. Let's get going before all the good spots at the pole are taken by out-of-towners and sticky-fingered six-year-olds!"

"There are no bad spots on the May Pole." I snicker. "And I'm not sure I want to participate this year."

Mina's head snaps around, hazel eyes going wide as she stares at me. "I'm positive I didn't hear you say that, Inoxia Freebairn."

"I'm positive it came out of my mouth."

"It's our tradition. One dance around the May Pole for a prosperous spring. It isn't like we're looking to take the crown."

I sigh in resignation as the last of my things go into the wagon. "Fine, okay. *One* dance and then we get to go back to my apartment and watch cheesy sci-fi movies until our eyes cross."

"Deal!" Her excitement is palpable as she claps her hands and jumps up and down.

The faster we get through the dance, the faster we can leave. The faster we leave, the less I worry about potential interactions with my ex.

～

There's a cheer from the crowd gathered around the stage as the pretty flower crown is placed on my head and the sash is attached at my side.

Who's got two green thumbs and just got crowned May Queen? This girl, unfortunately.

I glare daggers at Mina, who shrugs and smiles like a fool as she watches the scene from the ground below me. Normally, the town chooses an upstanding teenager to take the title. She gets escorted around town like royalty for the next couple of days by various public figures, is given a scholarship, and then gets sent on her way until next year, when she returns to crown the new queen.

Well, this year is apparently different. It's a leap year, so the committee has decided they need to crown an "unattached" woman. Something about encouraging the idea of marriage and fertility to boost the population after everything humanity has endured. They've also decided to throw a May *King* into this whole mess, and who should they decide on for that role?

Trent. He beams at me from his place on stage as the head of the festival committee gives her speech. He's wearing a loose-fitting white button-up with a brown vest over the top and comfortable-looking brown slacks. His boot taps out a rhythm as his gaze roves over me. A shiver runs up my spine, and I wish I were anywhere but here. The woman at the microphone is going on and on about the role of the celebration and how fertility has always been a major part of May Day.

My eyes dart to Trent, and I thank whatever gods are out there that we never had children together. The head of the committee wraps up and Trent makes his way across the stage. I spin away, hoping to make it down the steps before he gets to me, but there are already people blocking my path. I'm a second away from jumping into the crowd of people below me, hoping someone cushions my fall, when I feel a large, familiar hand wrap around my upper arm.

"Xia."

The sound of my nickname coming from his mouth makes my skin crawl, and my eyes narrow on his face. He had once been so handsome to me, with those dark brown eyes, jet black hair that curls around his ears, and a jawline so sharp you could cut your-self. The closer I look now, the more I can see the cruelty in his expression.

"You look beautiful today."

I jerk my arm from his grip and feel myself flinch when he steps closer. "Stop, Trent."

His eyes wander over the people mingling around us before he brings them back to me, running them from my bare feet all the way up until they lock with mine. "I was hoping I'd get to see you here. You look good." His tongue flicks out to swipe over his lips. "It's been a little while, hasn't it?"

"Not long enough," I murmur as I try to brush past him. He catches me around the waist, pulling me into his chest, and leans down to brush his lips against the shell of my ear.

"Come by the old house tonight. I'll let you help me with a little fertility ritual of my own." The lecherous curl of his lip makes my stomach drop and all of my senses go on high alert.

Never again, I promised myself. Never again was I going to let him get to me, let him hurt me the same way he had done before I got out.

As calmly as I can, I remove his hand from my body. "I'd rather chase parked cars."

His gaze turns hard, causing my heart to jump in my chest. I turn and rush across the stage, crouching down to slip from the platform onto the soft earth. I don't stop there, though. Someone calls after me, but the voice doesn't register to my mind.

Something inside of me has been triggered, and it's telling me to get as far from this man as I can. Therapy may have given me the tools to move past my trauma, but I'm not at all ready to face the person who caused it.

I realize as I'm running that I have no idea where I'm heading. I don't know why I didn't just find Mina and head home, but I can't even force myself to turn back. The shade of the trees envelops me once I make it into the tree line. Small twigs and thin branches snag my pretty dress, scraping at the skin on my legs, but I keep going.

Rocks and other debris dig into my bare feet and I stumble, catching myself on a nearby tree. Blood pounds in my ears, drowning out all other noises. My lungs feel like they're on fire.

When was the last time I ran this far? Or at all?

Never, honestly. When I finally catch my breath, I realize that the forest around me is silent. Eerily so. The hairs on the back of my neck and arms stand on end, and I glance around me, searching for whatever it is that has me on edge.

From my right comes a quiet buzzing noise. It races over me, growing louder and louder, like whatever is making the noise is getting closer. I push away from the tree, stumbling backward in an attempt to escape the mysterious threat. It's so loud now that I can't hear anything else.

Just as I slam my hands against my ears to block it out, something crashes into my legs and my whole world goes silent and black.

*a*quilian

Whispered words drift in along the bond in my mind, and I try my hardest to block them out. I don't have as much experience being around my tribe as Ettrian, my twin brother, does. Weaving through the massive trees that make up the village, my eyes locked on my destination, I push onward toward Safia's den. The front of her tree opens with the slightest nudge of my mind, welcoming me inside like an old friend. The beautiful Darkborn Taenov turns around from where she is mixing herbs together, her eyes turning white in surprise.

"Aquilian. I wasn't expecting you." Her silver quills rattle softly, sending a vibration along my *ilo* as she speaks along the bond.

"I need to talk to you." With my head bowed, I fan my black quills out and vibrate them in greeting.

"Such formalities are not required here. Tell me what you need." She sets her dried herbs down at the table and waits for me to continue.

It took me days to work up the courage to come to her with this, and I'm not going to back out now that I'm standing here. *"I* came to formally ask you to take Ettrian and I as your mates." I knew coming into this that I could—and most likely would—face rejection. There are very few who will even let me speak to them, let alone allow me the chance to propose a mating.

"We are not fated, Aquilian." The colorful swirl of her eyes tells me she is contemplating my words.

"No, but we could make a choice rather than wait for something that may never come. We are both Darkborn, Safia. It is unlikely either of us will ever find our fated matches at all."

"Aquilian…" There is hesitation, almost sympathy, in her voice. "I do not think you understand what has happened here." Something seems hidden behind her words. It causes my stomach to knot anxiously, but she shuts me out, keeping her secrets tucked behind her mental blocks.

"I know that we will never be able to give you what your fated males can, but we could be good mates to you. We don't even have to do the ceremony, so you face no risk."

She pushes her hand through her quills. "Does Ettrian know about this?"

I shake my head softly. "I haven't spoken with him about it. It seemed better to ask you first and then propose the idea to him." I feel myself reaching up to tug at my quills and force my hand back to my side.

Safia's eyes follow my movements before she turns her back to me. I wait anxiously as she runs her fingers over small clay bowls and jars that line the wall. "I will consider the proposal you have put forward, but only if you can successfully retrieve a cinsi bloom and bring it back here to me."

"Cinsi bloom?" I frown, not recalling having ever heard of this flower before.

"It is one of the most sought-after medicinal plants, but they require one to travel farther than many in my profession are comfortable with." Her gaze touches my face before she goes back to her table. *"The flower only blooms at twilight and is mostly known by its round, multicolored petals. There is a small stem that shoots up from the center, topped with a small cluster of tiny pods. If you can bring me at least one of these blooms, I will reward you with an answer."* I'm aware that she doesn't tell me she will agree to take us, but the possibility of it is enough for me.

I leave her den feeling lighter than I have ever felt before, and full of hope. I have lived most of my life in this forest, and this seems like the easiest task that has ever been put before me. *She didn't turn us down. She didn't say no.*

∾

I stare at the strange material before me. It's hard, transparent, and I cannot for the life of me figure out where it came from; this is nothing I have seen naturally occurring on my homeworld. My feet carry me a good distance along the perimeter of the barrier, and I'm starting to think that I've been caught in some sort of trap, like one of our nets. I'm used to being the hunter, not the prey.

I worry what Ettrian will do when he comes back to an empty den tonight. What will he think when he finds I am nowhere in the area we normally hunt? We have never spent more than a few hours apart. If I cannot find a way out of here, it seems like we are going to be spending at least this night completely separated. The thought alone makes my heart kick in my chest.

Surely he wouldn't have come as far out into the forest as I am. He had no idea I was coming here for the bloom, or even that I'd made the request of Safia. Ettrian is different than I am, not just in personality but also physically. His light coloring is pleasant, and he has a charming way about him that makes him more widely acceptable to our people. Well, as accepted as any twin could be here, at least.

Sun Father, curse it all!

A sigh fell from between my lips as I ran my fingers through my quill crest, testing the dome yet again with a kick to the glass. Solid. It didn't seem like there would be any breaking through and getting back to my den tonight. The only solace I took in this was that my twin brother would be safe from whatever—or whoever—had captured me.

My eyes drift to the massive planet that looms over Dimosia, its surface swirling slowly. I spent many hours as a child lying in the fields watching the patterns change above me, letting it soothe my worry away. One day, I had promised myself. One day I would meet the Sun Father in the blue waters of Loruta and ask why he had bestowed this curse upon Ettrian and me. Today is not that day, so instead, I watch as the sun falls behind Loruta, leaving the land in a twilight state. The only light now comes from the surface of the planet, from the plants, the animals, and even myself.

My ilo, the small tubes that line patches of my skin, begin to rustle as they pick up the oddest sensation, not quite a tickle against the sensitive tips but similar. It isn't anything I've ever felt before. Grasping the mental bond every Dauur possesses, I feel along it, reaching out to where I know Ettrian should be, but I get nothing in return. My fingers itch with the urge to tug at the quills that sprout out of the back of my crest, a nervous habit I've been fighting my whole life. *Control yourself lest you pull out even more quills.* The tickle is back again, pulling me in the opposite direction of where I had intended to go.

An ominous feeling settles over the forest, and I choose my steps carefully as I try to figure out what is throwing me off. I have been hunting these lands since I was old enough to walk and often lost myself in them when life became overwhelming. This place is as familiar as the back of my hands and it is how I know there is something in this forest that doesn't belong. The tickle continues, making my quills shiver in agitation. I step around large trees with trunks wider than my arms can open, moving over their roots that arch up all over the ground, all the while feeling the tiny sensations as they brush along my ilo.

I duck my head as I pass under another root, this one nearly as tall as I am, and my eyes fall on two of the strangest creatures I've ever seen in my entire life. The bigger one has its back to me. Long bright orange tendrils hang down from its head. It seems to be communicating with the smaller one, clutching its pale face between hands that shake. The larger one brushes back the nearly white tendrils on the head of the little one, allowing me a better look at the face. My quills shiver as I stare at the features in revulsion. A pointed nose sits above a small, thin-lipped mouth that opens and closes rapidly, liquid falling from big blue eyes as its little chin trembles.

What is *that?*

I step back, moving slowly, but I must have done something to call attention to myself because the little one's eyes lock onto mine and it emits a vibration that assaults my senses. The larger one spins around, revealing similar features, and it too begins assailing me with harsh vibrations.

Sun Father save me.

I stumble backward, baring my teeth at them as they continue. It's obvious I have startled whatever these things are so I try raising my hands, showing the pair I mean them no harm. In truth, I would rather not be anywhere near them. They are abrasive, unsightly, and don't belong here.

The quills at the back of my crest begin to rattle together, creating a vibration that seems to stop the harsh noises coming from the beings in front of me, and for the first time, I notice that at least one of them looks to be a female. An ugly female, but a female all the same. If this is her kit, then I need to be cautious.

Dauur females are ferocious when they feel like their kits are threatened. The kit moves toward me as if she is not afraid, which has me scrambling away even faster than before. There is no way in Dimosia I'm going to let *that* touch me. I attempt to reach out with the mental bond, but I need to be in close proximity to a new being for it to work the first time. My hands come back out, cautioning the little one as I speak through the bond, "*Stop! Don't come any closer!*"

There is no response from the small one. Instead, I am met with what feels like a blank wall. Darkness. *By the Sun Father, these being are as stupid as they are ugly.* The small one collides with my leg, her body pressed close against me. Her face tilts up and as her eyes lock with mine, big and blue, they do something strange to my heart. I attempt to *gently* shake her off.

"*Shoo. Back to your mama now.*" Still nothing. She reaches a tiny hand out and runs a finger over the horn on my calf. "*Hey! Do not touch there! It is very—*"

I don't even finish the sentence before she jerks her hand back with a sharp vibration. The mama emits softer, soothing sounds as she drops down to the little one's level, fussing over the small injury. Red liquid seeps from the tip of the finger, and the mama turns, shooting daggers my way.

"*I tried to warn your kit. You cannot place the blame for this on me, female. Perhaps you should teach her to behave.*"

A vibration runs through me when the little drops of clear liquid start to run down the little one's cheeks again, making me pause. What is the fluid? Why is it expelling it? I scent the air, wondering if this was some sort of defense, but all I can smell is the forest around me and the sweet floral scent of the female. She smells far better than she looks.

I take another deep breath into my lungs and feel a twist in my stomach. *Enough of that.* I look back at the little one, and panic shoots through me at the amount of liquid now spilling from her eyes. Was this too much to lose? What if losing so much kills her?

I certainly do not want the ugly little one to die. It's only a kit, after all.

I look around, snatching up some leaves from the quiltia tree nearby. Where is Ettrian when I need him? He is better at comforting others than I am. The mama doesn't seem concerned at all that her kit is spilling liquid at an alarming rate and this puzzles me. I shove the leaves at her face.

"Here. Stem the flow with these." But she only stares up at me in confusion.

My quills rattle in frustration and I push past her, dabbing the little one's eyes and face. The kit's lip trembles and the liquid seems to come to a stop. She stares up at me and an odd possessive, protective instinct comes over me. I've never really been around a kit before, and this experience has done nothing but show me that perhaps I should continue to avoid them altogether.

The female behind me begins her incessant vibrating again and smacks my hand away from her kit's face, her mouth moving strangely as her brow furrow above her eyes. Maybe it's some sort of warning. They have no male present to look after them, and the world I live in can be cruel to those who try surviving on their own. These two have no defensive qualities that I can see. They would not make it through the night if they did not receive help.

"Calm down. I am only trying to assist you."

I think maybe she understands me because her vibrations stop and she stares at me. *Finally.* Her eyes are wide and brilliant green, and if she were a Dauur female, this color would tell me she is happy. She vibrates again and her hand waves in my direction. I feel a tickle along the bond, and it makes my heart kick in my chest as the female points at my head.

"Will you please stop your vibrations? They are incredibly abrasive."

My quills shake and I reach back to run my fingers through

them out of habit just before I notice the amber-colored light coming from behind me. I spin around to find the source, but I see nothing aside from the trees and plants. The hand in my quills tightens, and I feel the telltale snap as one of them breaks off in my grip.

Sun Father take it all.

I curse and bring it around to make sure it came off in one piece, but what I see astounds me. A brightly glowing amber quill sits in my hand instead of the solid black one I was expecting, and my whole world tips as I stare down at the evidence that my life has changed without me even realizing it.

CHAPTER 3

*E*ttrian

A bright light blinds my sensitive eyes the moment I open them. There are not even lights like this on Dimosia. *Where am I?* I look down at my body and pull against the bindings that hold me in place. A rattle works through my quills, the vibrations growing in intensity as I fight harder against the straps that secure me to the table.

I try reaching out to my brother with my bond, or even another member of my tribe, but there seems to be something like a wall around my mind, cutting me off from the only people who can help me. A large creature with bulbous eyes looms over me. Its skin looks hard and is a putrid green. A slight vibration curls over my quills that seems to emanate from the thing standing before me. Hooked hands run over the side of my face, pressing on my skin as if it is searching for something. I'm not sure if there is anything of interest for it to find there.

Pain slices through my head as something sharp digs into the side of my skull. Everything blinks out as I try to fight off the pain and yank away from whatever it is the creature is using on me. Vibrations run through the space as my quills rattle louder and louder. I try again to press against the mental bond, but still there's no response. Agony claims my body as blackness begins to cloud my vision.

It seems like only a second has passed when I wake up again. This time, I'm outside in the familiar forest on my homeworld. Everything seems the same, yet something is different. I look around in wonder as the weirdest sensation rolls over me. It isn't exactly pain… but more of an uncomfortable feeling that won't cease. It threatens to overwhelm me. I watch as an anra, a creature with a neck that extends high up into the trees, opens its mouth, and this time actual pain slices through my head.

The anra turns to look at me, its head tilting to the side as it stares down at me through the darkness of night. I try reaching out along the bond to get a feel for its emotions, but the only thing I get is a strange sense of wonder and mild confusion from it. *I am right there with you.* Something scurries around my feet, the vibrations running along my ilo when suddenly the branch it's standing on breaks and the sharp pain shoots through my mind again.

What is happening to me?

It's like millions of explosions are going off on either side of my head. While I can still feel the vibrations that the animals normally give off when they open their mouths, I'm also experiencing something completely different, something that causes my body to seize and stumble with the pain. I catch myself on a tree as the world around me suddenly grows incredibly loud, like my entire tribe is trying to speak along the bond all at once.

I do not have a name for what's happening to me.

"So it is working then?" I spin around in the direction that the piercing feeling is coming from. This time I realize that it's not coming along the bond. It's something external.

"What has happened to me?" I reach out mentally to the

green creature in front of me. I recognize this alien as the same one who was in the strange place I woke up in earlier.

"You are experiencing what the rest of the civilized races call 'hearing.'" The alien buzzes, one clawed hand running along the snout that protrudes from its head. "I couldn't exactly get into your head the way you are able to get into mine. Doing this was the only way to make you understand what we require of you."

"Hearing?" I shake my head, trying to rid my mind of the pressure. *"What is it you think you can require of me?"*

"Yes, hearing, you dimwitted slime. I have given you the gift of sound. You should be grateful." The creature sneers before continuing. "Within this dome, we have left you a female. She is of kitbearing age. You will mate with this female and see if you are compatible for creating offspring."

"Why would I want to mate with an unknown female?" My lips pull back over my teeth into a snarl as I try to shake my head and dislodge the pain his words cause me. The gift he claims to have given me doesn't feel much like one at all. It is beyond simple irritation.

"It doesn't matter what you want, Dauur. You won't be leaving this dome until you have mated with the female and attempted procreation." I watch as the green alien plucks a leaf from a tree only to drop it carelessly to the ground. "I have also gifted you a translator with our language. No need to thank me. Given time, it will also learn the female's language so that you may communicate. If you decide not to cooperate with us, we will kill the kit she has with her."

At his threat, I push off the tree and attempt to grab him, only to collide against a glass barrier with a heavy thud. I slam my hand against it, trying to break through and dig my claws into the alien who makes an awful vibration that rakes against me.

"I thought that might upset you, hence the dome between us. I will give you one month from the moment you find her to accomplish your task. After that, we will step in and you will both suffer."

I want to stay here and find a way to get to the disgusting being, but a threat against a kit's life is something I cannot ignore. Why are they doing this to us? A rammit hops past me as I turn away from the barrier, its colorful feathered ears fluttering as it pushes through the underbrush. My kind doesn't have anything on our heads other than our quills and antennae, or at least all the Dauur aside from me. I run the tips of my fingers over the side of my head and startle myself when I reach a sensitive opening that was definitely not there before I was captured.

The night is warm but pleasant, and the sky is clear so I am able to see and do not complain. I can feel the tendrils of the bond between my brother and me, and my steps quicken in excitement. Aquilian is here somewhere! My mood is dark, but just the thought of finding my brother is comforting. The holes in the sides of my head ache again, and it worries me that he may have gone through the same thing I just did.

These beings want me to do something that is unthinkable among my kind—to attempt to mate with a female who may not want me, who won't even be able to understand me. I only hope that this translator the alien spoke of works and that she can communicate her wants or know that I am only doing this to save her kit. Mating a female without her consent is a severely punishable offense and rightly so. This mating is not right; I can feel in my heart. The fact that this is being forced upon us does not sit well.

But what choice do we have? The aliens know where we are. They have trapped us within this dome and threatened to harm a kit. The pain comes back again, and I 'hear' more sounds. Something is up ahead and this worries me. Am I ready to confront whatever this is in my current state? Peeking around the corner, I see Aquilian stumbling away from two strange creatures.

Is this the female and kit I was told about?

I move from where I am hidden and reach across the bond to my brother. *"Aquilian! I have finally found you! Are you all right?"*

"Ettrian!" His face is a mask of confusion when he whips his head in my direction. *"Why are you here? You should be back at the den!"* His eyes search the shadows, and when they finally land on my face, I see and feel something I never imagined would be directed at me from my own brother. His eyes are red with hostility.

My feet seem to move of their own accord, carrying me across the grassy ground to his side, and I take a moment to get a closer look at him. His quills… They are full of color.

"You have found our mate!" I pull him close for a second, wrapping my arms around him before he pushes me gently away. *"I never thought you would be the one to find her, but this seems to be a day for surprises!"*

I turn excitedly, looking around for the Dauur female we will spend the rest of our lives with, but the only other beings are the ugly creatures Aquilian was standing with when I found him. Surely our mate cannot be one of *them*. My twin looks hesitantly at the older female, and I feel my quills vibrate in horror.

"No, no, no! You finally find us a mate, and this *is what we end up with?"* I feel sick. *"How do you mess up a mating this badly? It is absolutely hideous!"*

"You can have it. I will not be touching it." Aquilian looks just as disgusted as I feel.

This is not at all like the colorful mate I had imagined we would one day have. She's not even the same species, and by the way she backs away, I can see she feels the same way about the two of us. If this is the female that the alien expects me to procreate with, then we may have more of an issue than I had originally thought.

Most Dauur families consist of two papas and one mama, though the males are normally those who fate chooses to be together and not usually siblings. Twins, however, are different. It is believed that they are like the Sun Father's own sons. They share a bond so strong that when fate was choosing their mates, it decided against splitting them up by giving them a mate to share. I've known since the day I was born that Aquilian would be a permanent part of me, my other half, but fate seems to be playing some sick joke on us considering the mate it chose to complete our family.

"Grattt, nao dere aroo two uff yoo." The noises the female makes are the first sounds that do not hurt my head. I'm still getting used to hearing as all of my neurons forge new paths, allowing me to learn how to cope with the new sensation. Out of the corner of my eye, I see my twin's quills rustle, and I am suddenly overwhelmed with his color. I want that too. The need to touch our mate is overwhelming, and I take a step forward, my hand hovering over her arm for a moment. As if I have committed some great offense against our female, Aquilian notches up his vibrations and grabs my wrist.

"Don't touch her, Ettrian."

"She is just as much mine as she is yours!" I say, my head swiveling so that I can meet his red gaze. A fire is burning inside of me at the thought that my twin does not trust me with our mate. How can he think I would ever mean to hurt her?

"Can't you see that she's scared? Even the kit is hiding from you."

The kit. I had forgotten about the little one, and when I look down at her, I find that she is, in fact, hidden behind her mama's body. She is an alien and perhaps she does not understand that, as her mama's mates, Aquilian and I are now her papas. I wish that I could tell her not to fear me, that I will do anything in my power to care for her, but I do not know their language yet. The other alien said the translator will learn for me, so I must wait until then. I debate whether I should share what I have been tasked to do with Aquilian and decide against it almost immediately.

I do not wish for him to have to share the pain it is causing me to know what is expected of me. He does not need the same weight on his shoulders that I am being forced to carry. Aquilian is a sensitive Dauur, and this would hurt him. To take a mate without first going through the ceremony is dangerous and puts her life at risk. If the Sun Father does not bless the union, then he could find it appropriate to take her from the two of us altogether. I glance at the female and kit and then back at my twin.

"What if they are hungry? Do you think they eat like we do?"

The look on his face tells me he had not thought that far ahead. He really does not have any experience when it comes to taking care of anyone but himself. With females and kits, my twin is hopeless. I suppose it is not much of a surprise considering his coloring makes him something of an outcast.

Safia is the only female in the tribe to ever take him into her sling and Aquilian was gone before the sun rose the next morning. Since that day, my brother has stayed as far from the village as possible, avoiding anyone from our tribe. I had been worried and wanted to ask him what had happened, to try to comfort him, but he never brought it up. I only hope that having a mate will help him to begin to accept himself and that he can find it within him to learn to love her and our kit properly.

CHAPTER 4

*I*noxia

There are colorful aliens standing in front of me. As if realizing I've been abducted and dropped onto a strange alien forest on a strange alien planet wasn't bad enough, I also find that little Kareen has been taken and left here as well. Alien planet, alien animals, alien men, and a six-year-old girl clinging to me like I'm her only hope. Yup, you could say I was definitely living out a nightmare.

Fuck my whole life.

We woke up in this place that was obviously not Earth and Kareen instantly began to freak out. Tears, snot bubbles, flailing arms, the whole nine yards. I don't know which one of us was more scared at that point. Kareen kept asking how we had gotten here, where were we going, and I had no good answers for her. I knew—or could at least guess—that we had been abducted from the forest back home on Earth and dropped here. The fact that I was also beginning to panic didn't help the situation, and it only made her cry even more because she realized I had no idea how to get us back.

When the huge, terrifying alien showed up, it had given her

something else to focus on. She seemed far more willing than I was to trust the stranger. Maybe her positive experiences with the Venium, the aliens who saved us from our war with the Grutex, had given her some sense of security. Kareen rushed to him as if he were our savior. The fact that he had gotten down on her level and wiped her tears away went a long way toward endearing him to her and making him seem far more trustworthy to me than the other male.

The first alien we met, Kareen's favorite, is so awkward that it's almost cute. He has a dusky aquamarine body with purple splotches and black stripes. The only white on his body is his crest and in small places along his torso. But this other one? This one has bright, vibrant colors. His body is brilliant jewel-tone colors—green, blue, orange, and purple—with metallic crimson stripes. His limbs have baby blue stripes that remind me of a zebra. The only dark coloring he has is the black on his hands, feet, and just at the top of his crest. His quills, unlike the first alien's, are white.

Both men are gorgeous in a very alien way, and they glow in the dark like beautiful moonflowers. There's no moon in the sky here, but there's no lack of light because it seems like every living thing here glows with its own bioluminescence. The massive planet that had been visible during the daytime had disappeared, taking its soft luminescence with it.

Kareen's hand is clenched tightly in mine as we walk along behind the aliens. Her wiggly fingers are a constant reminder that I can't run away, that it's not just my life on the line. Though we can't understand each other, they try to use other ways of communicating. They beckon with their hands for us to follow, which we do, but with a reasonable amount of space between us. I don't know if I can trust these guys with my life, much less Kareen's. She's distracted by everything around us, her eyes darting from one thing to the next, and I have to admit that I myself am a little preoccupied with the new plant life.

"Xia, my legs hurt! I don't wanna keep walking," Kareen whines at my side as she bends over and pants dramatically.

"Come on, baby, I'm sure it isn't too much farther." I run my hand along her back trying to soothe her. It has been a long walk, and I suspect we aren't even close to wherever it is these two are leading us. It's going to feel so much longer if she is already whining. I study the aliens out of the corner of my eye, noticing how they've stopped to stare back at us.

There are voices inside my head speaking in a language I've never heard and it makes me feel like I am going crazy. I can't understand what they're saying, but I hear my name among the unfamiliar words. Whatever they said was not Inoxia though, more like a growl and then "Xia" followed by more growls. If I weren't on an alien planet, I would probably think I was crazy. Maybe I am anyway. My alien guides haven't made any noises aside from the vibrating of their quills, and I'm starting to suspect that the strange noises inside of my head are their voices.

The second alien seems less wary and far pushier than the first. His coloring almost reminds me of a neon tiger lily, only I'm not sure even hybrids could pull off those colors. He's the one who keeps getting too close for my liking, and he makes me want to tuck Kareen protectively behind me.

"Hey, Prickly Thistle!" Mister Neon Tiger Lily looks back at me as if I have four eyes. "Hey, yes you!" I point to him before I move my finger directly in front of me like a game of charades as I try to make him understand that I need his attention. It must be clear what I want because it doesn't take him long to close the distance between us. My hand presses against my chest. "Inoxia." My hand moves to Kareen's shoulder. "Kareen." I then gesture to his chest. "And you are?"

A string of growls fill my head, and I think he notices that I'm confused because the words stop and he repeats only one. *Ettrian.* This only confirms I am not crazy and that the voices in my head are definitely coming from them.

"Et-tree-n," I try. It must be close enough because he nods in encouragement and his eyes seem to light up with pleasure. My hand moves to the darker alien, the one who was concerned by Kareen's crying. Again, he repeats a word to me until I'm almost sure I got it. *Aquilian.* "Ah-q-will-ian." The dark male tilts his head like he isn't sure about what I'm saying, but the light one nods again.

My mood lightens because the males obviously care that we know what to call them, unlike the Grutex, and my body is humming with satisfaction. Even though I don't want to trust them too soon, I'm crossing my fingers that these guys are like the Venium and will be our allies. Now that the names are out of the way, I just need to figure out how to get across that Kareen is tired and needs a break. I point my hand again at her little body and shake my head no.

Opening my mouth, I yawn and close my eyes and pretend I am sleeping. When I open them again, both men are looking at me in confusion. Right, so charades isn't as easy with aliens as it would be with humans. A sigh falls from my lips as I turn to Kareen and I crouch down, opening my arms to her.

"Come on, baby. I'll carry you for a little bit."

"Really? Are you sure?" she tilts her head.

"Yeah, I'm sure. I can do it."

She rushes into my embrace, and the way she wraps herself around my body reminds me of a baby lemur clinging to its mother's chest. My knees wobble as I stand, grunting under her weight. I didn't want to admit that I'm obviously not in the shape to be carrying a six-year-old around. How did moms do this all the time? I'm trying to not freak out because last time I did she had a meltdown.

We don't get very far before I'm lagging behind, and both males are starting to look at me with concern. Sleepy kids are dead weight. Once I catch up, Aquilian and Ettrian both shoot their arms out at the same time, offering to hold her, but Kareen recoils from Ettrian. Her fists clutch my now filthy dress as she looks between the aliens. Leaning her body to the side, she reaches for Aquilian and her eyes light with pleasure as he grabs her effortlessly from my arms.

Maybe it was a little obvious how much I was struggling.

Aquilian sends an almost triumphant look at the other male as he cradles the girl in his arms and a soft vibration runs through his quills. The moment is both sweet and unnerving, and I find myself fidgeting with my fingers as he turns and continues walking.

Is this okay? Should I be trusting him?

I watch as Kareen wraps one tiny hand around a quill that hangs a little lower than the others and closes her eyes. A softly whispered "good puggle" almost escapes my hearing, and I feel a grin tug at my lips. Aquilian seems to grow brighter than I've seen since meeting him, his steps light with his obvious pleasure.

On Earth, it would be a lot harder to travel at night, but here everything glows just enough that I'm not tripping over every fallen branch or large root. Without a moon, everything feels rather alien. I wonder how their people are able to sleep when there is so much light. Are they nocturnal? My mind wanders as more time passes and at this point, I'm starting to lag behind again. These guys have way longer legs than I do, and I can hardly keep up.

After the third incident of me tripping over my own clumsy feet, Ettrian swings me up into his arms with hardly any effort at all. Protesting, I try to wiggle myself out of his grasp. I'm used to men complaining that I'm way too heavy for them to be carrying, but a hand comes down firmly on my rear end, making me go still as an unexpected moan falls from my lips.

We both stare at each other, and my cheeks heat under his scrutiny. This is a horrible time for my body to respond. Spankings are something I've always been into, but the fact that I had such a strong reaction to a stranger—not to mention an alien— doing it shocks me. As I'm looking at him something rather extraordinary happens: his once completely white quills are now a powder blue at the base, white in the center, and topped with a deep red.

They're… beautiful. My hand moves as if it has a mind of its own and runs along one of the pointed tips. They shiver beneath my touch and a growl vibrates through his chest. It's such a serene moment that I press myself closer to him, not caring that my breasts are practically covering his face as I pet his quills. If he isn't going to make a big deal out of it, neither am I.

Is it normal for them to have quills that change colors? I've never heard of something like this happen. Then again, I've never seen aliens like these guys before. A shaking hand runs down the length of my back as he coos to me. The touch of his fingers is enough to bring me back to reality and remind me of what I am doing. I bury my face into his neck in embarrassment. Thank the gods that Kareen is sound asleep and didn't see me acting this way.

His hand doesn't stop rubbing my back, and I find it rather comforting despite the fact that I don't really know him. It's doing things to me that I'm reluctant to admit I might actually like. I have to remind myself that I don't want a relationship or even to fall in love again… not after the last time.

But sex doesn't mean love, right? You can have sex without it meaning anything, can't you? What if these aliens think that sex is the equivalent to signing a lifelong contract though? That thought alone stops me from taking things any further with Ettrian and I realize I have let myself go way too long without being laid.

Who am I kidding? For all I know, these two are planning on chucking us into a huge boiling pot and serving us up for dinner.

I must have fallen asleep in his arms at some point because the next thing that I know I'm being jostled awake. I look up at Ettrian's face, but he isn't looking at me. My head turns in the direction of whatever the aliens are staring at, and my eyes widen as the tree that we are standing in front of begins to open itself as if by magic.

The two of them look on like this is something completely normal for a tree to do. The tree is one of the widest ones I have ever seen, and it only seems to grow bigger before my eyes. As I'm watching, it hollows itself out and seems to make rooms out of thin air. The voices in my mind are nearly overwhelming now as they buzz around in my head just before Aquilian walks inside of the tree and disappears off to the left with Kareen.

"Hey, wait!" I yell as fear begins to consume me. Where is he going with her?

Ettrian runs his hand down my back again as voices collide in my mind. I don't understand the words, but I feel as if he's trying to tell me Aquilian is only looking out for her. We walk through the large opening and into a wide room before following Aquilian, and my anxiety only spikes as we move down the dark hallway. Just as I'm about to protest losing sight of them, Ettrian steps into a smaller room.

Here, there's a huge leaf-like sling that attaches to the wall where Aquilian settles my sleeping little girl down. Once he touches the side, it curls slightly around her like a swaddle. A soft glow lights up along his quills as he runs a careful finger over the side of her face and vibrates.

Aquilian looks over at me before he leaves the room, and Ettrian moves to follow soon after with me still nestled into his arms. I squeeze his forearm and shake my head as I slide down the front of my male companion until my feet touch the ground, blushing when desire shoots through me at the close contact. Trying to ignore the way his eyes light up with interest, I motion to the second sling, hopefully indicating I'd like to sleep. Nodding, he moves forward and shows me how to climb in, touching my cheek briefly before he steps back and leaves the room.

～

*T*he next morning, I rise early, even before Kareen, who slept fitfully. Tiptoeing out of the room, I go into the main part of the tree that we came into last night. I hadn't gotten much of a chance to look around between my worry over Kareen and my own exhaustion. The room I find myself in looks an awful lot like a kitchen with a counter that runs along the wall. There's a dip that makes me think this could be a sink, and there are shelves carved into the walls where small clay bowls and cups are stacked neatly. Ettrian walks into the room, pausing to look me over.

He takes my hand and pulls me toward the dip in the counter-top. There's a nozzle of some sort that appears to be part of the tree that hangs over. I watch as he runs his finger along the length of it and I jump back as water begins to trickle out of the opening. My tongue suddenly feels like sandpaper, my throat like a desert. I practically climb over him in my desperation to get a drink. I totally feel like a hamster as I lap at the nozzle, but it doesn't matter at the moment because they might as well be giving me the greatest gift ever.

I can feel myself perking up like a peace lily who's gone without water for too long. It doesn't occur to me that I have no idea how to stop the water until I pull back and it begins spilling all over. I touch the nozzle the way I saw Ettrian do it, and my eyes go wide with surprise when it doesn't stop. Why isn't it working? I move from the nozzle, letting it spill into the dip as my hand runs again and again over the length, trying frantically to get it to cease.

"Ettrian, help!" I yelp.

A light-colored hand moves around my body, caressing the stem and stopping the flow of water almost immediately. *How the fuck?*

"I just tried that and it didn't work!" I stomp my foot in irritation against the hard floor of the tree as I turn from him and walk to the other side of the kitchen. Looking around the room, I realize that Ettrian and I are alone and wonder if Aquilian is still sleeping.

Hands land on my hips, pulling me back against his hard body as he nuzzles his face into my neck. Panic fills me as I realize that he may have gotten the wrong impression from our earlier interaction. Or maybe it's the fact that my dirty white dress is now almost completely see-through where the water has soaked into it.

My fingers dig into the fabric of my skirts as I try to gently pry myself away, but he takes this moment to spin me around and press himself as close as he can get. A vibration rolls through the room as his quills rattle, his hands grasping at my sides. I only just met this alien yesterday and yet the thought of not stopping him flits through my mind.

If I were to let this continue, there wouldn't be anyone here to judge me like there would be back home. But again, I stop myself from following through because I can't even properly communicate with him to make sure we're compatible in this department. Ettrian presses his hips against my stomach, grinding against me, and I feel heat rush through my entire body.

Abort! Abort!

His tongue slides from between his lips as he licks up my neck, pulling a whimper from my throat as I push against his body. I need to get away and yet I only want to be closer. What's wrong with me? Fire lights up everywhere he touches, making my nipples harden against the thin cloth that separates us.

It's like he can sense my arousal because he takes in a deep breath and then begins to renew his efforts with vigor. A hand wraps around my thigh, pulling me off the ground until our hips are level, and he grinds himself into my pelvis, his quills trembling.

A small gasp from the doorway has my eyes shooting open and locking onto the six-year-old standing in the hallway. Her little hands fly up to cover her face and she turns away from the scene we're making. Ettrian seems to be too far gone to realize that someone has walked in as he noses at my breasts. My hands fly to the back of his head and I pull on his quills hard, accidentally yanking one out in the process.

This finally gets his attention.

He looks up at me, seeing the panic on my face, and lowers me to my feet. Ettrian glances around, eyes falling on Kareen. His quills seem to turn an even brighter red, and I watch as his jaw clenches just before he turns on his heels, exiting the tree. The wall of bark shuts behind him, and I realize they have effectively just trapped us inside.

"Are you okay, Miss Xia?" Kareen peeks out from between her fingers, making sure that Ettrian is gone.

"Yeah, I'm fine." I pant as I right myself. "Let's figure out how to get you something to drink."

CHAPTER 5

*A*quilian

A surge of rage spikes through me, halting my feet mid-step. I could feel Ettrian through the bond, broadcasting his arousal as flashes of what he was experiencing with our mate rolled through me. In a normal mating, this would not be cause for anger or jealousy, but for me, it was infuriating. Ettrian always seemed to have it so easy. There was never a struggle for him like there was for me. *He* never had to face being turned away just because the color of his skin wasn't what a female wanted or because he was seen as a plague that might one day consume all in its path.

He might be a twin, but he wasn't a Darkborn.

When I had attempted to touch our mate, she pulled away from me, and yet she so willingly went to Ettrian. I try to remind myself that she is alien, that she doesn't understand our culture. Maybe her kind only mates with one male. Perhaps they don't even have males. The fact that I'm so anguished over this is frustrating. The female is unattractive and makes unpleasant vibrations. I shouldn't care that she seems uninterested in me, but I do.

In a normal mating, there is no jealousy between males, but

this is nothing close to normal and I've struggled my whole life with these feelings toward my twin. Something inside of me craves to experience the same connection Ettrian has forged with her within the short amount of time we have known her.

It's a small blessing when Kareen, the little kit, interrupts them. Never have I felt such a sense of fondness for a kit before in my life.

Lifting up the bottom branch of the bush in front of me, I look underneath and find exactly what I am hunting for. An ojoo curls up into a protective ball as if it can hide from me. Pulling a quill from the back of my head, I use it on each ojoo to kill my meal and collect all four of the insects that are about as big as my forearm, carrying them back toward the tree.

Ettrian is standing outside, obviously waiting for me to return. Without a second thought, I drop my bounty onto the forest floor and lash out at my twin, slamming my foot hard into his chest. Every unfair moment, every ounce of my jealousy, is the driving force behind it. My grief, my rage, all of my frustrations are finally spilling over.

"What in the Sun Father's good name, Aquilian?!" he roars as he stumbles backward.

Without answering him, I pound my fist into the side of his face, pushing him further back. I send all of my rage through the bond to him and whirl around, storming across the space I have created between us. I know that he's not fighting back because he thinks that he can get through to me by just talking, but I don't care anymore. Instead, I grab his crest and yank several quills from where they bunch on the back of his head and continue to rip at my brother.

"Why?" I crash my fist against his chest in a feeble blow. *"Why is it always this way with you?"*

A vibration rumbles through my throat as my quills rattle in frustration. Ettrian attempts to hold my hands at my side as he sends calming thoughts through the bond, but I can't stand the pain anymore. I cannot continue living like this. My own mate has rejected me, and she is the only female I've actually ever *needed* to accept me. I held out hope my whole life that just one being other than my brother would be able to look past my coloring and see *me*.

"I only wish for acceptance, Ettrian."

"She has not accepted me yet either, Aquilian. We are all strangers to one another." He squeezes my hands. *"The Sun Father has seen fit to bless us. We are in this together, brother. If we give her time, surely she will accept us."*

I could feel the song of sadness welling up and rattling through my quills, my eyes surely glowing blue with my displeasure. My brother wraps his arms around me, soothing his hand down my back as he vibrates his quills in response.

"You don't know that, Ettrian."

"You are worthy of any female. If she cannot accept one of us, then she cannot accept either of us. We were born together and we will do all things in life together." His hand moves up to my crest to slide along the length of my antennae in the same soothing manner he has done our whole lives.

I shrug his hand off and snort derisively. I am not so gullible to believe that it works that easily. It is a comforting thought, but such thoughts do not warm one on a cold night.

My brother sighs wearily. *"Come, the kit is probably hungry."*

I scowl at him, but he's right—of course the kit will be hungry, and I am being selfish. Instead of thinking about the little one, I am worried about my own issues. I pick up our food and send out feelers to the tree to open up to me. Moving through the opening that is now cut into the bark, I walk into the most perplexing of situations. The little female is sitting at the bottom of the nozzle from which water is delivered directly from the tree itself and my mate is trying to coax the liquid from it.

It's obvious she doesn't understand that she needs to tell the tree that she would like water. Reaching my free hand out, I touch the stem and milk it while speaking to the tree with my bond. *"You have to tell the tree you are thirsty, my light,"* I tell her as I move my fingers to tuck a stray hair behind her ear. She bares her teeth at me, and I step back quickly. I've obviously done something wrong. The little one begins to suckle from the water, and once she is finished, I speak to the tree to stop.

My hand runs along the inside of the bark and a pocket opens. I deposit my kill within and watch as the tree closes over it. As a kit, I had been fascinated by the magic of the trees we called our homes. Some say that they are gifts from the Sun Father, a way to ensure we have the means to survive. When the pocket opens a few moments later, our meal is warm and ready to be consumed. Sitting on the floor, I use a leaf that I gathered before I caught the ojoo and place each one in separate spots.

"Xia, Kareen," I send along the bond, my hand waving them over to where I sit. The kit looks absolutely starving as she rushes to my side, sliding her tiny fingers over my quills. The vibrations she makes sends a shiver through them. Ettrian sends the sweet sound of her voice through the bond, and I look at him questioningly. *"How is that possible? She is not speaking to us."*

Flashes of a horrific experience flow through my mind from my twin, pain lancing my head. I must have made a noise because the little one is tapping my shoulder as she says my name. I can only understand her because of the open link with Ettrian and it takes a moment for me to realize what she's saying. "Quilian?" Her head tilts, making the blonde strands brush against her shoulder.

"I am fine, little one. Eat," I reply pointing to the food before me. The ojoo is still curled up in a ball, its body concealed within its shell. Xia reaches her hand forward and pulls the ojoo's black shell open, causing the legs spasm even though it is long dead.

Both females shoot to their feet in abject horror and run from the insect as a vibration assaults my ilo.

"I do not think they will eat ojoo, brother." Ettrian's quills vibrate with his laughter.

"What will they eat then?" Maybe they don't know this is food? I dig one finger into the soft belly of one of the ojoo and pop the meat into my mouth, chewing slowly to show the females how you consume it. Only instead of coming back to eat, both put a hand to their mouth while their other clutches their stomach.

"I will go get some fruit. Maybe they are not meat-eaters," Ettrian says, shaking his head.

Kareen takes a small step toward me and sits down. She watches as I eat and then, with a small hand, pushes into the stomach of her ojoo before bringing it to her mouth, hesitantly consuming her first bite. A smaller, more gentle vibration brushes against my ilo as she begins to tear into the ojoo like she has never eaten before.

She beckons to Xia, but it is obvious my mate will not give the food a chance the way her kit has. Even if my mate never accepts me, I think I can live with it as long as I still hold the favor of her kit. *Our* kit. I take my clean hand and run it over the silken light yellow strands that fall from her head, mesmerized that someone so sweet and small is not scared of me. It doesn't matter that she is not the kit of my blood, because she is the kit of my heart and she has chosen to accept me.

CHAPTER 6

*E*ttrian

My search for fruit close to the tree results in nothing edible for our mate and kit. It's obvious that I need to branch out further if I want to find enough to stock the home for at least a couple of days, but I'm worried about leaving Xia and Kareen alone for too long. Shaking my fear away, I decide to push on. Aquilian is more than capable of taking care of them while I find food. I am all too aware that he has next to no experience with females or kits, but I know I can trust him with our own.

My fight with Aquilian weighs on my mind, but I remind myself that I deserve his anger. I have done something that is unforgivable, all because I felt I knew what was best for him. Even though he doesn't know about it, and Sun Father willing will never find out, the memory draws to the forefront of my mind, turning my stomach.

"What did you just say to me, Ettrian?" Safia flares her quills as she turns toward me, her eyes flashing red in irritation.

"I meant no offense, Taenov. I only mean that you are Dark-born, like Aquilian." I bow my head in respect for her position within the tribe.

"What does our coloring have to do with what you are asking me to do?" The opening in the tree closes behind me, and she motions for me to come farther in.

"I thought you, of all people, would understand how he feels, the rejection and the fear he receives daily."

Her eyes narrow on me. "I understand all too well, but what you are proposing is dangerous, even for someone in my position."

"I am not asking that you mate us, only that you show him what being with a female can be like. To give him the opportunity to experience the pleasure he may never have again."

"You are asking me to open myself up to a bringer of death, not just a Darkborn, but also a twin, to risk my soul to the Sun Father twice." The red in her eyes deepens, her anger palpable.

"Please, you are the only Darkborn Taenov I can trust to keep this secret. He wouldn't forgive me for this, but he needs it. I watch him fall farther into despair every day that passes."

Her lips flatten into a thin line and she growls along the bond, her quills rattling. "Fine, I will do this for you. For your twin."

"Thank you, Safia." I put my hand to my chest, the tension seeping from my body as relief courses through me.

She shakes her head, her eyes swirling from red to bright pink. "You will thank me by worshiping me," she tells me huskily as she reclines back onto her mating sling, pulling up her skirts in obvious invitation. "Come, Ettrian." She brings her long legs up and lets them fall open.

I do not refuse her. How can I when I know what she will do for Aquilian?

. . .

*P*ulling myself from the memory, I shake my head and hope that Aquilian hasn't picked up on it through the bond. I need something to distract me from such thoughts. A hanging bloom, rarely seen on our side of the forest, peeks out from the spiraled trees, reminding me that I should see how far this dome actually goes. The alien never mentioned the size of it, but it seems important to know so that we don't run into anything or anyone unexpectedly while we're stuck here.

Aquilian and I reached out along the bond when we started looking for the tree, but we didn't find any of our tribemates near. It has been so long since I was captured that it is plausible someone may have come looking for us. Hours pass, the Lotura sinking lower in the purple sky as I reach the edge of the dome and rub my hands tentatively along the surface.

How did the aliens get in and out?

There has to be some way we can escape. If we can figure out how the aliens come in and out, then perhaps we can leave and I can be free of this burden the creatures have placed on me. Moving along the edge of the dome, I push forward searching for any sign of weakness that I might be able to exploit, but it seems solid.

My foot comes down on a branch, snapping it and sending a vibration racing over my ilo and through the holes in the sides of my head. I wince as a few small pagli take flight, their pretty orange and black wings taking them higher into the trees. Their colors remind me of the khali bloom Aquilian and I picked for our mama as kits.

I can still see us running through the open fields full of them, disturbing the tiny prina bugs so that we could watch them scatter into the sky before us. Those early days before we had realized we were different from the other kits are some of my most trea-sured memories. Life hasn't been kind since Aquilian's color darkened and people from the tribe began avoiding us. My emotions are so great that I'm pulled back in time to one of many sad moments.

I watch as yet another one of our friends is tugged away from us, his mama's voice echoing in my head, "What have I told you about those two, Ethmos?"

"But they are my friends, Mama!"

"Not anymore." We watch in confusion as he turns to look at us one last time, his sad eyes a reflection of our own.

"Darkborn ..."

"The Sun Father has cursed them..."

"Bad enough to have twins, but to have one so dark? What a shame..."

The voices of the village swirl through my mind as we walk back to our home. I look over at my brother and see Aquilian's brows are furrowed as he stares down at our interlocked hands, my soft white skin in stark contrast to his deep black. I see nothing wrong with him; he is my brother, my twin, and he is the most wonderful being in the whole wide world as far as I am concerned.

I squeeze his hand tightly and bump my shoulder against his. "Mama says not to listen to the gossip of others." He shrugs and shakes his hand from mine, bringing it up to his quills where he begins tugging at them in his absentminded way. Papa Eldav told Mama and Papa Ekaz a few nights ago that if they did not get this new habit under control soon, Aquilian was going to yank every quill out of his head. As I watch, one snaps off into his hand and he merely drops it to the ground.

"Stop that!" I yank his arm down and he turns to me in shock. "You will have no quills left if you do not quit."

Aquilian shrugs and continues walking, his feet scraping

along the ground. A female up ahead sees us coming and takes a
detour, giving the two of us a wide berth. Although he pretends
not to notice, I see the hurt in my brother's eyes, and it makes me
furious...

*T*he recollection reminds me that there is an old legend
in our culture, a story about the twin sons of the Sun
Father. The brothers, Nebol and Semol, fell madly in love with a
woman, Yssa, and brought her before their papa to receive his
blessing. In order to gain this, she needed to drink the nectar from
an Oya bloom to show that she was their fated mate. Alas, she
was not and breathed her last breath while walking home to the
mates of her heart.

The elders say this was the curse of Nebol, who was so dark
that his mate needed to shine the way for future generations.
Semol, who was Lightborn, suffered from the same curse only
because he was born with his Darkborn brother and their bond
was forbidden. The twins wanted no other Dauur to ever suffer
the same heartbreak and gifted our people with a physical sign
upon finding a fated mate. Our quills change color, the same way
mine and Aquilian's have.

As with all Dauur, Aquilian and I were born a dusky gray, and
the glowing patterns running over our skin were the only way for
our parents to tell us apart. We were perfectly normal kits, with
many friends among our tribe's young, and we were happy.

As we grew older, we began to notice changes in our skin
tones. Instead of becoming lighter like I had, Aquilian started
getting darker, turning from our original gray to a deep, dark
black like the burnt-out coals of the bonfire in the center of the
village.

That was when the talk started.

It was little things at first, fewer friends to play with, adults avoiding him, but then it got worse. Members of our own tribe spoke harsh words to him, shooed him away from their homes or families as if he carried some sort of illness they would catch.

To them, his dark skin was a bad omen, a curse from the Sun Father. It had been bad enough we were twins, but now we had a Darkborn. Although Aquilian was not the only Darkborn among us, he had the misfortune of being the only Darkborn twin. While I had been on the receiving end of more than a few taunts, Aquilian was always their main target. Our parents staunchly ignored the gossip. *"They speak from places of fear. Do not let their worries into your hearts."*

A drop fruit tree towers over me, twisting and curling upward, glowing blue fruit hanging from its thorny limbs. My mind drifts back to Xia and the kit, and my heart races a little with the knowledge that they are ours. We have a mate who does not fear my twin, who seems to not hold any bias. This is something Aquilian and I have hoped for our whole lives, something neither of us thought would ever happen.

And I am being told to risk it all.

I close my eyes for a moment and let her face appear in my mind. She's just as alien to me as I am to her. Even though I found her appearance rather ugly, I was not repulsed when I touched her. The thought of what happened between us earlier makes my cock ache behind the protective plating.

Perhaps performing this duty will not be as horrible as I had first imagined.

When she had been in my arms, she felt right, like she belonged there. I would never wish to hurt her, not even before I knew who she was to us. If I do as the green aliens demand, I would not only hurt Xia, I would hurt my brother, and I would hurt our kit. The same kit I was so desperate to keep safe in the first place.

I can feel the pull to my mate slide along the bond already and

44

my anxiety rises. I have no idea how I'm going to keep her safe. I'm terrified to love her, and I'm terrified of not loving her. A mate is supposed to be a gift, something to be cherished, and while Aquilian wants to fawn over her, I am trying my best to put distance between us. Not because I do not want her—Sun Father knows I more than wanted her while she was in my arms—but because I cannot live with the thought that I may hurt her in the end.

Pulling myself onto the limbs, I climb until I reach the branch that holds the fruit. Plucking a quill from my head, I shoot one at the hanging orbs, successfully dropping a couple. It's a mindless task, one that clears my mind.

From my spot in the tree, I can just make out a nolfira nest. The members of its family clan snap at one another restlessly as they nudge their pups around. The sleek white animals have long pointed ears and big innocent eyes. They are extremely loyal to one another, usually only fighting among themselves for dominance. The best thing to do right now is to ignore them.

I descend from the tree and gather the fruit that has fallen to the forest floor before I head back toward our temporary den. It's getting late, and my mate is sure to be hungry if she has not eaten the ojoo. Later, I will finish my inspection of this prison we are stuck in.

CHAPTER 7

*I*noxia

While eating and drinking is great, I could really use a bathroom right about now. I've been holding it for a little while, not really sure how to ask about the facilities, and it's getting harder and harder. Each time they let the water from the faucet run, I feel like my bladder is going to explode. It isn't like I can just go outside with the tree sealing itself back up, and I have no idea how they even open it in the first place. Kareen walks up beside me, fisting my skirts and tugging to get my attention. Looking down at her, I notice that she has her legs crossed and is hopping from foot to foot.

"I need to go," she whispers, glancing sideways at the aliens who are busy in the kitchen area of the tree.

"Fuck."

"Did you say fuck?" she looks around as if she's going to be caught using the word before turning those big blue eyes on me. "That's a bad word, Miss Xia."

"You know what? You're right. I'm sorry I said that." *Goddammit.* I'm not used to being around children in stressful

46

situations. Normally, I don't have much interaction with the younger kids outside of their visits to our greenhouse, which is where I'm the most comfortable and calm.

I debate on which man I should ask for help, Ettrian or Aquilian? Looking over at their backs, the answer is clear. While I had interacted with Ettrian more, Aquilian was actually way easier to talk to. Well, to *try to* talk to, since we still don't understand one another yet. My teeth bite into my lower lip as I softly lay a hand on his shoulder. He turns to me, his eyes flashing with color so fast I'm not even sure which one it was. "Umm, we need the bathroom."

His head tilts in the universal sign of "what the fuck did you just say" and I worry that I'm not going to be able to get my point across before Kareen and I pee our pants. Hopping from one foot to the other, much like Kareen, I move my hands between my legs and clutch myself. I'm hoping beyond all hope that they too need to relieve themselves somewhere. This only seems to confuse him further. So, with burning cheeks, I squat down and flick my fingers as if there is something coming out of me. Light seems to dawn on him, and he looks horrified. Turning his face from me, he holds out a hand, as if afraid to even look my way. Reaching forward, I take his hand and nod at Kareen.

"Come on. Let's follow him." The sound of her feet racing across the floor has him looking back at her in a perplexed manner, like he isn't sure about my decision to bring her along. "She needs to pee too."

Aquilian gives a very human-like shrug and pulls us deeper into the tree, which seems to be reforming itself as we walk. A new room appears to our right, and he leads me inside. There's a sling in the middle like the one he put Kareen in earlier, only this one has holes in it. Does he expect me to pee in that? The pee would get all over me and the floor!

The male sits me in it, grabbing my hips to place me just right, and then pulls my dress up. I want to push his hands away, but maybe there's something special I don't know about—and if I don't pee soon there will be a mess. But instead of doing anything further, he crouches down and mimes for me to remove my underwear.

"Uh, no. I've got this," I say, but he only ducks his head and tries to peek beneath my skirts as he holds his hands out like he's getting ready to catch something. What. The. Actual. Fuck.

"Miss Xia?"

"Not right now, Kareen. Aquilian and I are trying to figure this out."

"I don't have to pee anymore."

"What?" My head snaps in her direction at her words, and I notice a little puddle at her feet. *Oh, no. Nononononononono.* How do moms deal with this stuff?

Aquilian looks over, and I think he finally understands what I've been trying to say. A rattle works its way through his quills and his eyes change to a sickening yellow. Kareen looks like she's about to cry, but Aquilian—ever her hero—walks over and runs his hand through her hair. He motions for both of us to follow him once more, his head hung slightly. The puddle disappears right before my eyes, getting absorbed into the tree. I sure hope that doesn't get recycled into our drinking water.

The next room he brings us to is quite obviously what we needed. There's a small bowl that I assume is used for waste and a large basin that I am hoping is where we can take a proper bath. Over the large basin is a nozzle much like the one in the kitchen.

Aquilian reaches out his hand, running it along the stem to make the water flow, and stands with Kareen as they watch it begin to fill up. The sound of rushing water does me in. Since their backs are to me, I hike up my skirt, shove down my panties, and relieve myself in the bowl. The alien either doesn't seem to hear me going, or he respects my privacy because he keeps his back to me. Poor Kareen still stands beside him waiting to be helped. Once I finish, I move over to them both to see that a decent amount of water has collected. Aquilian strokes the stem and the water comes to a stop.

He moves across the room, reaching into the tree to pull out two pods. Pretending to run one over his quills and the other he rubs over his body, Aquilian says something in my mind, like he's telling me this is what these things are for. Handing them both to me, he leaves the room.

Okay, so… no towel?

But just as I'm worrying about what Kareen can wear now that her clothing is soiled, he comes in with a soft length of something that looks similar to silk but feels far more absorbent. I take it from him without a second thought and shoo him from the room. With a little bit of work, Kareen and I figure out this whole bathing a kid business. When she's finished, I fashion her a makeshift dress as best as I can out of the silky material, wrapping it around her before taking her clothes and throwing them all into the tub.

"Sorry, sweetie, you're going to have to use that until I can get your clothes dry," I tell her, washing them by hand and wringing the water from them. Once I'm positive I have gotten them as clean as I can, I hang them over the side of the basin. I'd love to bathe, but it looks like I'll have to wait a bit. Ushering Kareen from the room, I lead her through the kitchen and into our makeshift bedroom.

"Come on, you. Let's get you into bed." A sigh falls from my lips as I ruffle her hair. "You didn't get much sleep earlier."

"I was worried." Her hand tucks a ringlet behind her ear.

"Worried about what, honey?" The moment reminds me of my mom, who always listens when I'm upset, and it makes my heart lurch in my chest. I miss her so much, and I'm sure she would know exactly what to do right now.

"We're never going home, are we?" Her little lip trembles, and again, I fear that I'm woefully underqualified to handle this parenting thing.

"Baby, it's okay. We've got this. I need you to keep being brave for me."

"Brave for you?" Her little eyebrows come together as she frowns.

"Well, of course! How am I supposed to deal with those knuckleheads out there if I don't have you to help me?"

"Aren't adults supposed to be the brave ones?"

"Oh, sweet girl, anyone of any age can be brave—and you've been doing it so well today!"

The look of pride that spreads across her face makes my heart flutter. *Maybe I'm not so bad at this after all.* Her eyes light up with pleasure and before I know it she is wrapping her arms around my waist in a pint-sized bear hug.

"Thank you, Xia," she whispers. "You're the best mama ever."

Tears threaten to spill from my eyes as I pick her up and tuck her into her little cocoon, pressing my lips to the top of her head.

"Get some rest, Kareen." My voice only cracks a little with emotion.

Back in the kitchen, I find both males standing at opposite ends of the long counter. They look up as I approach, slipping between them to snag one of the cups from the counter. A smile curls my lips as Ettrian reaches over, running his finger along the spout so that the water spills into the small depression below. My mouth feels like cotton after speaking with Kareen. That kid certainly knows how to tug at my heartstrings, and it took every bit of emotional strength I still had not to burst into tears.

A hand brushes my shoulder, and the cup nearly falls from my hands as I jump in surprise. My whole body tenses up, and I can feel the panic attempting to take over as old, awful memories assault my weary mind. The hands in these memories aren't gentle; they grip me with shocking brutality. I can feel my chest tighten as I recall being jerked around, my back slamming into the granite of the countertops that had been in our kitchen. I hear the phantom crack of Trent's hand on my cheek, and a whimper falls involuntarily from my lips as I pull away from the touch.

You aren't there, Xia. Trent is gone, and he can't hurt you anymore, I remind myself as I close my eyes and take deep, calming breaths. *You got away. You're safe from him.*

Before I open my eyes again, I count backward from ten, willing my body to relax. Aquilian is watching me, his blue eyes filled with concern and sadness. The quills on his head rattle as he extends his arm slowly toward me and I almost cry when I see the length of silk that hangs from the tips of his fingers.

"Oh... Yes! Thank you!" Snatching it from his hands, I take off running to the bathroom. Nothing else in that moment matters as much as having the chance to feel clean. I grab Kareen's wet clothes and look around the bathroom for somewhere to put them. Ettrian reaches around me, taking them from my hands before disappearing through the doorway, but Aquilian stands just inside, waiting expectantly.

"Soap?" I mime washing myself the way he did earlier.

He opens his palms to show me that he's already thought of that and even the tub is already full of fresh water. *Well, okay.* I try to take it from his hand, but he closes his palm over the little treasure and takes a step back.

"Aquilian, I'm really not in the mood for a game. We've already played an unsuccessful round of charades and I just want a bath."

More of his growly mindspeak fills my head as he begins to nudge me toward the water.

"My dress is still on!" He seems to have already thought of that too because he is attempting to figure out how to get the garment off. "Okay, no!"

Turning on my heel, I push at his body until he's standing in the hallway. I know that I am only able to move him because he allows it, but still, I feel triumphant. I hold my hand out once again, curling my fingers in a gimme motion. With great reluctance, Aquilian hands over the soaps and turns to leave without so much as a growl or protest.

"Wait—" I lean forward, my hand resting on his arm to get his attention. He looks down at it and I snatch it back, curling my fingers into my palm as I press my hand to my chest.

Once again, I'm frustrated by our lack of communication. I'm sure I'm sending him all sorts of mixed signals, and if I'm being honest with myself, I don't even know exactly what I'm feeling either. "I just wanted to say I'm sorry about the way I reacted in the kitchen. It wasn't anything to do with you. My ex... he was horrible to me. He hurt me, and there are times where I get sucked into the past. Therapy can only help you so much, and I'm still working on it."

He doesn't give me any sign that he understands what I'm saying. Instead, he curls his hand into my hair, much like he did with Kareen, sliding his long fingers through the strands before he walks away.

With a small shrug of my shoulders, I spin back around toward the tub and sigh in relief.

Finally!

I get through washing my body, scrubbing the dirt and sweat away, and am halfway through washing my hair before I break down and give in to the tears. I curl my knees up to my chest and wrap my arms around my legs as the sobs take me. I've been putting on a strong face for Kareen ever since waking up on this planet, and I just need to recharge with a bit of a pity party.

My soft wails fill the room as I think of possibly never seeing my parents again, never curling up on my couch for movie night with Mina, and never ever getting to work in my greenhouse again. It's heartbreaking and absolutely terrifying. Life has thrown me a massive curveball, and I suddenly find myself a mother—at the very least a temporary one—to the little girl I adore but who I had been told would never be mine. I'm on an alien planet where the forest is full of trees that morph into houses, giant bugs are *food*, and alien men rock heads of colorful glowing quills. No sane person should be expected to take all of that in stride for this long.

A gentle hand lands on my shoulder, making me jump and jerk my head up. Ettrian is crouched down outside the basin, his face full of concern as he looks at me.

"I'm okay," I hiccup.

His hand curls under my chin and tilts my face up so that he's looking directly into my eyes. The soft growls play through my mind just before he brings his forehead down to rest against mine. Unlike the last couple times he's touched me, I don't feel the pull of arousal. This is only meant to soothe me, to bring comfort. His other hand rubs over my still soapy hair, and the softest rattle comes from his quills as he rubs his face against mine. It is the strangest and oddly sweetest thing anyone has done for me in a long time.

Trent never did stuff like this. He never cared when I was sad or upset. All Trent had cared about was himself and his needs. He shamelessly cheated on me, brought women home to guilt trip me into threesomes, and berated me anytime I went against what he wanted. Ettrian and Aquilian have been far more considerate of my wants and needs than the man I had once loved ever had.

A broken sigh falls from my lips as I take a moment to lean into the comfort he is offering. *All right, Xia, you've had your cry. Time to get it together.* Pulling my head back gently, I give him a brave smile which sends him stumbling backward. Right, aliens are so strange. I wave my hand at him. "Shoo, shoo. I need to rinse and that doesn't require an audience. I've already had to kick Aquilian out." I know he doesn't completely understand me, but he inclines his head and leaves me to it.

CHAPTER 8

*A*quilian

The rammit shoots to the right into the underbrush just as the quill leaves my hand, sailing through the space between us and embedding itself in the ground where my prey had just been. *Sun Father curse it!* My breath huffs out as I snarl in irritation. I don't think I've missed a rammit since I was a kit just learning the skill from my papas. I run my fingers through my quills, just barely stopping myself from tugging any out.

I may not know how to be a great mate yet, but I've never failed at hunting. *Until today.* Apparently, this is a day of firsts. I'm distracted, and it's not just this situation with our mate that has me feeling off.

At the start of my hunt, I swore I caught a glimpse of another being, one who seemed familiar, but the flash of soft light was there and gone so quickly that I couldn't be sure. I searched the brush and the ground and found no signs of the offworlder who claims to reside on Lotura. We'd grown close over the course of his visits, and for a moment, I let myself believe that help had arrived, that we might be able to get our mate and kit to safety.

"A trick of the light," I tell myself as I grab the quill I threw

and stalk off toward the tree where Ettrian and I decided to keep the females until we can figure out how to get out of here. The only things I've gotten for food are fruits and some root vegetables I can remember my mama making. Maybe Xia will like those more than the ojoo, although I'm pretty positive she likes nearly anything more than the ojoo.

My mind drifts to Xia as I walk, and I cannot help the embarrassment that seeps into my very soul. I had thought she was telling me she was giving birth. Shocked, I naturally set about preparing to help her whelp her newest kit. I wanted to bang my head on the nearest hard surface at the memory of her confused face as I had crouched down in front of her.

Stupid, stupid, stupid.

It had taken poor Kareen soiling herself before it had dawned on me that they needed to relieve themselves. My stomach drops at the memory of her reaction when I placed my hand on her shoulder in the central room of the tree. She had seemed disgusted, frightened by my presence, and that sentiment had only been strengthened when I attempted to be a proper mate and take care of Xia by bathing her. She had ushered me from the room, shooed me out like some pesky kit. *Can you blame her?* I was stupid enough to mistake her needing to relieve herself for her giving birth. It must be clear to her that I am not fit for this. I close my eyes and take deep, calming breaths, reminding myself that I have no experience with these things, but that doesn't ease the shame that wiggles its way into my mind.

"He is a Darkborn twin. You cannot expect good things from him."

"He will never be worthy."

My throat tightens as I replay the words of my tribe. I want to be worthy of this female. She may not be what the Dauur consider beautiful, but I want her to have everything she deserves and will do anything it takes to provide that.

I wish I could experience her voice the way Ettrian does. Although her language is unknown to me and we cannot communicate in the same manner, I understood the fear and pain in her expression as she stood before me. Perhaps I am merely pushing my own emotions onto her and she was actually telling me what a massive fool she thinks I am, telling me not to not touch her again.

Telling you she wants Ettrian instead.

It isn't healthy to think this way. I know it's wrong, but I find it incredibly difficult not to after all of the experiences of my life. With a rattle of my quills, I open up the front of the tree and immediately dodge the cup that comes sailing through the air at my face. The hardened clay shatters against the wall of the tree as it closes behind me, and the pieces scatter across the floor at my feet. Clearly, I have missed something. Xia clasps her hand to her mouth, her eyes going wide, and she vibrates frantically.

"What is she saying?" I ask Ettrian who blinks in confusion.

"I am not sure. I cannot understand her," Ettrian replies before he sends her strange words to me.

"Osside." she demands, clearly frustrated that we are not comprehending her needs. Her foot stomps against the floor as she looks up, emitting an angry vibration.

"Do you think she is hungry?" I hold out the assortment of fruits and roots I was able to collect and watch with a satisfied rattle as her eyes light with interest.

Xia presses her palms together and rushes forward, her delicate fingers tracing excitedly over the blooms I didn't bother plucking from the fruit. Soft vibrations tumble from her lips and roll along my skin as she touches the pink petals, motioning for her kit to join us. Kareen scurries forward, her tiny, blunt teeth bared in a manner that makes me stumble backward involuntarily.

"Have I misinterpreted their needs again?" I ask my twin, dropping the fruit into Xia's hands in an effort to avoid the kit.

The little one looks at me, her brows dropping slightly before she turns to her mama. Xia shrugs in answer to whatever it is Kareen has said before snapping the bloom off the fruit. She crouches down, gently tucking the pink petals into the golden strands atop the little one's head, baring her teeth.

"I am beginning to think this may not be a form of aggression among their kind," Ettrian murmurs as we watch them.

Kareen spins around until even I am dizzy, and I glance sideways at my twin, praying to the Sun Father that he is correct. For the Dauur, this display of aggression is baffling, especially between a female and her kit. Once again, I am reminded that our mate is alien and that her mannerisms will most likely reflect that. Still, it unnerves me.

Xia stands, picking the rest of the blooms from the fruit in my arms before she spins around, making her way across the central room where she stretches up for one of the remaining cups. Ettrian follows, filling the cup with water from the tree when she motions toward the nozzle. The corners of her lips tug up as she places the blooms into the cup, setting it on the counter, turning it this way and that as Kareen bounces around her legs.

I nearly drop my bounty to the floor in shock when our mate rushes toward me, wrapping her arms around my waist as she presses her cheek to my chest. Her warmth seeps into me, and for a moment, I can do nothing but stand there with my mouth hanging open like a fool. I bring my hand up and stroke her head and back with soft, slow movements. This moment is worth all of my struggles, all the shattered cups. I would pick her blooms until my fingers bled just to know this was my reward. For once, it seems as if I have done something right.

a few days pass in much the same fashion, with both females staying safely tucked inside the tree. They may be safe, but the kit has begun to practically bounce off of the walls. She makes the sharpest vibrations when she's upset, and even her mama seems to be floundering in her attempts to calm her. I did not think much of her outburst until my sweet little Kareen lobs a woven basket at the side of my head. Perhaps it is just my inexperience with young ones, but how can this be the same kit who snuggles up to me before bed, the same kit who runs her tiny fingers through my quills while she vibrates at me?

Ettrian has shown me bits and pieces of what happened when he was captured, but I know in my heart that he is keeping secrets. There is something weighing heavily on his mind that he is not ready to share. The thought that these creatures may try to take Xia and Kareen sends a surge of protectiveness through me. I know the females do not like being kept inside, but the image of them in the hands of those monsters is more than I can bear. I would rather die than see any harm come to them.

Glowing liquid drips down Inoxia's chin as she devours the fruit Ettrian and I gathered for her. I have the overwhelming urge to lick it from her skin, but I turn away, afraid she will see the desire in my eyes and reject me. Pushing up from where I have settled down on the floor, I hold my hand out to our kit. If I cannot show her affection in the way I wish, I can at least give her a reprieve from the responsibilities of caring for her kit.

"Time to sleep, my little Kareen. Let us give your mama a break." Kareen bares her teeth at me, but I hold my ground. If Ettrian is wrong and this is some sort of aggressive behavior, I should demonstrate that I am the one in charge. Right? I gently tug her up into my arms as she waves at Xia and take her down the hall into the sleeping quarters she shares with her mama. The fact that she only allows me to do this routine with her gives me a

great amount of joy. The last time Ettrian tried, she fussed until I relieved him. I think she can also tell he is hiding something and behaving unlike himself.

"Sleep, little one," I tell her as I tuck her into the sling, hoping that soon the bond will allow us to understand one another. Both she and her mama seem to pick up words here and there, and while it is not uncommon for the bond to teach a female the language of her mates, I do worry that it may not be extended to her kit.

When I leave the room in search of my brother, I do not find him with Xia where I expected him to be. She points to the room we have taken for ourselves when I say his name and I make my way to him.

"Ettrian?" He is sitting quietly in his sling, his eyes distant, and he looks like he might fall over at any moment. My quills rustle as I step closer.

"I am sorry, Aquilian. I know it is not fair to lay the responsibilities of their care on your shoulders, but whatever these monsters have done is exhausting me. I cannot seem to keep my eyes open tonight."

Increasing worry for my twin curls in my belly, and I try not to let it engulf me. I try not to let him know that I have heard the sorrow in his voice over the last few days. *"Are you sure you are all right?"* He nods softly but says nothing. *"Kareen has gone to sleep. I will make sure Xia is taken care of tonight."*

Out in the main room, I lay my hand on the wall of the tree and speak to it, sending images of the blooms that grow on the fruit I gathered earlier. Tiny buds begin to form on the smooth bark, their pink petals unfurling as they grow larger. Xia looks up from her spot on the floor, her lips curling as she watches. The dullness in her eyes fades for a moment, and my heart clenches as she reaches up to brush a finger over a flower.

"I know you do not understand me," I tell her when she turns

to me, *"but I am worried about Ettrian. Every day since we found ourselves trapped in this place, he has become weaker, the shell of who he was."* Xia watches me as a step away from her, lowering myself to the floor. *"I am lost. What do I do? How do I make sure he does not crumble while still protecting you and Kareen?"*

We stare at one another for an awkward moment, and I see her cheeks redden in what I have come to understand is her embarrassment. With a frustrated rattle, I rake my hand through my crest before I feel the warmth of her hand on my arm. Xia tugs, forcing me to release the quills as she slips her hands into mine. I look down, enthralled by the sight. We are different in so many ways, but I count her five small fingers as she squeezes my hand, and for the first time I stop to appreciate our similarities.

Her head moves from side to side, strands of red falling into her face, and she is vibrating in such a soft, gentle way, as if she cares that I could have harmed myself. Pleasure pulses along the bond between us as she continues, and I find myself leaning forward, looking up into a face I had found unattractive mere days ago. Her unusual features have become almost endearing, beautiful in a way unique to her.

I find it comforting that, like me, she is different.

Her green eyes pierce me, and I move closer to press my crest against the top slope of her head in the way my kind shows affection. Instead of leaning into me, I feel her lips press against mine, a soft pressure that causes my entire world to tip.

All too soon, she jumps up, her lips curling slightly as she looks down at me. *"Night,"* she mumbles before running off down the hall to join Kareen. It is the first time I have ever understood one of her words, and I want more.

*a*quilian

Setting up the snares to capture the little animal is the easy part. Not killing my catch right away is harder than I thought it would be. For Kareen, I am willing to try. If the kit had quills, she would have been pulling them out right about now.

I'd been thinking of ways to relieve her boredom, and lessons in being a proper Dauur kit seem like they might be fun. My papas used to take me hunting when I had too much energy and taught me the ways of our people. Since I cannot bring Kareen out to hunt, maybe I can bring home a live rammit and teach her how to kindly kill and clean it. My hand throbs as the rammit sinks its teeth into my skin for at least the third time, trying desperately to get out of my grip.

The feathered ears beat against the air as if it can just fly away from me. Sometimes I wonder if rammits are really as stupid as they seem. The glowing pink fur is puffed up, making it look more like a ball of fuzz with wings than an actual animal. The tree opens with a little prodding on my end, and I am nearly taken out by a basket as it sails through the air past my head.

"Kareen!" I frown down at the kit as she comes running up to

me. The rammit in my hand jerks, and I hold it up like some great prize. A sharp vibration jolts through my ilo, and the kit nearly tackles me in her excitement to see what I have brought home.

"Patience, little one. I will show you how to finish it off soon enough," she bares her teeth and it makes my quills tremble. *Fierce little things. "Calm down. I promise I am working on it,"* I tell her as I pluck a quill from my crest.

I bring the sharp end to the neck of the rammit, crouching down so that she can see how to end its life quickly and with as little pain as possible. She is baring her tiny blunt teeth at me again, and with the way she looks at the rammit, I'm starting to worry she may not have gotten enough to eat. Two intense vibrations pulse through me as the kit snatches the rammit right from my hand and Xia clutches the one that holds the quill. Horror rushes at me along the bond from both of them and makes me stumble backward. Xia is still holding my hand as she tries to calm Kareen, who is once again leaking fluid from her eyes.

"What did I do?"

Ettrian laughs uproariously in my mind, his eyes creasing and quills beating together fiercely as he takes in my bewildered face.

"Bunnyfly!" Kareen yells through the bond, her bottom lip sticking out as she runs her hand gently over the rammit's fur. It snuggles its whole body beneath her chin and peeks out at me.

"By the Sun Father..." I do not even know what a Bunnyfly is, but she seems to think she has found one. Still, she spoke along the bond and that warms my heart. She is learning.

"The next time I think bringing home dinner will be uneventful, please remind me of this moment." Ettrian pats my shoulder as he moves past us, his laughter echoing after him.

When I attempt to get near Kareen, she makes a strange vibration and shouts something along the bond, halting me. She looks like a mother defending a kit, dangerous and protective. The fire in her eyes is the only warning I need. The rammit belongs to her now. I glance down at Xia's hand where it is still resting on my forearm and watch as her cheeks flush a familiar red before she snatches it back. Our mate steps toward Kareen, bending over to run her fingers through the animal's soft fur as I turn toward Ettrian.

"I assume we are no close to escaping this place than we were yesterday," I remark, nudging his foot as he watches the females.

"I will try again in the morning." Kareen's harsh vibrations make him wince. *"We have to get them as far from here as we can."* His eyes dart around the interior of the tree as if it can understand our conversation, like it is watching him.

"Is there something I should know, Ettrian? Something you have not shared with me?"

His eyes lock on mine before he quickly averts them. *"I have told you the truth, Aquilian. Why would I keep anything from you?"*

That fact that he does not actually answer my question is not lost on me, but I decide to leave him be for now. I know from experience that pushing him will do nothing but create conflict. My jaw clenches as my gaze falls on our new family. Ettrian may keep his secrets for the moment, but I will not allow him to put them in further danger.

With a murmured pardon, my twin brushes past me, disappearing down the hall toward the room we share. When I return my attention to the central room, Xia has taken up her pacing again. Our mate's attention is normally occupied by Kareen, but in the moments when the kit is sleeping or busying herself, I have noticed she has started this habit. I know there are only so many places in a home to clean, and even the blooming wall she seems to love so much loses its appeal when you cannot leave the tree.

The baskets Kareen broke are stacked near the entrance to the tree, and I grab two of them before picking a spot on the floor, tucking my legs beneath me as I loosen the fronds I secured around my waist while I was hunting. Xia is watching me, her head tilted to the side as I begin to break the fronds done into strips.

"Come. Sit with me." I beckon her over with the crook of a finger, imitating the gesture I have seen her use to call Kareen, and am pleased beyond words when she takes up the space across from me. She waits as I prepare the strips, helping me lay them out between us. With slow movements of my fingers, I demonstrate how to weave the new fronds into the hole, repairing the damage. To my surprise, Xia doesn't need much instruction, and she has soon found a groove, soft vibrations flowing from her lips as she works.

The day passes slowly, and as it comes to an end, I am captivated by the way Kareen and Xia seem to be a little more at peace. Hope wells up within me, and I pray once this nightmare is over, they will come to love my homeworld.

~

ttrian

The gentle sound of singing pulls me from the blackness of my depression and has me creeping from my room to investigate. I know it's Xia. I have stopped to listen to the sound of her voice too many times to count. It calls to me, and it seems like the longer I fight the bond, the more I find myself drawn to her. The more I try to avoid her, the more I catch myself watching her from the shadows like the predator the aliens want me to be.

Xia is so enthralled with her work that she doesn't notice when I step into the central room with her. In her hands is the cup of water Aquilian leaves out for her every night, but she isn't drinking. She is carefully dribbling the water onto the blooms that are growing from the walls. My eyes turn green with amusement as I watch her for a moment longer.

"There is no need for that. The tree sustains them." She jumps a little, but to her credit, she keeps hold of the cup as she spins toward me. I know she is still having trouble understanding us, so I reach for the cup to show her there is no need to waste her time, but she refuses to release it, mumbling something I don't entirely comprehend. *"Let me refill it for you."*

"Stahp it," she argues, her brows drawing down above her eyes. "I want to."

"What was that?" I'm stunned for a moment. This is the first time I've been able to understand an entire sentence. Leaning in, I pull harder in an attempt to bring her closer.

"Fine!" She releases the cup, and before I can catch myself, I jerk my arm back, splashing the cool contents onto my face. Her eyes go wide as the water drips onto the floor at our feet. "Oh ghods." I hear her gasp before a sound as warm as embers fills the room, stopping abruptly when she slaps her hand over her mouth. It's one of the most beautiful things I've heard since the aliens cursed me with the ability.

"Again," I tell her, pulling her hand away. *"I want to hear it again."* It reminds me of the noise our kit makes when Xia pokes her sides, and I wonder if this will have the same effect on her. With slow movements, I reach out toward her, giving her ample time to scurry away if she does not wish for me to touch her. *"Please."* I slide my palms over her sides, watching as her breath catches just before I squeeze, mimicking her play with Kareen. I rattle in satisfaction as the sound bursts from her again. She tries to dance away from me, but I follow, renewing my efforts.

"Stahp!" she screeches. "Agh! Can't. Breathe!"

Sun Father, help me. I snatch my hands away, terrified that I have hurt her. Is this some sort of strange punishment she was handing out to our kit? Have I accidentally punished our mate? She is doing that strange baring of teeth that unnerves Aquilian, but she takes my hands in her own, squeezing my fingers as she looks up at me and blinks only one of her eyes. *"Is there something wrong with this one?"* I question, pulling my hand free to probe at her cheek and temple.

A few moments alone with her, and you have broken your mate.

Xia throws her head back and releases another burst of the warm sound before she launches her attack on me, running her fingers along my ribs and torso, stretching up on her toes to flutter them across the sides of my neck. I'm not sure what reaction she was hoping to draw from me, but it's obvious it was not the confusion I'm currently feeling. She looks... playful.

My quills rattle with my laughter as I look down at her, and it suddenly dawns on me that perhaps that is what I have been hearing: her laughter. I want to lose myself in the moment, in her joy. I want to hold onto this feeling I haven't felt since I was a kit playing with my mama and Aquilian on the floor of our tree. I was happy then, as happy as Xia looks right now.

The pain of my heart clenching in my chest has me stumbling backward, pulling away from her as her laughter dies. I feel like a coward as I hurry away, but when she looks at me that way, it makes me feel like a monster.

She is learning to trust you. You are letting her think you are not a threat. I shake my head as I retreat to the darkness of my room.

Liar. Monster.

I cannot betray her.

CHAPTER 10

*E*ttrian

"Do not touch her! No!" Our kit is pulled from the arms of my mate, both of them screaming as the disgusting green alien wraps his arms around Kareen's throat. I struggle against my bonds, jerking as hard as I can.

"Stop!" I hear myself roar over the sounds of Kareen's strangled cries as her life is slowly extinguished before my eyes. I cannot breathe through the pain in my chest as I fight. "Please do not do this."

Her little body falls to the floor, and that's when I notice Aquilian is lying lifeless next to her. My brother, my twin, the one who has been with me every single day of my life, is gone. I have lost both of them. My world is spinning and I look up in despair to see that they are now holding Xia.

She is glaring at me in disgust, blaming me for their deaths, and she is right. This is all my fault. I should have done something, anything to save these females who count on me to protect them. I should have done something to save my brother, who has always looked to me for answers. I failed them all.

"Please, spare her!" I beg.

"It's too late now." Xia's head jerks sharply to the side and she makes no sound as she crumbles.

I shoot up in my sling, panting as sweat rolls over my skin. Squeezing my eyes shut, I try to shake the image of my family lying dead at my feet from my mind, but it continues to haunt me. When I finally look up, Aquilian is staring at me from across the room, concern filling his eyes. *"Spare who, brother?"*

"It is nothing. Just a dream," I lie and cut off all access to my mind that he has.

Sun Father, forgive me for my deception.

A mostly uneventful week passed without interference from the aliens. I say "mostly uneventful" because Kareen has decided that what should have been our dinner is now a part of our family. I glance over at the kit. Her light-colored hair has been pulled back into a braid, and she has the rammit lying in her lap, its feet up in the air as she rubs its soft, fluffy belly while she sings.

I'm learning more and more about having hearing, and I find that I love listening to Xia and Kareen when they speak aloud or when they attempt to teach me and Aquilian songs from their homeworld. My twin cannot hear them, but he watches intently as their mouths move while I project their voices to him. I know their company has done more for him in mere days than I could have ever hoped to do in our lifetime.

Hope curls deep in my belly that perhaps our captors will leave us be. Maybe they assume I am breeding her inside of the tree. Xia has not allowed me or my brother to get too close to her for days, but she seems to be more relaxed than she was when we first met. Aquilian is sitting beside me repairing one of the baskets that Kareen used to boost herself up on last night. Her foot went clear through it and she cried huge tears, which is something very new and terrifying that we're trying to get used to. A lot of explaining on Xia's part and broken translations on the alien technology in my head taught me what the liquid was. It had taken a comforting embrace from each of us to soothe her and stop the leaking.

"Thank you," Kareen had whispered against my chest, and I felt my entire being light up. It was the first moment that she had sought me out for comfort, and I knew it was now etched into my mind for the rest of my life.

Xia sits next to Aquilian, watching as he weaves dark, flexible leaves into the broken section of the basket. She catches me looking at her and the corners of her mouth tip up as her cheeks start to turn a deep pink. I can feel my cock trying to push past the plating that protects it, and I realize I need to leave the tree and get myself under control.

"I'm going to scout a bit more. I should not be long."

Aquilian does not look up from his task. *"Grab more tear fruit while you are out. Kareen snuck the last one last night and thought I did not notice."*

"Of course." My quills rattle softly in amusement.

Leaving the tree is as simple as opening my mind to it, something that only Dauur can do, I suspect. Xia has complained that she cannot make it open the way we do, which is a blessing considering what could be waiting outside in the forest. It keeps her safe, though she does not realize it.

Climbing the spiral tree is not as hard as it looks, but reaching the tear fruit is a task within itself. If I did not have my quills to shoot at it, I doubt I would even be able to reach them thanks to the large thorns that surround the fruit to protect it from scavengers. Pulling a quill from atop my head, I send it sailing at the nearest blue treat and grunt triumphantly when it falls. I've had a lot of time to practice gathering these.

A shiver runs through me. The forest grows quiet and even the air feels off somehow. Climbing down the trunk, I ready another quill and cock back my arm as I scan the foliage. The predators that got caught in the dome have become more desperate, coming closer to the tree with each passing day, and the silence makes me worry that a nolfira and its clan may be stalking me. Both Aquilian and I are big enough to usually be ignored by these predators, but Kareen and Xia would make the perfect meal.

Instead of the great white beast I feared had tracked me down, I come face to face with the green alien from before. The same one from my nightmares. My caution does not seem so silly now that I'm staring down the disgusting being.

"Have you done as I asked? We have not seen the female nor the kit in quite some time."

I suspect something on my face gives away that I have not followed through, because he seems to grow agitated. *"I cannot do that to my mate."*

"Even with my gift you choose not to speak? If it were not for your uncanny ability to procreate, we would not even be here." A buzz fills my ears as he starts to pace just a few feet from me. He is in the dome this time, I realize. It is the perfect chance.

I slink across the leaves that litter the ground while he is distracted, a quill held tightly in my hand. A hissing sound of irritation falls from his unnatural mouth. Pulling my hand back, I strike at his neck, but instead of hitting his skin something stops me in mid-air. Like an invisible wall. The wings on the alien's back flutter as his head turns sharply in my direction.

"You would dare attack me? You think that I am stupid enough to come without protection?" His voice grows louder with each word, his tongue licking his lips. "For this you will pay. We know where you hide, Dauur." The threat in his voice has me backing up, nearly tripping over the overly large roots. "We also know the location of your tribe."

There is no mistaking what he means. *"There are kits!"* But I know even as I say it that he doesn't care. My tribe has many warriors, but even I worry for their safety when he so easily deflected my blow.

"I am feeling generous. I will give you one more day to do as I asked you," he says before he walks away from me.

Collecting the fruit from the ground, I hurry back to our den, scared of what is to come. If anything, Xia is warier of me than she was the first day, and I do not know how I am going to accomplish this. Making my way through the forest in record time, I call out to the tree to open. It is taking too long and the room is not revealed fast enough. This den is not nearly as responsive as the one we have near the village.

"Open!" I growl just as the hole forms and the sight of Xia greets my eyes. The floor is covered with leaves she had us collect, because she says the wood was too cold for her feet. The sound of Kareen and Aquilian come from deeper inside the den, but I deposit my fruit into the basket we weaved the day before and rush to my mate before the tree even has time to close. I pull her against me and rub my face along her neck when she speaks in her exotic voice.

"Ettrian? You okay?" she asks quietly.

"Mine." My quills rattle so harshly that it is almost painful, and I run my tongue along her neck. I need to be lost in my mate; I need her to accept me now. Even without the ceremony, I have to believe she will be able to survive it. So much depends on this.

"What was that?"

Satisfaction rushes through me at the thought that, between the translator and the bond, it is getting easier to understand her. My tongue slides along her throat as my hands bury themselves into the soft strands that curl around her face.

"You are our mate," I tell her for what feels like the hundredth time, but as with every other time we've spoken the words to her, she only scrunches up her face in confusion. The garments she wears to cover her body have been washed in the water of the tree and yet the same floral scent she had when we first met her still clings to it. A soft whimper falls from her lips as

she moves her hands to cradle my head and attempts to dislodge me.

"Ettrian, no."

I know these words, but they do not stop me this time. Her life, our kit's life, and even the lives of my tribe are on the line. I am so lost in her that I do not notice when Aquilian enters. Only when he throws me clear across the other side of the room, quills rattling as if I am a threat, does my mind clear.

"She said no!" he snarls.

"I cannot afford to wait any longer, Aquilian! The time for that has passed!"

"We have plenty of time to ease her into this. She is not like us. She does not understand!"

Kareen clings to Xia as liquid falls from our mate's eyes. *What have I done?* I should have just told them. Even if Xia couldn't understand, my twin would have.

"He will kill you all if I do not do this." Bile rises in my throat just at the thought of it.

"Who?" he asks.

But I cannot find the words to tell him, so instead I replay the memory for him, letting him see for himself the being who haunts my dreams. I know the moment he hears what the alien has commanded I do because pure rage flashes through him, and he pins me against the wall with his hand on my throat.

"You should have told me! We do not keep secrets!"

"Aquilian!" Xia says, her hands gripping his arm as she tries to pull it away from where it cuts off my airway. "No!" She tugs at him, the liquid falling from her eyes flowing faster.

It's the agony that is sent through the bond from her that has him releasing me. *"Get out."*

Aquilian lifts her up into his arms and crosses the room to Kareen, grasping her hand in his before pulling them both deeper into the den. I stumble back through the opening in the tree and run blindly into the forest, putting as much distance between my family and myself as possible. Being separated from them is agony, but it is preferable to what I almost did. I broke her trust. I would have gone against my own mate's wishes if Aquilian had not stopped me, and the thought turns my stomach.

I'm sickened by my own actions, by the fact that I let my fear control me. Aquilian was right. I should have told him everything from the very beginning. Wandering the forest aimlessly, the things I've done play over and over again in my mind and shame consumes me. I never wanted to hurt Xia. Hurting a mate is the last thing any male wants to do. My heart clenches painfully at the memory of the fear in her eyes and the way our kit looked at me. I deserve whatever punishment the Sun Father deems appropriate.

A rammit hops across the pathway in front of me before darting into the bushes. A sharp pain pierces my back, making my steps falter. The world around me grows dark, and my vision narrows as I drop to the forest floor. Just before unconsciousness consumes me, I look up to see the alien standing over me.

"You just couldn't listen, could you? I see I will need to intervene after all."

My whole world fades to black.

CHAPTER 11

*I*noxia

In the week since Kareen and I were abducted, so much has changed. I find that I'm able to communicate with my two aliens better and better each day, though I still can't understand them very well, and yet I still sit here wondering how I've given Ettrian the wrong idea for the second time. I have been careful to not even touch him lately so it confuses me how he could still misunderstand. He's been a nice enough guy—up until he tried forcing himself on me.

At first, he was so caring, so quick to make sure I was fed and felt wanted. Before today, I worried that something was wrong with him. He'd been sleeping more and more, becoming more distant not just with Kareen and I but also with Aquilian. The fact remains that I still like him, still find him attractive, and still wish that I knew what was going on. He'd been trying to tell me something for the last couple of days and I just couldn't understand.

"You okay, Xia?" Kareen whispers as she snuggles into my side.

"Yeah, I'm okay, sweetie. Ettrian and I just had a hard time understanding each other. That's all."

"I want to go outside," she sighs.

The guys have kept us locked away inside this tree for days, and I swear if I have to stay here any longer even I'm going to start bouncing off the walls. Being without sunlight for so long is unnatural for the two of us. I've already been coming up with a plan to get us out of this tree for at least a little while. The men leave us alone to go get food and supplies, and it isn't like we're *actually* locked up in here. While they're gone, I have been practicing "talking to the tree," as they call it. It opens further each day, and I think that I am starting to get the hang of this tree whisperer stuff.

"Soon, Kareen," I whisper back.

They assume that I tell them the truth when I say I cannot speak to the tree, and under normal circumstances, with a normal tree, I can't. These trees are different from the ones on Earth though, and I'm learning from the way they get inside my head how they communicate with it. Whatever their reasoning, they don't guard us to make sure we stay inside. This gives me time to learn, and the more I learn, the easier it becomes.

I don't have any weapons to use against animals we may come across, but I've been collecting the quills that Aquilian seems to have a bad habit of pulling out of his head. They're sharp enough that I'm confident I can defend myself and Kareen if the need arises.

Even if it is just for a few hours, I need to get out of this damned tree. I never thought I would hate nature, but right now I feel pretty resentful. Hours pass and still, Ettrian hasn't come back. I know it's been too long when even Aquilian starts to become antsy. I can't help but feel affection for him as he crouches down to where Kareen and I sit and cups my face, pressing his lips to mine the same way I did to him before bed a couple of nights ago.

"Stay." His voice is like silk in my mind, and I find myself almost wishing to hear him out loud, but it's become clear to me over the last week that Aquilian is deaf. This seems to be his only form of communication, and I would never ask him to be anything but himself.

"Now?" Kareen asks as the tree closes behind him.

"Just a little bit longer. Let him get far enough away that he can't stop us."

After a moment, I get up cautiously. I'm not sure where we will go, but I know that we need to be in the sun and feel the cool breeze against our skin. I worry a little. What if they return and find us outside and Aquilian feels betrayed? What if he's so angry he casts me out like he did Ettrian? I shake the thought out of my mind, knowing that he wouldn't do that over something like this. Once a little time has passed, I grab Kareen's hand and nod my head. "Let's go."

Time to get out of here for a little bit. Fear nearly consumes me, but I push past it. What if some alien animal attacks us and I can't get the tree open in time? What if whatever abducted me and Kareen comes back? *Everything is going to be okay*, I tell myself as I try to calm myself down. If I stay inside, I'm going to go crazy. I'll never know if I can do this if I don't at least try.

I move to the front of the tree where the guys always open it and lay a palm against the smooth bark. There's a slight hum that moves through me, and I think as hard as I can, picturing it opening in my mind. The clearer I picture it, the more the tree responds before it opens fully and exposes the world outside. It's almost dusk as I step into the fresh air, Kareen following excitedly behind me. Leaves crunch beneath my feet and sounds of the local wildlife fill the air around us.

"I thought I would never see outside again!" Kareen shouts dramatically as she begins to run around the trees.

"Try not to go too far!" I shout after her, laughing when she bends down and grabs a bunch of the fallen purple leaves before throwing them in the air.

Clutching one of Aquilian's quills, I scan the forest around her to make sure there's nothing dangerous as I follow close behind. Giggles fill the air as she dances around another tree, and then another as if she hadn't a care in the world. I watch as she bends over to grab a flower and quickly scold her.

"Don't touch that! You don't know if it's safe. Some of the most harmless-looking plants could be deadly, Kareen!"

"Sorry, Xia." Her lower lip juts out and I feel awful for over-reacting, but Bunnyfly—her rabbit-looking pet—soon has her attention, and she chases it through the bushes as if nothing has happened at all.

I tilt my face up toward the sky and let the warmth of the last rays of sun, or what passes for it on this planet, caress my skin as it filters down through the leaves of the strange, twisted trees, sighing in pleasure. This is exactly what we needed. The world that surrounds me is even more amazing in the waning daylight. The plants here are unlike anything I have ever seen before, and honestly, the gardener inside of me is screaming with joy. The only thing missing is my mother's soft hand on mine as she shows me how to care for each new plant. I'm still holding out hope that my alien roommates might have some sort of technology to get us off this planet. I wish I could ask them why they took us, but we're not exactly there yet. Only a few words have been trans-lated between us so far, but I hope that soon we'll learn how to communicate better. Until then, I have Kareen to talk to.

The silence is suddenly overwhelming, and I realize I no longer hear her or Bunnyfly. *Where did she go?* My heart pounds in my chest, my stomach dropping as my panic rises. I shouldn't have let her go off on her own! I know better than to let a child do that. What in the world is wrong with me? The week of screaming, tantrums, and throwing objects at the tree must have gotten to me. Sure, I wished for a little peace and quiet, but now I'm terrified at what the silence means.

"Kareen?" I call, hoping she's close by and just playing with me. "Come out, baby! It isn't the time to play hide and seek."

A loud rattle fills my ears, and I take off running around the tree so fast that I nearly trip over a root. What if she's been caught by the alien version of a cougar? Or a wolf? Or a rattlesnake? Terrifying scenarios I never even knew existed before I was put in charge of a six-year-old on some other planet play through my mind. I clutch Aquilian's quill tight in my hand ready to defend my little girl. There's so much more to being a mom than I ever imagined.

I clear a small bush and stop dead in my tracks at the sight before me. There's a tall male who looks similar to Aquilian, the only difference being that he has a base forest green color rather than the darker gray-blue of my guy. His partner is much brighter and covered in neons, much like Ettrian. The darker male is holding Bunnyfly out to Kareen as she cautiously steps toward him, arms outstretched.

"No!" Both males look up at the sound of my voice. "Kareen! Stop!"

The way they respond makes me think they, like Ettrian, are able to hear, and I wonder absently if Aquilian being deaf is uncommon. Right now, I'm more focused on the fact that these two strangers are way too close to my little girl. *This must be what people mean when they say 'going mama bear.'* I insert myself between Kareen and the males, hoping my sneer looks ferocious enough to keep them back. Bunnyfly is putting up a decent struggle and I reach out and snatch the little beast away from the dark one just as it sinks its sharp teeth into the male's hand. The quill I brandish like a knife only trembles slightly.

Good job, Bunnyfly!

"Female—" the lighter one begins, but I take hold of Kareen's hand and make a break for our home, Bunnyfly clutched tightly against my chest.

I don't trust anyone other than my males.

"Xia, I'm s—"

"Not right now, Kareen," I tell her, ushering her back to the tree.

We should have stayed put like we were told. My mind is reaching out for the tree to open as soon as it's within my sight, and I'm practically shoving her through the opening the moment we get to it. *Close!* It snaps shut quicker than I thought it could and I crouch down in front of Kareen.

"Are you okay? Did they hurt you?" I rub my hands over her hair and cup her cheeks.

"No, they were really nice to me. I found this flower that reminds me of the one you showed me at the greenhouse… They said it was safe to pick."

I look down at the flower she holds out to me. She's right. It looks a lot like the hibiscus plants I told her about the last time she came to visit me at work. We talked about how much I loved the tea that's made with them. Hibiscus normally don't have a rainbow of colors on their petals though.

"You're right. It does look like a hibiscus," I tell her.

Even though I want to scold her, I also don't want to make her scared. Her moods have already been up and down after everything she's dealt with since coming here.

"So we can make your tea and you can be calm?" She looks so pleased that my heart melts. It's so sweet that she was thinking of me.

Sighing, I take the bloom from her little fingers and place it on the counter. "I know they said this is safe, but it's better if we wait for Aquilian or Ettrian to come back so we can ask them. Or maybe I'll try first and see for myself."

"Okay, Miss Xia."

"Let's get you and Bunnyfly the Brave some water."

CHAPTER 12

*I*noxia

It isn't until after I get Kareen down for bed that I realize we have nothing left in the tree for her to eat. I need to go back out and see what I can find nearby. With a little bit of luck, she'll stay asleep while I get us something. Bunnyfly is curled up on her chest and I tiptoe past them. I don't want to risk taking her out again, not when I know that there are two strange males waiting somewhere in the forest. I was able to get her to snack on some of the roots that our guys showed us were edible to fill her tummy for now.

Opening my mind to the tree, I ask it to allow me out. I'm thankful Kareen doesn't know how to do this yet and that there isn't anything she can get into trouble with inside if she wakes before I come back. Focusing on staying aware of my surroundings, I close the tree and move out into the darkness. Everything looks different at night, but no less beautiful. I don't know if the males followed us back here, but to be safe I don't want to go too far out.

"I'll get some roots and some of the insects and be right back," I mumble to myself, trying to chase away my fear.

A shudder works its way through me at the thought of eating those giant bugs, but at least Kareen likes them and it's got to be a good source of protein. I'm so thankful that Aquilian weaved some shoes for my feet. Without them, moving over the forest floor wouldn't be too comfortable. The sound of something snapping to my left has my head whipping around so fast that I feel a pain zing through my neck. It feels like I'm being watched, but I see nothing in the vegetation around me.

Where are you guys?

I turn away from the direction of the sound and nearly trip over the large leaf on the ground. The blue fruit Aquilian and Ettrian collect for us is sitting on top of it. Maybe one of them made it back and left this for me to find. I bite my lip and wonder if I should take the offering, but my stomach growls and I know I can't let Kareen go hungry. If it stays out here any longer, it may get snatched up by the other animals prowling around out here.

I hurry back through the forest toward the tree. With this much fruit, we should be fine until lunch tomorrow. The moment I'm inside, I deposit my bounty and run to the room Kareen and I share to make sure she's still tucked in and safe. The tightness in my chest begins to subside, and I release the breath I hadn't realized I was holding in until I saw her still curled up with Bunnyfly. I tuck a tiny blonde ringlet behind her ear as I watch her sleep.

Admittedly, I had initially been terrified of being responsible for the welfare of a child. When I started the process to adopt her, it had been with the knowledge I wouldn't be in it alone, and I definitely wouldn't be trying to protect her from an alien world. She's exactly what I've needed. Kareen has taken one of the worst situations of my life and made it seem not so bad. I could be married to Trent, so there are worse things.

Jerking up in the sling, I rub the sleep from my eyes and I realize the tree is literally shaking. It reminds me so much of the unpredictable weather back home, of the severe storms that started after the war ended, that I shoot up from my sling in alarm. The weather on Earth is dangerous, and some people are even talking about how they believe it will force humanity to move to a different planet or perhaps even under Earth's oceans pretty soon.

Not too long ago, there were scientists on the news talking about how the government had shelved research that would have aided plans for an underwater city. I'm sure they regret that right about now. I move into the main part of the tree, wringing my hands. Worry for Aquilian and Ettrian who, for some reason, are still out in the forest creates a pit in my stomach.

Another rumble vibrates through the massive tree as I open a small portion of the smooth wall so I can peek outside. I'm hoping to catch a glimpse of my males, but instead, I see the ones I ran from earlier today. They are curled in on each other not too far from our tree. Their quills are rattling so bad in the blasting winds that I actually start to feel bad for leaving them out there.

Nope. Not falling for it.

I shut the tree and turn my back to the wall. Definitely *not* going to feel bad. I stop halfway across the room and sigh heavily. *Oh, for gods' sake!* Turning around, I wrestle with myself. I don't know these guys. I have no idea if they're dangerous, and I can't risk letting them near Kareen again. Last time was too close.

At the end of the day, without Ettrian and Aquilian here, I'm the only person who can protect Kareen. The storm is raging outside the tree, but the only thing that matters—the only person I should care about—is safe and sound in our room.

I run my hands through my hair, tugging at the strands as I turn back toward the kitchen to snag a cup of water. A sudden gust of wind and rain slash at my body, and I whip around in confusion. "What the hell—" I scramble away from the entrance that's opened up, gaping in horror as two massive figures barge into the room. "*Hey!*"

"Female—" one of them starts as he rushes out of the storm.

"Get out! You can't be in here." *Oh, great argument there.* I reach behind me for Aquilian's quill, pointing it at them in what I hope seems like a threat. The tree closes behind them, blocking out the storm, and I watch as two pairs of eyes flash pink as they fall on me. I've caught glimpses of the color before in Ettrian and Aquilian's gazes, but I haven't figured out the meaning yet. "Out. Both of you."

"We ask for shelter from the storm," the dark one grumbles. "We may not be as delicate as you, but the rain still stings our skin."

My eyes skim over his body, noting the tiny raised bumps. I don't suppose I actually have a choice in this. I'm one woman armed with a quill against two giant aliens, each with a head full of equally deadly weapons. "You'll stay on *that* side of the room, you hear?"

"Your generosity is appreciated, female," the light one says, nodding his head toward me as he sidesteps to the corner farthest from the hall where I stand guard.

"No funny business from either one of you or I start poking out eyeballs." I sit down in the middle of the floor, my back to the hallway as I keep a careful eye on my unwelcome guests.

Long minutes drag by, turning into even longer hours. The two males hardly move. Their backs are pressed up against the wall, and they sit with their eyes closed as if they are sleeping, but I can feel them watching me every time I adjust my position. Now that I'm getting a better look at them, I realize there are a lot of differences between my guys and these strangers. Mr. Green Bean has gold in all the places that Aquilian is purple, and his quills are solid black. The one I thought looked similar to Ettrian has a base color of baby blue and his stripes are gold instead of crimson. When I look at his head, I see that he has white quills.

Exhaustion is tugging at my eyelids, but there's no way I can fall asleep now. *Maybe it's time to brew that tea.* The bloom Kareen found for me earlier is sitting on the counter, its pretty petals creased from her death grip as we ran. I pick it up, pursing my lips as I consider the males.

"You said this is safe, right? That's what you told my kid when you let her pick it?"

"It's used to aid in relaxation among our people. A calming brew," the dark male, or Mr. Green Bean as my brain has deemed him, tells me.

I've been able to eat and drink everything offered to me on this planet so far, even the things I never ever want to eat again. *Looking at you, giant pill bug.* I can't imagine brewing this would be any different, and with the way my anxiety is beginning to mount, I could use something calming.

After an embarrassing minute of jerking on the nozzle in an unintentionally suggestive way, I fill one of the clay cups with water, trying not to notice as their eyes follow me. I place the bloom into the water and watch as it spins on the surface before it dawns on me that this kitchen has no stove. *Well, shit.* Where had Aquilian touched to open the oven thing? After a few minutes of rubbing my hands along the wall with no luck, I turn and glance sideways at the males, who are still watching me intently.

"Do either of you know how to heat this up?"

The lighter male stands and walks toward me. I feel every hair on my body stand on end as he gets closer. These guys, like my aliens, are at least eight or nine feet tall and tower over my five-foot-six frame. Intimidating doesn't quite describe the feeling I get. He extends a long arm and rubs his hand along a spot on the tree I *swear* I just touched and watch as a pocket opens. He plucks the cup from my hands and sets it down inside the wall before running his hand along the seam to close it again.

"Thanks."

He just nods and takes a step back, but he doesn't return to his spot beside the other guy. I place my palm over the pocket and feel the warmth it's creating. I have no idea how this tree operates, but it's amazing.

The pocket pops open with a hiss, making me jump as the steam rises out of it. The lighter guy, aka Mr. Neon, rattles in a rhythm I've come to understand, thanks to Ettrian, is humor. He reaches into the wall and lifts the cup out, setting it gently on the counter in front of me.

"Be careful." His voice is soft, and it occurs to me that these are the only people, aside from Kareen, who've spoken out loud to me since I woke up on this planet. Even Ettrian only speaks to me within my mind.

I wrap my hands around the clay and realize it's not hot at all, just pleasantly warm. There is steam rising from the surface of the tea so I blow on it a couple of times before taking a tentative sip, moaning quietly as the liquid plays over my tongue and rushes down my throat. This may be the most delicious thing I've ever tasted in my entire life and I take another longer swig.

"Oh my gods," I sigh, clutching the cup to my chest. "Thank you so much. This is amazing."

Mr. Neon nods at me and turns around, walking back to Mr. Green Bean, and takes a seat on the floor. I fidget with the rim of the clay cup and wonder what I should do now. Kareen is sleeping, and as much as I would love to join her, I can't just give these two free run of our home. It shocks me that I think of it as our home, but that's what this tree has become to me. I slowly move back to the hallway so that my body is between the strangers and Kareen again. They seem to be able to communicate far better than Aquilian and Ettrian, so maybe I can get a few answers while I wait for my males to get back. "Well, I guess we could start with names." I take another sip. *Gods, this is good.* Warmth spreads through my chest as I settle my palm over my heart. "I'm Inoxia."

"I am Yssig, and this is my twin brother, Doxal." He gestures toward the darker male, who nods at me.

"Nice to meet you." I watch as their eyes change to a soft pink, the same way I've seen my guys' do. "I'm sorry if it's against some social norm to ask, but what's with the color-changing eyes?"

"The colors represent different emotions," Doxal speaks up first. "Dauur do not express with their faces like your kind seems to do."

Although we were still having problems understanding one another, Ettrian had been able to explain that much to me. It was clear that my facial expressions often confused them, especially smiling. "Who or what is Dauur?"

Yssig tilts his head, and contrary to Doxal's claim about not showing emotion, his brows draw together in a frown. "We are Dauur. They are the people of this planet, Dimosia."

"Ah." I take another sip and I can feel each of my muscles, from my head down to my toes, go loose as my body heats up. My lips curve into a silly grin all on their own, and I hear myself laughing. *What's wrong with me?* I straighten my face and try to remember the other things I've been curious about. "One of the males who live here, Aquilian, he's deaf, I think. He only speaks to me in my mind." I frown into my tea. "Well, Ettrian only speaks in my mind too, but I know he can hear me."

"Dauur are not born with hearing. We feel vibrations along our ilo that allow us to identify movement in our surroundings, but we communicate through the bond we share with everything in our world. I assume this is what you are hearing in your mind," Yssig explains.

"If you aren't born with hearing, how are Ettrian and the two of you able to hear me?"

Doxal reaches a hand up to the side of his head and caresses the small hole there, and I realize it's nearly identical to the two that Ettrian sports. "We were given a *gift*." He practically spits the word. "The aliens who took us created these wounds that enabled us to hear the way they do."

Yssig rattles next to him, his eyes turning red. "It was extremely painful in the beginning. The noises around us were loud and confusing, and it took us many days before we could start forming words with our mouths."

I feel a painful tug at my heart. Poor Ettrian was probably still in the first stage of learning to cope with hearing. That would explain all the times he snuck away when Kareen cried or got too loud. I'd mistaken it for him just not wanting to deal with her or finding her annoying, but now I see that it may have been physically painful for him to be around her during those moments. "Who did this to you?"

"They called themselves Tachin. We were not familiar with their species before we were taken," Doxal tells me.

Yssig nods. "It sounds as if one of the males here was also altered by them before being placed with you. I do not know why they left the other untouched."

My mind is starting to feel foggy, and my body is so heated that I'm tempted to start stripping off my dress despite my strange company. I take another drink, hoping the tea will help, but it only seems worse once I swallow it. I look down into the cup where the bloom has settled to the bottom and frown. *What the fuck? Is it the tea?* I know they said it would relax me, but I didn't expect to feel drunk. My eyes narrow slightly and I feel my whole body sway. *This is not good!* My mind is screaming at me that this was a stupid idea. My face blanches as I glance toward the strangers. There was no way he could have slipped anything in there with me watching him like a hawk while he prepared it, right?

I screwed up not waiting on my guys to come home and assure the bloom was safe.

I don't even notice when the two males stand and walk over to me; I'm far too caught up in my panic until I feel a hand on my shoulder. It's gentle and oh so cool against my burning skin and I hear myself moan hoarsely. *Nope! No, no, no, no.* My eyes shoot wide open and I stumble backward, but my legs are unsteady and instead of carrying me away, I feel myself crumble to the floor.

"Calm down," one of them—I think Yssig—hisses.

Large hands pull at my arms and I start to struggle against him, but my body is a traitorous bitch and I feel need wash through me as I'm pulled up against a hard chest. "Let me go!" Another moan escapes me, and I bite down hard on my bottom lip. *Damn me!*

"We are not trying to hurt you, Inoxia. Stop fighting and let us help you. Something is wrong. The tea should not affect you this way." The voice is right next to my ear and I feel a shiver run through me. My mind flashes back to all the times Ettrian has held me, all the times he's breathed softly against my skin, or the way Aquilian presses his head to mine before he places the softest kiss on my lips.

"Please," I plead pathetically as I arch into him. I want *my* aliens, not these two. "I need…" My voice trails off and I hear two sets of quills rattling around me. I feel helpless, weak, needy, and I'm terrified. I'm scared they don't understand me, that they will take advantage of this situation. Tears fall down my cheeks as a hand caresses my face and I feel my fear choke me, even as my body thrills at the contact.

How did I let this happen? How could I have put not just myself but Kareen in so much danger? I had only wanted to calm my nerves, to keep myself from descending into panic. As I'm pulled tighter into the alien's arms, I pray to any gods that might be listening to keep my little girl safe, to allow her to sleep through whatever might happen to me.

CHAPTER 13

*E*ttrian
A few hours earlier...

There is an overwhelming pounding, piercing pain inside my head as I slowly regain consciousness. Groaning, I try to turn my head, but I find that I'm unable to move it. Panic shoots through me as I try to adjust my arms and legs. My eyes snap open and I glance frantically around the familiar metal room. "Ah, there you are."

The voice makes my stomach twist anxiously and I jerk even harder against the bonds. *"You lied! You told me I had more time! I still have three weeks!"*

A chilling laugh fills the room. "I did indeed tell you I would give you more time, but we found you running from the female like a coward. The tests we ran on her indicated she is within her most fertile period now."

My lips pull back over my teeth at the insult. *"You expect me to do something unspeakable to the female! I could have hurt her!"*

"You Dauur and your misplaced sense of chivalry," he chides. "I gave you a chance."

The panic is all-consuming as I realize what he will do to Kareen. I have to find a way to delay this. *"Wait! You did not give me a fair chance!"*

There is silence for a moment before he speaks again. "Not fair? I place you and your twin in an enclosure with a fertile female and this isn't considered fair? Explain."

"Dauur cannot reproduce like this. We..." Think, dammit. *"We need to communicate our desire to mate. In a way the female can understand."* I'm grasping desperately for anything that will give me more time. *"The device you gave me does not work properly. She does not understand us and will not permit us to mate with her."*

More silence. A moment later, the door to my right slides open and the bastard himself walks in, followed closely by another of his species. "We will check the device. If it is defective, I will allow you more time. If we find no fault in it, we will bring in the kit and she will die for your lies." He gestures for the alien behind him to come forward and takes the device from its shaking hands.

I pray fervently to the Sun Father, begging him to intervene, to do something to protect Xia and our kit. The alien presses something on the device before he waves it over my head, brushing the holes they created the last time I was here. His large eyes narrow and he growls, slamming the tool into the chest of the creature behind him. "I give you a task and you fail!" The being stumbles back, shivering and cowering against the floor. "Fix his translator, now!"

It takes only a moment once the alien pulls himself together. There are pops and clicks inside my head; they aren't painful, just strange. The one in charge is glaring the whole time, watching every move the other one makes. When he is finally finished, he waves the device over my head again and this time there is a small chime. By the look of sheer relief in his eyes, I assume he has succeeded. Without any warning at all, there is a loud blast, and the one who had been standing in front of me jerks to the side, a massive hole in his chest as he falls lifelessly to the floor.

I stare at his corpse as black liquid gushes from the open wound.

"Thanks to his error, you will be given four days. However…" The green alien puts his weapon back on his hip. The door slides open again, and three similar-looking aliens walk in, two of them grabbing the corpse and dragging it from the room while the third comes to a stop at my side. "The game has changed for you and your brother." My stomach sinks. This was never a game for me, or Aquilian. "Two other males were released into the dome a moment ago. I assure you it will not take long for them to seek the female out and complete the task you could not."

Rage surges inside of me, and I fight against the bonds. *"NO!"* The alien's lips curl at the sides.

"*If* you and your brother can keep her for yourselves, you may take the four days. If not, the other males will be given your time and I will take the kit as promised."

Before I can even respond, the room around me spins so much that I feel my stomach rise. My eyes slam shut, and when I open them again, we're back in the forest. My feet are on the ground and I'm no longer strapped in place. The alien I assume is in charge jerks his head to the one at my side.

"You will be escorted back and watched closely. Do not mistake this extension for kindness, Dauur." He disappears in the next moment, and I turn to the one who has been left with me. I don't want him anywhere near my home or my family.

A significant amount of time has passed since I left the tree, at least a few hours. I have no idea how long it will take the other males to find Aquilian and Xia, but I need to deal with one threat at a time.

"Move, Dauur," the alien hisses.

"This way." I have a plan, but I'm not sure if it's smart or completely insane.

~

 he alien stumbles behind me for the hundredth time in the hour or so that we've been walking, and I laugh in my mind as he curses. He grumbles again and then shoves at my back. "Where are we going? We should have been at our destination by now."

My head jerks to our left. *"We just have to make it over this hill and the tree will be visible."* He growls again but nods and waves at me to continue.

They know we are coming. Like the Dauur, the nolfira rely on the vibrations around them to hunt and to be able to sense when something is drawing near. With the way the alien behind me is stomping through the underbrush, the nolfira clan has probably been on alert for some time. I slow my steps, allowing him to catch up to me. All around me I can feel the shift in the forest. The smaller animals will not come anywhere near here knowing there's a nest. It is quiet, but my ilo picks up the subtle vibrations of the large predators that stalk us through the trees. *"Almost there."*

We make it to the top of the hill, and I know the moment has come. As the alien comes up next to me, I round on him, grabbing his arm and twisting it behind him. Unlike his leader, he has no invisible wall to protect himself from my attack. He tries to grab onto me with his other hand, but I yank hard on the delicate wings on his back, throwing him off his center and making him flail wildly as he tries to right himself.

Taking advantage of this, I shove as hard as I can, propelling him down the incline. There's a heavy thud when he lands at the bottom, and I scramble to get to higher ground. A muffled buzz rolls up from his throat as he begins to push himself up, but a loud growl drowns him out, fear dominating his face as the massive female nolfira emerges from the nest in front of him. She is guarding pups and he is an intruder.

The alien's eyes go wide in alarm, and he lets out a piercing scream as he tries frantically to get to his feet. There was never a chance for him, though. Nolfira are fierce in the very best of circumstances, and with pups to protect, this female will not allow him to escape.

I turn away as she grabs him in her strong jaws and begins to tear him apart, hoping this will keep the clan busy so that I might make a dash for the tree, but I know I've made a major miscalculation when I come face to face with one of the clans younger males.

Curse the Sun Father!

Baring my teeth, I rattle my quills in a display of dominance, but this male is young and yearns to prove himself to his clan. He will not back down so easily. I curse. With no weapons on me aside from my quills and no one to aid me, the need to think quickly about how to get myself out of this is apparent.

The nolfira lunges for me and I drop to the ground so that it sails over my head, snapping its jaws with a loud crack. Flipping over, I kick up, driving the sharp horn on my calf into its soft belly. It hardly makes a scratch on the beast, but it stuns him enough that I'm able to jump to my feet and get some distance between us before he takes off after me. There is loud crashing behind me as the nolfira tramples bushes and downed branches. I dodge trees and rocks, trying to evade him, but he's fast. I'm forced to a sudden stop when he cuts in front of me, his fangs bared as he pants, eyes gleaming with something that looks like victory. He thinks he's won, but I'm not giving up that easily.

Yanking two quills from the back of my head, I hold them like daggers and square off against my opponent. Again, he lunges for me, and this time I'm not fast enough. His front paws slam into my chest, and I find myself pinned beneath him on the ground. His claws dig into my skin and his weight knocks the breath from my lungs.

Sorry, but I have no plans to die today.

I swing both of my arms as hard as I can, burying my quills into the sides of his neck, and yank down, opening bigger wounds. The shrill screech that erupts from it makes me wish, not for the first time, that I was not gifted with the ability to hear. I take a deep breath as he jerks backward and the weight is lifted from me, but I cannot seem to get up fast enough.

Before I know it, he has me clamped in his mouth and flings me across the small clearing we stumbled into. Pain shoots through my whole body as I connect with a tree and land in a heap on the ground. I've broken something—I know it. Strong jaws close around me again, and I'm flung against one of the large boulders along the edge of the clearing.

This time, I cannot even attempt to rise. My body hurts all over, and a groan slips past my lips when I open my eyes and see the nolfira watching me. It knows it has won, that I am exactly where it wants me. My eyes are heavy as they droop shut and I conjure up an image of Aquilian mending the basket, Xia next to him as she watches intently and Kareen sitting in the corner with her rammit in her lap. The last thing I want to see before I'm eaten is my family, not the nolfira as it paces toward me. I am making peace with my death when the sound of a sharp, angry screech comes from the beast and frenzied rattling surrounds me.

Someone has come to my aid by the sounds of it, but I cannot seem to force my eyes back open. The sounds of the fight barely reach me as the darkness threatens to pull me under, my body is going numb. Someone or something is moving me, shaking me. A voice is in my head, but I cannot make out who it belongs to.

"Ettrian!" is the last thing that reaches me along the bond before I am pulled under.

CHAPTER 14

*a*quilian

"Get out."

The look on my twin's face as I walked away from him with our mate in my arms and our kit at my side had hurt me more than I cared to think about. I had been furious at what I saw him doing, and after he showed me exactly what those aliens who had mutilated him wanted him to do to Xia, I lost my temper. Why had he not told me the moment he had found us in the forest? Or even after he realized she was our fated?

Although I know my twin did not mean to hurt her, the thought of what he had looked close to doing to Xia is still unbelievable. Spending my whole day looking for him wasn't something I had planned to do, and the nagging memories I had to endure weren't helping my mood. They pushed in on me when I was alone, bringing back some of the most humiliating moments of my life. They overwhelmed me and reminded me that I did not deserve Xia. No matter how much I told myself she was meant for me, that the Sun Father himself had brought her to us, my brain refused to see it. One of the worst of these memories had taken place not too long ago, and the wound it had created inside me was still fresh.

*S*torming out of Safia's den, I ignore her cries for me to come back.

"Let me explain!"

It does not matter that she is the only one who has ever touched me, that she allowed me to be with her when no other female would even look at me. What she said in there is the only thing that matters at the moment. She moaned Ettrian's name at the moment of her pleasure, while I was still inside her, still chasing my own release. It stopped me dead to hear it roll through her mind along the bond, to know that she was thinking of him while we were together.

"Please, Aquilian, hear me out!" she begs as she follows closely on my heels.

"No, he is always the first choice. I am not desirable." my quills rattle with irritation. "Did you mate with me out of pity?"

"It is not what you think!" I don't need to see her face to know she is not being truthful.

"Is it not?" My emotions are overflowing as I turn to face her, sure that my eyes are blue instead of the red she expected. "What is it then?"

"I... I cannot tell you. I swore an oath." Her eyes shift down to her feet.

"I do not want any more of your lies, Safia. You were with my brother before you sought me out?" There is guilt in her eyes. She nods softly, and that is all I need to know.

Leaving her where she stands, I make my way deep into the forest to work through my jealousy. The fact that I should never be jealous of my bondmate crosses my mind more than once, but I cannot seem to help it. He has never been subjected to the same rejection, never had his hopes crushed in the ways that I have. It is not fair.

"Life is rarely, if ever, fair, Aquilian."

I can still hear Papa Ekaz tell me as I shake the memory from my mind. He's right, but that does not mean I have to like it.

It took me some time to come to terms with the fact that Ettrian had been with Safia first, although I am not sure why I was ever surprised. He had always been popular among the females, despite the fact that he was a twin. Even so, I would have been willing to work past the jealousy had she accepted us, taken us both as her mates, and ended my uncertainty. Surely, if she had taken us both into her bed, she would not be against the idea of taking us on as mates.

A sense of relief fills me when I think about how she refused to accept my offer right away. If she had not sent me out here to find the bloom, I would never have found Xia and Kareen. There would have forever been a gaping hole in my soul where the two of them were meant to be. Only the Sun Father knows what would have happened to them out in the wild if we had not found them.

Turning back to the tree, our mate crosses my mind as dusk approaches, but then the worst kind of vibration works its way through my ilo. I know that vibration. Any Dauur would recognize it immediately since we are taught from a young age how to differentiate them.

Darting through the trees, I reach out with my natural bond, trying to get a feel for all the creatures that are in the area. *There.* Ettrian's presence is fading. Worry shoots through me, causing me to nearly fly across the ground in my bid to get to him. As much as we disagree and fight, as much as I hate that he is so easily accepted when I am not, he is a part of me I never wish to have taken away. I cannot lose him; I will not lose him.

Pain laces my throat as I open my mouth and try to make the sound little Kareen makes when she is angry, though I fear it is not as fierce. My quills rattle hard as I swing my leg at the creature, sinking my horn into the soft skin at its nape. The loss of the young male's life, while unfortunate, is of no concern to me. There will be others born to replace him, but no one can ever replace my twin. That thought is as freeing as it is terrifying.

The Nolfira still has fight in him, I realize, as he swipes at my free leg, knocking me to the ground. This doesn't stop me as I yank a quill from atop my head and stab it into his eye as he lunges. The beast twitches for a moment before going still, its dead weight falling over me, making it hard to breathe. I shove its body off of me, not worried about the blood that soaks my skin. My legs propel me across the space to my fallen twin. Ettrian's wounds are seeping violet blood all over the forest floor. My ilo squirms with distress as I stumble to him.

"Ettrian?" I touch his face and then his shoulders, shaking him gently.

There is no response from him, and his body goes slack as I call out for him to wake. We cannot stay here. The other members of the nolfira clan will seek the young male out soon, and if we are found anywhere near him, they will finish us off.

Hefting his weight onto my back is a difficult task, but I eventually manage. I move in the direction of the tree, careful to keep my balance as I make my way. My eyes are also peeled for the cinsi bloom, the same one I was supposed to retrieve for Safia. It will not heal him, but if she was telling the truth, it will help to ease his pain.

All that really matters right now, however, is that I stop the bleeding. I can feel it dripping down my back and it fuels my anxiety. If we can make it back to the tree and get him into the seed pod, it will help with regeneration, healing him far faster than he would be able to on his own. The longer it takes me to get him back, the less likely he is to survive, and I refuse to think about that.

As luck would have it, I happen upon an elder tree and snatch a couple leaves from its branches. I lay Ettrian down gently and press the leaves to his wounds and send up a prayer to the Sun Father that they staunch the bleeding until we make it home. We have both been injured before on hunts, but neither of us has ever had to deal with wounds this bad before.

"I will not let you die!" I whisper along the bond as my emotions threaten to overwhelm me. The sky above us seems to reflect them and rain begins to pour down from the dark, swollen clouds. A clap of thunder rolls over my senses as lightning zigzags through the darkness. The storms here often come out of nowhere. Ettrian and I have been caught many times in them, but never so far from shelter.

Wind assaults my body, pushing and destabilizing me as I try to pull Ettrian onto my back again. *We're not going to make it tonight,* I finally concede. We will have to wait out the worst of it and try again. *"If the Sun Father wills it, it will be."* I can hear Mama's voice in my mind, and a mixture of fear and disgust turns my stomach.

I will not allow him to take my brother. I will fight his will tooth and quill if that is to be Ettrian's fate. The Sun Father took Yssa from her mates, but I will not allow him to take Ettrian from Xia and Kareen. He is needed *here*. A large fungus up ahead catches my attention and I rush forward. We can take shelter beneath its top where it will at least keep the rain from soaking us to the bone and I can tend to Ettrian properly. Memories of my mother dominate my thoughts as I tend to my twin.

. . .

"*A*quilian?" *Mama's voice is gentle through the bond, but I pretend that I can ignore her as I curl up tighter in my sling. I feel her hands lightly caress my quills and she hums to me. "Have you been plucking these again?" she asks gently.*

"No," I lie even though I know she cannot be fooled. Many of my quills are missing, more than is necessary for hunting, and no amount of lying can cover that up. They will grow back as they always do, but the open wounds are uncomfortable and I know it worries her.

Mama tsks. "You are going to pull them all out soon."

"What does it matter? Quills or no quills, I will always be passed over."

I feel her perch on the side of the sling, tipping it to one side so that I roll to face her. "Why would you think that?"

"Why?" I shoot up, rattling the quills I have not yet yanked out of my head. "Look at me!"

"I am looking at you and I see no reason you should be passed over."

"You are my mama. You are not supposed to see it," I grumble, and she vibrates her quills with her humor softly.

"That is true. Kits are perfect in the eyes of their parents." Her eyes flash blue briefly before settling back to black. "The ones who will matter the most in your life will not care about your coloring, Aquilian. Until you find a female who can look past what the others cannot, you have the love of your parents and the unending loyalty of your brother." I look away at the mention of Ettrian. He is once again the cause of my bad mood. "You may not see it right now, but your brother is your greatest supporter. He'll always be by your side on your journey."

. . .

*H*er words ring through my mind, and I look down at Ettrian where he rests on the ground. His wounds have already begun to heal, but they still require close observation. We will need the assistance of the pod to completely mend his body. As time goes by, the storm slows and I decide I can make a run for it. With Ettrian thrown over my shoulder, I wait for the next flash of lightning and then bolt from under the protection of the fungus' top. Rain pelts us still, but the wind has calmed and it makes my journey a little easier.

The tree appears before me, looming over the forest around it and I have never been so relieved to see one of the giants in my entire life. My muscles strain under my twin's weight, legs shaking as I force them to move across the distance.

"Open!" I tell the tree, but nothing happens. *"Sun Father curse it all, open!"*

Slowly, the bark begins to separate, parting for me as I rush through into the main room. Ettrian slides from my shoulder as I stumble across the threshold. A flash of red that I have come to associate with my mate is the first thing I glimpse, and it's a more than welcome sight. I turn toward her and feel my lungs seize in my chest as my eyes fix upon her. She is in the arms of another Dauur male, her legs wrapped around his torso, hands gripping his quills, while his bondmate stands at her back. A murderous, possessive rage consumes me, and I feel my quills rise and rattle out a challenge.

CHAPTER 15

*I*noxia

"What do you need, Inoxia?" Doxal asks me, his rough voice sending shivers up my spine.

The question is simple, but I can't seem to find the right answer. Instead, I wrap my legs tighter around him and bury my hands into his crest of quills. My mind is full of images of Aquilian, of how he touches me and the way his eyes light up when he's close.

I press my lips firmly against the ones in front of me and gyrate my hips, grinding against Doxal's body. *Yes!* I think as pleasure surges through me, radiating out from my core. Vibrations flow through my fingers as his quills begin to rattle and it pulls a moan from deep in my chest. A pair of hands take hold of me and try to pull me away, but I latch onto Doxal with all my strength.

"Inoxia, you are not in control of yourself," Yssig tries to tell me, but that's a stupid statement. I know I am not in control. I would never *choose* to do this with a man I didn't know if I was in my right mind. I would have stopped just like I did with Ettrian.

A hand runs from my hip and up the side of my body, making my pussy clench in anticipation. The soft touch is igniting fires in its wake and my nipples harden painfully as someone's hands brush the sides of my breasts, but instead of lingering, they move to my armpits.

My body is so, *so* hot, and I tear frantically at my dress in an attempt to get closer to the coolness of his skin, but a hand covers mine. *No problem*, I think and throw myself into the kiss, running my tongue along the tightly closed lips. He doesn't taste like Aquilian and I whimper sadly at the thought. A growl flows through the chest I'm pressed against, and I feel a hand grip the hair at the back of my head tightly. Instead of deepening the kiss like I'm anticipating, I'm yanked backward.

No! I need this!

"Inoxia, stop! I will not allow this while you cannot make the choice for yourself!" Doxal and his stupid logic. "We were sent here to breed you, but I will not do it this way."

That stops me in my tracks. I lean back in his embrace, my eyes searching his as he holds me against him, one hand still clutched in my curls.

"You were sent to do *what*?" The fire in my core diminishes some but doesn't quite go out.

"Breed you," Yssig answers. "If we do not do as they say, the aliens will kill our sister. She is your kit's age."

Goosebumps rise all along my skin as a cold breeze rushes into the room. We all spin toward the massive opening in the tree, and my heart kicks hard in my chest.

My guys!

Aquilian is standing in the threshold, rain falling onto the floor at his feet as lightning flashes behind him. Instead of his usual green-eyed welcome, I'm met with a blood-red stare that sends a jolt of dread through me.

"Put my mate down." His voice is colder than the winds that whip through the forest. I'm so busy trying to breathe through my panic that I'm only vaguely aware of the fact that I can actually understand what he says.

Yssig gently pries me from Doxal, and the friction from my body sliding against his makes me moan, causing my cheeks to flush fiercely. The sight of Aquilian before me overwhelms all of my senses, and I swear I could come just from the way his gaze rakes over me. *"You choose these males over us."*

"No!" I deny the accusation vehemently, but I feel shame wash over me.

"We did not know she was mated," Doxal says apologetically as my feet touch the floor next to him. *"She is not in her right mind. It seems that the cinsi tea she brewed is having a strange effect on her. We were only trying to help."*

"Help?" His quills rattle menacingly. *"Yes, I am sure that is what I saw when I walked in."* He crouches down and pulls something along the floor, but I don't have a clear view.

"Your brother? Is he hurt?" Yssig asks.

"Ettrian!" I feel like the worst kind of person for not realizing he hadn't been standing with Aquilian. Stumbling over the floor, I grasp for my other male, clutching at his limp hand before he is pulled out of my reach. I can see the males moving forward out of the corner of my eye, but Aquilian rattles his quills in a manner I've only heard once. When Ettrian attacked me.

"Back off."

"We are just trying to help," Doxal tells him.

"Why are you here?" Aquilian asks, his eyes roaming over me.

I can feel myself sobering under his gaze and look away, shame washing over me at what he must have seen when he walked in.

"We were sent here by the aliens," Doxal answers.

"Why? For what purpose?"

Doxal's head tilts as if he is confused. *"To do what your brother was not strong enough to do."*

I don't miss the look he throws my way, and from the sound of Aquilian's quills, I know he hasn't missed it either. I turn to watch him as he crouches down, lowering Ettrian's head to the floor of the tree a split second before he charges forward. His shoulder slams into Doxal's torso, and I watch in horror as they fall, a tangled mass of neon-colored limbs rolling across the floor of the central room. There's no sign of my shy, calm Aquilian as he lashes out at Doxal, slamming a fist into the other male's face before pinning him to the floor. The sound of their angry rattling fills the room, and I'm stunned, frozen in shock by the violence I see in my sweet male's eyes.

Yssig curses, jumping forward to wrap his arms around Aquilian's chest as he hauls him backward. *"Enough!"* he shouts.

Doxal sits up slowly, wiping the blood from his face as he catches his breath. *"I suppose I deserve that."*

"You deserve far more than a bloodied face for touching her," Aquilian says, glaring at the male as he shoves away from Yssig.

"We were not told she was mated," Yssig tells him, watching him carefully as he walks over to Ettrian, brushing his hand over his brother's cheek.

"Is he dead?" I whisper, blinking the tears from my eyes as I watch Aquilian try to lift his brother into his arms.

"No. He will live," Yssig tells me. Doxal moves forward, picking up Ettrian's legs so they don't drag along the floor. "The seed pod will hasten his healing; replenish the blood he has lost."

I scramble up as they move into the hallway, not wanting to be out of Aquilian's sight again. I know he's upset; I can feel the anger rolling off of him in waves as we enter into one of the rooms toward the back of the home. The two dark males lift Ettrian higher as a segment of the wall detaches, moving out to form a deep nook. It looks eerily like a casket, and I step up as they lay him within it, feeling the tears gather as I lay my hand over his. Aquilian nudges me back as the pod begins to seal.

"We passed cinsi blooms along a path on our way here," Doxal says. *"Yssig and I will retrieve them."*

Aquilian merely nods in acknowledgement, staring at the opposite wall as the brothers retreat. Out in the central room, I hear the front of the tree open and close with a soft woosh that tells me they have left and a shiver works down my spine.

Without a word to me, Aquilian turns, stepping out into the hallway. *"Aquilian?"* I call after him, but he ignores me.

He stops in front of the room Kareen and I use, stopping in the doorway. His body seems to relax a fraction when he sees she's sleeping, snoring softly, completely unaware of anything that has occurred tonight. Bunnyfly's head pops up over the edge of the sling, his eyes big and unblinking. The doorway begins to close, slowly blocking my view of my little girl and her companion. Once it is sealed, Aquilian marches toward the room he shares with Ettrian and I'm left to run after him, barely keeping up with his long strides.

I want him to say something, anything, and at the same time I'm terrified for him to speak. Terrified to hear what he's thinking. I stand silent as he closes off the room, trembling as I stare at his bare back. The effects of the tea have worn off completely at this point, and I cringe at the mess I've made.

"Do you remember the journey here?" he asks, still facing away from me.

My face scrunches up in confusion. *"Yes."*

"Do you remember what Ettrian did to you when you insisted on squirming in his grasp?"

My cheeks heat at the memory. *"Yes. He spanked me."*

"Disciplined you," he corrects.

"I remember it." I shift, feeling warmth spread through me, welling up in the pit of my stomach as I recall the sting and the thrill it had sent through me.

He turns, moving around me to perch himself on the edge of one of the slings. With a small crook of his finger, he beckons me forward. *"Come."*

I step into the space between his spread legs, and even with him sitting, we are face to face. A minute passes before he finally looks at me and what I see in his eyes makes my breath catch. There is obviously hurt, but there's also fear. I want nothing more than to wipe it all away, to have my brooding, sweet Aquilian back.

"I want to discipline you," I hear him say along the bond. His fingers reach out to tuck my hair behind my ear, trailing over my skin. *"Will you let me discipline you, Xia?"*

"I—" Let him spank me? My skin tingles with excitement. *Yes. Let him,* my mind encourages. *"Are you angry with me?"*

"No." His eyes close as he presses our foreheads together, rattling his quills softly. *"I am not angry with you, Xia. I would not discipline you in anger."*

"Aquilian," My hands skim up his chest to rest on his shoulders. I want this. I want him. *"Please."*

"Tell me you want to be disciplined, Xia."

I know he can't hear my moan, but rings in my ears. *"I want it."*

"Remove this." He gestures at my dress.

I'm not sure I've ever stripped for anyone before. The majority of my sexual encounters happened in the dark and were nowhere near as exciting as this already is. With my lower lip trapped between my teeth, I clutch nervously at the hem of my dress.

"If you do not remove it, I will tear it from you."

My eyes fly to his face in shock. It's not a threat. It's a promise, and it makes my heart thunder in my chest. My hand drops away from the fabric in a silent challenge.

I'm completely unprepared for the speed with which his hand shoots out toward me. The sound of the delicate fabric ripping, giving way to his long fingers, echoes in my ears, and I gasp when the cool area touches my bare skin. His gaze roams over me, skimming from my chest all the way down to my toes.

He pats the top of his thigh, and I lower my body, pressing my torso against his legs. *"Do you know why this is happening?"*

I press my lips together and nod. *"I made a mistake."*

He pulls back his arm and brings his hand down on my bare ass. *Thwack!* A yelp bursts from my lips, and my flesh burns beneath his palm.

"You left the safety of the tree." Thwack! It isn't a question; he doesn't need my answers or excuses.

"How did you kn—"

But he cuts me off. *"You put yourself and Kareen in danger." Thwack!* I moan against my hand and bite down on my bottom lip. *Holy shit, yes.* I've always been a bit of a masochist, but it's been so long since I let myself experience this. I was only able to trust Trent for a short time before he took advantage of me.

He gently rubs my heated flesh, soothing the sting. *"Invited strangers into our home." Thwack!*

"Please, Aquilian… I didn't invite the—" I say breathlessly, shifting against him, trying to relieve some of the pressure I'm feeling between my legs.

"You could have been taken from us. Both of you." Thwack!
"We could have lost you and Kareen forever." Thwack!

A groan of pleasure is ripped from me, and the slick of arousal paints my thighs as I dig my fingers into his leg. *"Again,"* I beg, and he gives it to me. Two more slaps, one right after the other land on my ass.

"Do not ever *do that again, Xia."* The cool slide of his fingers between my thighs has my breath catching in my chest.

This is what I've been waiting for, what I've needed so badly. Aquilian's middle finger brushes my folds and I whimper softly, shaking with desire. *"What about Ettrian?"*

"He is regenerating. Now that he's in the seed pod, he will be fine."

His voice is not as harsh as before, like punishing me has centered him. I never thought that I would like this sort of thing, but I find myself hoping he isn't finished with me yet. *"Aquilian?"*

"Yes, Xia?"

"I'm sorry." I feel the tears well up in my eyes and spill over my cheeks. *"I didn't mean for this all to happen."*

"Why did you let them in Xia? If I had not come back when I did, you may have been harmed." His hand soothes over my bare back and up into my hair where he fists it, tugging my head back so that I'm looking into his eyes. There's no anger there, just a calmness that speaks to every anxious part of me.

"I didn't let them in. They opened the tree on their own."

Aquilian tugs my hair, and I crane my neck even farther back to look into his face. *"You have no idea the terror I felt when I walked in and saw you with them."*

"I'm so sorry." The need he has built inside of me feels like it is overflowing, seeping from my pores. It is so different from the need the tea inspired within me. *"I need you."*

His body seems to thrum beneath me, the little bulbous tendrils that extend from his crest wiggling freely. *"I cannot give you the mating marks without the ceremony. I will not risk you. Do you accept this?"*

I'm not really sure what he means by that, but my arousal is peaking again and consumes my thoughts completely. My body feels like it's burning from the inside out.

"Yes."

The sound of my panting fills the space between us as he pulls me up from his lap and flips me onto my back inside the sling. I frown at first because I'm so far from wanting to sleep that it's almost laughable, but it vanishes the moment he climbs in with me. Aquilian wedges himself between my legs and leans down over me, drawing in a deep breath against my skin.

He reaches down between us, pressing his hand against his lower abdomen, and I jolt a little when something that I assume is his cock springs out and brushes against my thigh. I can't see much of it with how closely we're pressed together, but what I do glimpse is neon pink and glistening and it makes my mouth water. It wiggles like it's got a mind of its own, seeking out my core, and the sight both terrifies and arouses me. A finger traces over my jaw, bringing my attention back to Aquilian's face, and his glowing pink gaze bores into mine.

"I will not hurt you," his voice caresses my mind.

With tender care, his hand wraps around the column of my throat, squeezing the sides with just enough pressure to have me arching beneath him. His head tilts in question as he watches me for my reaction. *"Yes!"* My whole body trembles as his free hand spreads open my slick folds and his twitching cock prods at my opening. A finger moves along my slit, stopping on the pearl of my pleasure as Aquilian rattles again.

"What is this?"

"My clit," I manage. *"Rub it, please."* I'm only briefly aware that I sound whiny, but I can't even find it in me to care.

He doesn't need to be told twice and sets straight to stroking me, his cock still only barely touching my core. I need more, but when I try to move against his hand, he squeezes my throat a bit tighter. *"No."*

"No?"

"This is your punishment. You will be still."

Whimpering as I struggle to obey him, I move my hands up the sides of his torso and hold on. Never in my life have I wanted someone as badly as I want him. I need him more than I need my next breath. The alien looks at me with deadly focus in his eyes. It's something I can deal with now that the coolness has left his voice.

One strong hand still remains wrapped around my throat and the other moves to caress my thigh, pulling it up onto his hip as he pushes forward just a little more. He only keeps his hand there for a moment to make sure that I don't move my leg before moving it back to my clit. What little of his smooth cock he allows inside me sends a thrill rushing through my veins. Aquilian sinks into me with an agonizingly slow thrust of his hips, the tip of his cock roaming along my inner walls. Every nerve feels like it's exploding as he pulls all the way back out and thrusts again. A soft groan falls from his lips, the sound only driving my need higher.

One day I'll need to get a better look at what he's got going on down there, but right now all that matters is that it hits all the right places. And boy does it hit *all* the right places as it moves within me. I want to meet his thrusts, I want to disobey him, but I am reminded that he can take away his gift at any moment. The despair of being the focus of his disappointment has been transformed into pleasure, and I'm now so enticed by his cock that I feel like I am losing control all over again.

Instead of fighting to keep a tight grip on myself, I push against him, grinding myself into his body. His hand tightens a little but he doesn't pull himself away. Instead, his thrusts become more erratic, pushing me higher and higher with each slide against my swollen folds.

I'm so close that my whole body is trembling beneath his

touch, the pressure on my throat only bringing me closer to the cliff that he's gradually pushing me toward. I need something... more. My mind goes blank, stars dancing behind my eyes as the head of his cock hits just the right spot inside of me and the hand lodged between our bodies rubs zealously over my sensitive clit.

My climax hits me like a tidal wave as it raises me higher into bliss. I moan uncontrollably, enjoying the sound of my own rapture as it fills the space around us. Aquilian reaches his own peak a few thrusts later, hot cum shooting into me as my walls clamp down on his thick girth. His hand squeezes my neck as his head falls back in absolute euphoria.

It doesn't matter that I can't breathe because just the sight of him coming undone would steal the air from my lungs. He's beautiful, his whole body glowing with a light that I've never seen before, the rattle of his quills caressing my skin like a physical touch. When I wiggle beneath him, he slowly lets go of my throat, dropping over me and nuzzling into my neck.

"Aquilian?"

"Yes?"

"We understand each other." I can't believe I'm just realizing this. *"How?"*

I feel him sigh, his warm breath tickling my skin. *"It must be the bond. There have been instances among our people where they find themselves mated to a female or males from other tribes who have languages of their own. With time, the bond allows mates the ability to communicate. A gift from the Sun Father."* Aquilian pushes himself up, the lean muscles on his arms bunching as he holds himself above me. *"It hurt me to think that, because we could not understand one another, could not tell you what you meant to us, that we might lose you."*

"Aquilian..." I want to pull him back down to me, but he pulls back, sliding free of my body before standing. I glance down, but his cock has hidden itself within its cover once again.

"You should rest, Xia." His finger caresses my cheek. *"I will retrieve Kareen and stand guard."*

I open my mouth to argue, but it turns into a yawn. My eyes drift close as I watch him walk away, and I realize I never want him to leave. I want this, Aquilian and Ettrian, always.

CHAPTER 16

*I*noxia

Little tingles of pleasure still roll over my skin as I make my way into the kitchen wrapped in the silky material. My dress was a lost cause, a casualty of hot, sweaty sex. Aquilian kept trying to apologize, but after the soul-melting orgasm he gave me, there really isn't anything to apologize for.

Cheeks blazing, I shake my head to clear my thoughts as I snag a cup from one of the shelves and fill it with water. Aquilian has taken up his post in the central room where I know he's keeping a close eye on the other twins. I only saw him long enough this morning for him to hand over the material and then he was gone, back to his guarding. The nozzle closes at my request sent along the bond, and a flush of satisfaction rushes through me. I feel proud at how fast I've gotten the hang of this.

The smile on my lips instantly fades when I glance down at Kareen and see her bringing the cup of tea I made last night up to her mouth. The cup and its questionable contents go flying across the room as I swat it out of her hands.

"Hey!" she whines. "I just wanted to taste it!"

"That tea is *not* for kids."

Kareen frowns up at me, her small hands fisting on her hips. "Oh, so it's a grown-up drink?"

A snort escapes me as I retrieve the cup from the floor, setting it down on the counter. "I'm not even sure adults should be drinking *that*."

A laugh has my eyes narrowing on Doxal where he sits in the middle of the room, twisting a bloom between his fingers.

"Is that why you got punished?"

"Hmm?" My brows furrow and my head whips back toward the little girl. "What was that?"

"Did you get punished for drinking the tea? Or was it because you talked to strangers?"

My eyebrows nearly climb to my hairline and I can feel my cheeks start to redden again. "What do you mean?" I ask with a nervous laugh.

"I heard you get punished last night." Her gaze is curious as she watches my face, her little foot tapping the ground as she waits for my answer.

"That's a conversation for when you're bigger," I manage to choke out.

She huffs, folding her arms over her chest just as Aquilian walks over to where we are. "You told me we could talk about anything!"

Doxal laughs at my discomfort again, drawing Aquilian's gaze. Quills rattle softly as my gentle alien scoops Kareen up into his arms. He presses his face into her ringlets and she giggles when his crest vibrates against her cheek. Her little hand wraps around one of his quills, something I've seen her do often when she's seeking comfort, and she snuggles into his chest as he settles himself on the floor. "Why can't we talk about your punish—"

"Kareen," I warn softly. She's a kid, and they're curious, but I'm not ready to have a conversation about my spanking and subsequent activities with my six-year-old charge. "We can talk about anything, but let's save this conversation for when you're older, all right?"

She looks like she's about to argue her case some more when a soft rumble—not quite a snore—comes from Aquilian.

"Is he sleeping?" she whispers, trying to twist her head to see his face.

"Aquilian is really tired." I crouch down next to them, brushing my fingertips over his crest. "He stayed out all night and found Ettrian hurt in the forest. Let him sleep a little longer." I decide not to mention that he stayed up to watch the other males, keeping us safe from any threat they may have presented.

Kareen's blue eyes widen. "Is Ettrian okay?"

"He's going to be fine, little one." Both of us turn to Doxal as he pushes away from the wall he had been resting against.

She smiles, her little teeth flashing, and I try to pretend I don't find it funny when Doxal shudders. Bunnyfly scurries over, pushing its head beneath Kareen's hand in a silent demand for attention. I can feel Doxal's eyes on me most of the afternoon as I sit next to Aquilian, weaving the strips of fronds into baskets in the way I've been taught. It makes it hard to focus on everything Kareen is saying next to me, and I'm relieved when she burrows her way under Aquilian's arm, sighing softly before she falls asleep.

"Inoxia?"

The sound of Doxal's voice within the room is strange. I've become so used to only hearing Kareen that the deep rumble startles me for a moment. "Yes?"

"Could I speak with you?" He glances down at where Aquilian and Kareen are curled up. "Outside."

"I shouldn't leave the tree." I don't want Aquilian upset with me again for leaving. We still don't know if these two are trustworthy. These males were sent to breed me, and though they have been honest about their intentions, the confession makes me incredibly uncomfortable.

"The tree can remain open," he promises. "I only wish to have a word. Nothing more."

With a glance at my sleeping male, I nod, pushing myself up from the floor. My skin is immediately assaulted with the tiny pinpricks that tell me I've been sitting for far too long and my limbs have fallen asleep. I grit my teeth against the discomfort and limp out after Doxal, barely stepping out of the protection of the open entrance. The assurance that I can easily fall back into the tree or shout for help does little to ease the tension in my body.

He must sense my wariness, because Doxal puts more distance between us, nearly standing within the tree line that hides the entrance. I keep my eyes trained on him, blocking out the beauty of the warm afternoon breeze on my skin. I can't afford the distraction.

"I want to apologize."

"What?" My eyes dart to the trees, scanning for any signs that Yssig may be hiding.

"I apologize for not telling you our intentions from the moment we entered your tree." His eyes stray to his feet as if he is ashamed to meet mine.

"I guess it was hard to get a word in when I was crawling all over you," I mutter.

His eyes flash darkly. "I swear to you we did not know it would have that effect on you."

"It's okay." Aquilian had confirmed that this morning when he had brought in the fabric. As far as he knew, the tea had never caused such a reaction before. My brows draw down as I remember something he said. "You told me last night that the aliens who sent you here have your sister."

"Yes," Doxal practically growls. "She is their prisoner."

"I don't have actual siblings, but I have a best friend who's as close to a sister as I've ever had, and I have Kareen. If someone threatened them, took them away from me, I know I'd do anything I could to save them." The look he gives me has me taking a step backward.

"We were given time," he says as he watches my retreat.

"For?"

"They have given us a week to mate you."

A sardonic laugh fills the air. "Yeah, that's not happening."

"Even if we truly wished to, it is no longer an option for us, Inoxia. You have your fated mates. There is no changing it."

I knew about the concept of mates from having lived among the Venium for so long, but I didn't know what exactly it meant here. I make a note to question Aquilian later. "The aliens had Ettrian there?" Doxal nods his head. "What do they do there?"

"They experimented on us." His fingers brush over the holes on the side of his head. "They used us in ways I am not comfortable talking about." Doxal looks toward the tree line, his breathing becoming uneven.

I want to ask more questions, but my words die in my mouth when two little arms wrap around my waist. I look down at Kareen, who stares up at me with comically wide eyes and a pout that could melt the coldest heart. The giggle escapes me before I can contain it. "What is it, baby?"

"Can we play outside? Please?" Her lower lip juts out even further.

"I'm not sure that is safe right now, Kareen. Let's go inside and ask—"

"Kareen!" Aquilian's voice feels warm across the bond as he rushes from the tree, his eyes falling on us. *"Xia?" His gaze slides toward Doxal. "What are you doing out here?"*

"I'm fine," I tell him, reaching out to trail my hand over his

arm. *"Doxal just wanted to apologize for the misunderstanding without waking the two of you up."*

His eyes narrow on the male, but he addresses me. *"Come back inside, Xia."*

I smile down at Kareen as she huffs, taking her little hand in mine as we slip back into the tree. The rest of our day is spent in the room where Ettrian rests within the pod. Kareen talks to him, convinced that he can hear her and that it helps him recover. If he can actually hear her, I'm sure the constant chatter will be enough to wake him at any moment. Yssig brings us food, setting the tray on the floor near Kareen. Before she can even bend to grab her favorite fruit, Aquilian has snatched the tray, taking small bites from each of the offered fruits and roots before he allows her to collect what she wants.

Yssig only shakes his head, quietly retreating down the hall. He still doesn't trust them.

The days crawl by, one fading into another as we create a new norm. Doxal and Yssig continue bringing food into the room that we have made into our living quarters and Aquilian tests it, waiting to see if this is the day they will try to poison us, but it never happens.

My big broody male has finally agreed to let me help keep watch so that he can rest, but he insists that I do it with him curled tightly around me, Kareen's small body sandwiched between us so that she is protected. On day four of Ettrian not waking, I fall asleep with my hand pressed to the outside of the pod, hoping it won't be for much longer.

"Time to wake, sweet one."

My eyes flutter open when firm lips press against mine. Pleasure curls in my belly and I reach up to hold Aquilian, tugging him closer.

"Eww, gross!" Kareen throws herself between us dramatically, and I laugh as we break apart.

"Do you understand the meaning of privacy, young lady?"

She giggles, shaking her head from side to side before she jumps into Aquilian's arms. As I sit up, my eyes fall on the pod, and my heart stutters when I see that it has remained closed.

"He will not wake yet," Aquilian says. *"Ettrian's body used a fair amount of energy trying to heal before he was placed in the pod. It will take time for him to regain his strength."*

This isn't the first time he's reminded me, but I wake up every morning hoping all the same. *"I know. I just miss him."*

"So do I." He takes my hand, tugging me up from the floor. *"Come. We will go get food with Yssig and Doxal."*

"All of us?" Kareen asks, turning hopeful eyes on him.

"All of us."

"Is it safe to go?" I ask as Kareen dances around my legs.

"There will be three of us to protect you both, and our kit needs the fresh air. I do not want the two of you to feel the need to sneak out again."

"We wouldn't do that again, Aquilian," I protest, but the look he sends me makes me smile. *"We sneak out one time and you can't just leave it be."*

"Come." Aquilian rattles his quills as he moves from the room and I follow after him, not willing to miss an opportunity to get myself and Kareen out of the tree for even a moment.

CHAPTER 17

*a*quilian

Four days of living with these strange males, and I am still not sure I can trust them. In truth, they have done nothing to try to harm Xia or our kit, but I cannot overlook the fact that they were sent here to take my mate away from me. Within Dauur society, violence against females and kits is practically unheard of, but if what they said to Xia is true—if they have been experimented on and threatened—then they may not be in their right mind.

Even so, the hatred I feel for them is something that surprises me. I had imagined that meeting another set of full-grown twins, especially ones so similar to Ettrian and myself, would be comforting. I had expected to feel sympathy and kinship for them. I, more than most, know what it is like to be driven away, to live on the edges of your society for something you cannot change.

Kareen skips next to Xia as we walk through the forest, and I try not to show how much this is all weighing on me. My female does a wonderful job of distracting me without even trying. My eyes travel along the curve of her hips as she moves, and my mind conjures up the image of her writhing beneath me in the sling. I want to drag her back to the tree. My body burns with the need to feel the soft vibrations she makes when I caress the sensitive spot within her, to hear her whisper my name along the bond as she tightens around me. I'm jolted from daydream by the feel of my quills rattling.

Stop that, I tell myself sternly. *There will be plenty of time for that once we are safe.*

There's a print in the soil that I recognize as one of the younger nolfira. This is one of the reasons I decided to risk bringing them out here. The males informed me that they found some closer to the tree, and I could not leave the females behind to investigate for myself. Although nolfira look vicious and have the potential to be dangerous to the younger kits, they are normally not a threat to the Dauur. I need to know what has caused this nolfira to stray so far from its den. If Kareen were to leave the tree on her own... My heart lurches in my chest when I think about what could happen to her.

"Stay in the middle of the group, little one," I remind her.

"I know, Quilian! You don't gotta keep saying it."

She is probably frustrated with my constant worry, but she is safer between us than anywhere else. Her rammit, Bunnyfly, hops beside her without a care in the world. Her small hand runs over the tops of fungi as she moves past them, leaving a trail of color in her wake.

"There should be some fruit trees up ahead. We have mostly picked the ones close to your tree," Yssig, the Lightborn twin, tells us.

The fact that they speak our common tongue, even without the aid of what they called a translator, tells me that the twins are from a neighboring tribe. Unlike many of the males our age, Ettrian and I avoided mingling with them. The females from the other villages may have been interested in letting my brother warm their slings, but they were not willing to be mated to his twin.

My gaze turns to the trees, and I'm not surprised when I notice that many of the fruit bearing ones have been picked clean. In this part of the forest the trees are more mature, having already lived through their fruitful years. This means that our food supply is limited, especially since we are in competition with any of the other animals who rely on the fruit as a source of nutrition. This might also explain why the nolfira has strayed so far into our temporary territory.

Doxal stops up ahead, pointing skyward. High above us, at the very top of the trees, hang Kareen and Xia's favorite food. The teardrop fruit sways in the breeze.

"I will get them," Yssig says as he begins to climb the thick trunk.

Doxal starts up a second tree, and just a little further down is a third. I put Xia and Kareen at the base, plucking one of my quills and handing it to my mate. *"Keep this with you just in case. Stay right here. I should be able to drop down if there is any trouble."*

I have been navigating these trees my whole life, but I suddenly find it hard to concentrate on my hand and footholds when I know my family is below me. Once I reach the teardrops, I pluck a few more quills, flinging them at the fruit so that they fall to the ground.

"Kareen! Get back here! Aquilian!" Xia's words stop my heart cold as I look around for our kit.

She has taken off after Bunnyfly, who has darted from her side. My stomach drops out from beneath me and I feel my grip slip. There's movement in the underbrush around her, and I know I will not make it to her in time. A flash of white passes to her left, and I begin to drop through the branches. The nolfira.

"Kareen!" My whole body jolts as my legs bend to absorb the shock of my landing, and my feet are immediately carrying me

across the distance. A shrill vibration scrapes across my ilo, and I shout her name again.

When I break through the brush, I prepare myself for what will surely be the worst moment of my life. Xia is wrapped around our kit, her whole body shaking as she scrambles away from where Doxal is fighting off the young nolfira. I stumble forward, my entire being numb as reach for my mate. The dying vibrations of the beast along the natural bond we share hardly registers within my mind.

My hand shakes as I brush Kareen's head, but nothing prepares me for when she turns toward me, her eyes huge and glassy with fear. *"Sun Father, save me."* The air rushes from my lungs as she begins to sob. The vibrations are unpleasant, but they let me know she is alive.

"Aquilian told you to stay! He told you!" Xia is trembling, crushing the kit to her chest as she rocks them both back and forth.

"I know, but Bunnyfly—"

"I can replace your rammit, kit. I cannot replace you." My words do not seem to help, and she begins to cry even harder.

"I'm sorry!"

I pull them both into my shaking arms, holding them tight against me. Xia looks up at me, the fear in her eyes echoing what I feel within my heart.

"I have you now," I tell her as I rub my hand over the red strands of her hair. *Our kit is alive*, I tell myself, trying to stop the trembling in my limbs.

"Is she okay?" Doxal asks. His arms and chest are covered in bright blood from his fight, but I can see the fear in his gaze as it sweeps over Kareen.

Xia pulls free, turning to the other male. *"She's fine. A little shaken up."* My mate wipes the liquid from her cheeks before placing her hand on Doxal's forearm. *"Thank you, Doxal."*

Maybe I have judged the twins too quickly. The Darkborn risked his own safety to protect my kit. He looked after her as if she were just another member of his tribe, of his family.

Our eyes meet and I nod, thankful, for the first time in a long time, that I am not alone.

CHAPTER 18

*I*noxia

"Do you think Ettrian will wake up soon?" I ask Doxal as we all rest in the central room. Aquilian has relaxed around the twins since they saved Kareen's life.

"I do not think it will be much longer, but it is hard to know when the pod will release him." He stretches his arms into the air, rattling his quills as he stands. "I will go out and gather more of the cinsi blooms in preparation."

"Can I come with you? More hands to help gather will cut down the time it takes."

"If Aquilian gives his blessing, then it is fine with me. I will wait outside." I watch as he disappears through the opening in the tree.

I crouch down, tapping Aquilian's shoulder. He's curled up with Kareen for her afternoon nap, and the sleepy look he shoots me makes my body tingle. *"Doxal is going out for more of the cinsi blooms. I thought maybe I'd go help him."* I know he wants to object, but he nods instead.

"Be safe." He tells me as he runs a finger along my cheek.

"I promise." I look directly at Kareen, making sure she's

listening. "You're going to stay here and take care of Aquilian, okay? Make sure he gets some sleep." She nods, her eyes following me as I stand. "Do not leave his side, Kareen. Got it?" Another nod. "Good." Bunnyfly bounces into the room, zeroing in on the snuggle pile at my feet.

"Where are you going?" she asks, her free hand brushing through Bunnyfly's fur when the little beast jumps up into her arms.

"I'm just going to help Doxal. We won't be far." The tree opens for me, and I pause just outside to look back at them, feeling my heart squeeze a little. I may be on an alien planet, but I know in my soul that I have finally found a family to call my own.

~

*I*t feels like I've been walking for hours behind Doxal, maintaining a safe distance between us in the hopes that he doesn't feel overwhelmed with my presence. I can see his black tipped quills when they rise in response to each little noise. Keeping up with Doxal's long stride is forcing me to acknowledge just how out of shape I am. Sweat drips from my brow, down the side of my face, and I use my forearm to wipe it away. "Keep up, little female." He taunts.

The path isn't easy to follow and it makes me wish I hadn't left my woven shoes back at the tree. Each time a twig juts up between my toes, I seriously consider burning the forest down, or at least giving up and turning around.

I need to know what kind of aliens these brothers are. They admitted to being sent down here to "breed" me, but I'm still not sure exactly what that means or who the aliens are that sent them here for that purpose. Doxal saving Kareen was something that had been completely unexpected. Neither Doxal nor Yssig have been anything but helpful since that first night, but there's still something in the way they look at me that puts me on edge.

Another sharp jab to my foot has me gritting my teeth together against the pain. *I love plants. I will not burn the forest down. It's my own stupid fault for not grabbing my shoes.*

"Are you okay, Inoxia?" His head whips in my direction and I gasp, stumbling backward as his black gaze lands on me. Unlike Aquilian, who couldn't hide his emotions if he tried, Doxal is hard as hell to read. I can't tell if he's genuinely concerned for my wellbeing or if he's annoyed that I can't keep up.

"Sorry," I pant. "I'm just a little out of shape." He takes a step toward me and every cell in my body shivers at the feeling of danger that radiates from him. Something is different.

"Why are you looking at me like that, Inoxia?" he questions, his voice low and deadly.

"Looking at you like what?" I stammer, turning to face him head on as he prowls to my left.

"Like you are ready to flee."

I shake my head, trying to find my footing among the exposed roots. "I'm not—"

"Why are you lying to me?" The stare he pierces me with makes my hair stand on end.

The forest around me is filled with strange noises and even stranger creatures. While following Doxal, I've kept my eyes and ears peeled for anything that might try to sneak up on me, for any beast that might be waiting to attack, but now I see that I was following the real beast the whole time. Where's the Doxal from the past week? Where's the Doxal who told me he was trying to help me? Everything around us has gone silent and I'm standing across from an alien who knows I'm lying, and what I see in his eyes terrifies me.

The only thing I can hear is the sound of my heart thundering inside my chest, and the soft rustle of the leaves as the wind pushes through them. There is hardly a breath of space between us as he comes to a stop in front of me, our feet almost touching as he stares down at me. The tension between us is palpable. It reminds me of an article I once read about what it's like moments before a tsunami hits, when it feels like the whole world holds its breath as the wave looms over the shore. Instead of a wave crashing down on me, Doxal's strong arms clamp around my body, pinning my arms to my sides as I struggle against his chest. His face drops down close to mine, his lips brushing against my hair as his quills rattle loudly.

"I am sorry," he whispers. "They will kill her if I do not do this."

His sister. "Wait! No! What are you doing?" I try to dig my feet into the ground only to realize I'm no longer able to feel it beneath me. "Put me down!"

Doxal grunts and shifts me in his arms. "I cannot. You do not understand them."

"Then help me understand! Tell me who they are, what they want from you, from me!" He ignores my plea. *"Aquilian! Help! Aquilian!"* I reach out along the bond.

This gets Doxal's attention and my neck jerks to one side as I'm yanked in front of him. "You can shout along the bond all you want, but you will accomplish nothing aside from drawing every predator in the area to us." His lip curls up in a sneer as he watches my face. "Aquilian may be your mate, but you are not Dauur and have not yet learned how to control your thoughts. He cannot hear you from this distance, but …" He pauses, something sinister and unstable flashing in his eyes as he leans down to whisper to me, "my brother is still with your mates and your kit."

The threat is unmistakable. If I don't listen to him, Yssig will harm the people I care about, and there's nothing I can do to stop it. I can't reach Aquilian and Ettrian is still healing. There's no way for me to warn them that they shouldn't trust Yssig.

"Please…"

His grip on me tightens again as I'm lifted higher. "This isn't what we want either." He sounds exhausted.

I want to feel sympathy for them, but I'm finding it difficult. Sure, Doxal makes it sound like he doesn't have a choice, but don't we all? They're taking away what little freedom I've had since coming here. Taking away *my* choice. *Just like Trent did.* I feel the old panic surge inside of me. So many therapy sessions and medications, so much hard work to heal from his abuse, and I feel all my control slipping away.

Breathe. Get control of yourself so you can figure out how to get out of this situation and back to the tree. I try not to think about the fact that I may never see Kareen, Aquilian, or Ettrian ever again. Even not seeing Bunnyfly has me choking up a little. I push all of those thoughts aside because I *will* find my way back to them.

"Kareen will be safe?" Doxal nods. "And Aquilian and Ettrian? They won't be hurt?"

"You're the one they need," is his only response.

Well, fine then. He carries me under mushrooms taller than he is, through trees that twist this way and that, and around animals that I don't have names for. They look like they have scorpion tails, talons like a bird, white fur, and deceitfully innocent looking eyes. They're absolutely terrifying!

Doxal walks until he reaches a solid wall of what looks almost like glass. His hand moves along it until he finds something that I can't see and a light glows beneath his palm. The glass slowly breaks down, seeming to dissolve into a doorway just big enough for us to fit through before snapping closed behind us. Has this been keeping us in or out this whole time?

Then something even more upsetting occurs to me. If the other males had the ability, does this mean Aquilian and Ettrian do too? Have they been holding Kareen and I captive? Before the thoughts take root, my mind is rebelling. I know the truth. My males would never have kept us locked away inside some sort of cage. Call me naïve, but I know in the deepest part of my soul that they're innocent.

My eyes are searching everywhere for something to slow him down, but there's nothing I can do. If I kick, I'm only going to piss him off, and I don't know where Yssig is at this point or if they can still communicate from this distance. Me fighting him could put everyone at the tree in danger.

My eyes travel over the shrubs as we pass by them, and I'm startled for a moment by what I see. Hiding just between some trees is an actual Venium warrior. His long white hair hangs loose around his shoulders, black skin blending in with the bark on the trunks of the trees, and scars cross over his body as his green fushori glows softly. I turn away, not wanting to alert Doxal to what I've seen. *Think, think, think!* As quietly as I can, I wave at the male, my eyes locking on his. *Please help! Please don't be a part of this.* The Venium cocks his head to the side and narrows his gaze before I lose sight of him.

Aliens, trees that you can talk to, strange animals, some sort of barrier keeping us in, and a Venium warrior who I'm not sure is native to this planet. At this point, I'm not sure much else can surprise me. I'm proven wrong when I glance up and my mouth drops open. Where there was once just a forest of trees and the hint of massive mountains in the distance, a structure is visible that must have been cloaked before. The white building forms a hexagon, and little pods branch off from the main segment topped by a large dome. My heart pounds against the inside of my chest as the doors at the front begin to open. My first look at the aliens who apparently sent Doxal and Yssig to breed me drains all the blood from my face. Disgust rolls through me, and I clutch at Doxal's arms in panic as we draw closer.

"What the fuck?" These guys are giant freaking houseflies!

CHAPTER 19

*E*ttrian

Someone is crying out for help. The sound of their screams bounce around inside of the dark depths of my mind, clawing, and hammering at me relentlessly. *Xia?* Why does she sound so distressed? My fingers reach out to the shadow of her but come back with tendrils of smoke instead. Why can I not reach out to her? The bond, which is already weak, is growing weaker and weaker by the second. I cannot tell if this is another nightmare or if I have been captured again. Suddenly, a familiar, soft voice breaks through the darkness as I struggle to push myself toward consciousness.

"Ettrian?" Kareen whispers. "I don't know if you can hear me inside the tree, but I want to tell you I'm really scared."

Again, I shove against the darkness trying to rise above the sea of emotion that floods me. The need to be free and help my mate is so strong that I feel overwhelmed by it. Everything within me screams to reach out to her, but I find nothing when I try. She is not there, and that terrifies me more than anything. The fear in my kit's voice breaks my heart and I fight harder, swimming up through the gloom that pulls at me.

"Xia told me she was going out to get more blooms while Aquilian took a nap. She said he was really tired." She sniffles quietly. "I'm sorry you got hurt. The other guy is being weird and Xia isn't back yet. I don't want Aquilian to leave me here to go look for her, but I want her to come home."

Other guy? Sweet Sun Father, the other males that were sent by the aliens must have discovered my family before I made it back here. *I am going to tear them to pieces.* Again, I shove at the darkness. I will not let Kareen be afraid another moment longer.

"Please! I don't want anything bad to happen to Xia. She's the best mom I've ever had." Her voice breaks, and I hear her begin to cry. "I don't remember my real mom, but I remember the first time I met Xia. She has a really, really big garden called a green-house and she showed me all of her flowers and how she plants them. Her mom and dad are super nice, and I wanted them to be my grandma and grandpa, but now we aren't on Earth anymore."

The urge to comfort the kit is overwhelming. Warmth works its way through me and my muscles begin to twitch. *Get up! Wake!*

"I don't want you to be gone either. I like having a mom and I really, *really* like having two dads. I don't know anybody who gets to live with *both* their dads. Please don't leave us, Ettrian. Please come back so we can find Xia."

I can never leave her. Not even when my body grows old and frail do I think I will be able to part from her. Everything that I am is my mate, my partnership, my family, my kit. *My kit needs me.* My body starts to respond, my fingers flex, my toes wiggle. From what my kit has said, she's been alone for too long already. I will not let her down again... I will not let them down again. My eyes fly open and I gasp for breath. I am inside the seed pod. Aquilian must have gotten to me in time. Outside, Kareen gasps as the entire pod shakes from the force of my struggle.

"Ettrian?"

"Move away, Kareen!" Her little footsteps retreat and I slam myself into the side of the pod once, twice. On my third attempt, the seed pod shatters and I fall to the floor of the tree.

"Ettrian!" she screams before launching herself at my body.

I catch her and pull her tightly against my chest, squeezing as I rock her in my arms. *"Shh, no more tears. We will fix this."*

Her raw emotions beat against me stronger than ever before as she clutches at my neck. Terror, love, and sadness wash through her so fast I have a hard time latching onto any of them. "I missed you." Her little hand snakes up to wrap around one of my quills in the way I have seen her do so many times with my twin.

"I missed you too, daughter."

"I thought you were going to die in there," she sniffles.

"The seed pods make you better. They won't hurt you." My quills rattle softly as I grab her delicate hand. *"Besides, how could I leave you alone? You would tear apart the whole tree."*

Kareen pulls away to touch my face before she plants a tiny, soft kiss on my cheek. "I want my mama back."

My throat constricts at the sight of the big tear that rolls down her cheek, and I know I will do anything in my power to keep her from feeling this way ever again. *"We will find your mama."*

"Do you pinky promise?"

"Do I what?" I shake my head, not knowing what 'pinky promise' means, but it is not important. I need to know what has happened in my absence. Speaking out loud for the first time in my life is an odd feeling. "Tell me everything."

$\sim$

"*A*nd then she got punished by Aquilian, but she wouldn't tell me why. She said I have to wait 'til I'm older." Kareen's lower lip pokes out in the same way Xia's does from time to time. Since the day I met her, I've never heard the kit speak so many words at once. Even when she is upset and 'throwing a tantrum' as Xia calls it, she never talks this much. Especially not to me. Aquilian has always been her favorite, and it is not hard to understand why. My twin has endless amounts of patience and love to give, and it makes my heart happy to know she loves him just as fiercely.

The last thing she says finally filters into my mind. *"Punished?"* By Aquilian?

"Yeah! She got in big trouble for talking to strangers. You aren't supposed to do that." she adds in a whisper.

Anxiety eats at me, and I feel the overwhelming need to find my twin and get the rest of the story. I am beginning to think that something terrible has happened to Xia. What concerns me the most is that, according to Kareen, my mate and one of the other males have gone missing. Worry settles like a stone in my stomach, and I ruffle the kit's head fur, holding her close to my chest as I stand and follow the pull of the bond to the main room where I can feel Aquilian's presence.

Aside from my twin's sleeping form, the central room is empty. I stomp over to Aquilian, annoyed and frustrated that he could possibly fall asleep while two strange males are in our dwelling with our kit and mate, but I stop short. He looks like a kit himself, one arm beneath his head while the other curls protectively around the rammit Kareen has adopted. I do not remember the last time I saw him look so at peace, and I almost feel bad for having to wake him.

Nudging his curled leg with my foot, I reach out along the bond, prodding his mind. Kareen's little hand is still clutched in mine and she flexes it gently, rubbing her thumb along my skin. She might not be the daughter of my blood, but she certainly is the daughter of my heart, and I cannot imagine my life without her or her mama in it. Panic surges within me, and I kick Aquilian a little harder.

"Brother! Get up," A frustrated growl tears from my throat when he merely turns over, ignoring me. *"Aquilian, our mate is missing! Wake up!"*

His eyes shoot open and he bolts upright, sending the rammit fleeing in a panic from the room. A rattle works its way through his quills as his eyes dart around the room before they land on me.

"Where did she go, Kareen?" he asks groggily.

"She said she was going to get blooms. I was supposed to stay right next to you, but I got scared." She ducks her head meekly into my neck as if she's afraid Aquilian will be angry with her.

"She asked to go with Doxal." He looks around the room as if we have somehow overlooked her. *"She has not returned?"*

"You let her go on her own with another male?" The astonishment I'm feeling drips from each word.

"The male is trustworthy," he argues. *"He saved Kareen's life."*

A breeze as soft as Xia's breath whispers against the back of my neck, and I spin around toward the hole that has opened up in the tree. Standing just outside, in the spot where I had hoped to find my mate, is a younger Lightborn Dauur male. We stare at one another for a moment before I hand Kareen to my twin.

"Ettrian?" Aquilian calls as I walk toward the opening, but I do not respond.

Anger courses through me, causing my quills to quiver as I approach the younger male. *"Where is she?"*

"Who?" The mocking tone of his voice pushes me over the edge.

My hand shoots out, wrapping around his throat, and I slam him against the wall of the tree. Our quills are rattling out warnings to one another, but I ignore him and squeeze tighter. Aquilian has not beaten these males to a pulp so I gladly will. They were sent here for my mate. They were sent to do something because I could not stomach the thought of following through with the command from the aliens.

Rationally, I know these males have no reason to hurt her. The aliens want her alive, want her to be bred. If she is injured, that could jeopardize their plans. Dauur males, under normal circumstances, would never try to force a female. Even if a pair did, our females are more than capable of defending themselves against unwanted advances, but Xia is not like them. My female is small, soft, and was not born with anything she could use to fight.

I have good reason to be concerned for her safety, and if Aquilian knew the things that I did, he would be fearful as well. *"Enough lies."*

"I am not lying to you!"

I am surprised when he decides to speak out loud instead of through the bond. I should have known the aliens would have done the same to him as they've done to me. His claws have dug into my skin where his hands grip me and blood drips from the wounds. "Tell me where my mate has gone and I may not strangle the life from you, Lightborn."

His eyes narrow on me, quills rattling louder. "I have already told you! I have no idea where she ran off to. Neither my brother nor I have hurt her! We have done nothing but help since we came."

I hear his words, but my mind is on Xia. She is out there somewhere, most likely with this male's twin. I would kill for this female, tear this Dauur apart if it would help me find her. Xia is everything to me. I see her holding Kareen close as she whines and fusses over having to be inside the tree all the time. I see the way she gifts Aquilian with touches that light up his entire being. Guilt rips through me when the memory of her gentle kiss against my lips flashes through my mind. Xia kissed me, touched me, even without knowing what she meant to me and Aquilian.

You tried to force her into acceptance, I remind myself

bitterly. *You do not deserve her after what you did.* I know it is the truth, and yet I hope that someday she will find it within her heart to forgive me. I acted out of fear and lost the very thing I was trying to save.

"Release him, Ettrian!" I hear Aquilian command. *"Yssig has done nothing but aid your healing. He has brought back cinsi blooms."*

I glance down at the floor and see the sack of blooms he must have dropped when I attacked him. That does not matter to me. I know what this male was sent here for. It's obvious my brother does not because he would never have allowed them to stay within our home, this close to our kit and female.

"I have already told you, Ettrian. We have done nothing to her, I swear it."

I open my mouth to tell him I do not believe him, but a sharp pain in my calf causes me to stumble backward, releasing the Lightborn so I can catch myself. I spare a glance at my wounded leg. There's a gash from his calf horn, but it is not bad enough to keep me from going after him again. A snarl rips from my throat as I launch myself at him, ripping a quill from my head. We collide and a moment later I have the younger male pinned beneath me, the quill in my hand is pressed against his throat.

Blood trickles from the small wound on his neck as he resists. The farther the quill digs in, the harder he fights. His chest heaves as he pushes up against me, struggling to throw my weight from him. I position my leg, aiming my calf horn for his side, but Aquilian makes a sound of distress followed closely by Kareen's gasp. My gaze flies up to where they're standing. Kareen's tiny bottom lip is trembling and large tears are trailing down her cheeks. Her hands are wrapped so tightly around my twin's quills that I see two of them release from his head.

"Stop!" she cries as Aquilian scowls at me, his arms wrapping around her tightly as she buries her face in his chest. "No more. No more." Her panicked whispers break my heart.

Even the male beneath me has gone still as he watches the kit, concern pinching the features of his face, his eyes going from the red of battle to blue. He's sad that my kit is upset.

I pull my quill back slowly and frown down at him. "Are you going to tell me the truth now, Lightborn?"

With a deep sigh, the male turns his eyes to me. "She has been taken to the alien's lab." His jaw clenches, and I know he must find that thought as distressing as I do. "I will take you there."

I stand slowly, reaching my hand out to help him to his feet, my eyes locked on his. "What was your name?"

"Yssig," he grunts, rubbing at the blood on his throat.

"Thank you, *Yssig*, for the blooms." I cannot help the snarl that pulls at my mouth. With the way he watches me, I know I do not have to tell him I do not trust him, that I know why he is here and it is not to help me. Kareen sniffles again, and I move toward her, keeping the Lightborn within my vision. My kit reaches out to me and I scoop her up into my arms, my hands brushing her tears away. "I'm sorry," I whisper into her hair.

"I don't like when you fight. It scares me."

If I did not feel awful before, I absolutely feel it now. I nuzzle my face against her wet cheek and rattle softly, trying my best to soothe her. *"I have never been a papa before, Kareen. I am trying to learn to be a good one, but sometimes I need help."*

"I can help you! I'm a great helper." She wiggles in my arms and I set her down, watching as she bounces excitedly. Her little hand clutches Aquilian's and she smiles up at him. *"I'll help* both *my papas!"* That she whispers this along the bond so he's included squeezes at my heart.

Through our bond I feel his joy and the love we share for our kit and although I never would have admitted it all those days ago

.when I first came upon the females with my twin, I am grateful to the Sun Father for choosing Xia for us.

"We will find your mama now. Stay in the tree until we return."

Our daughter's little head whips my way, and she stomps her foot against the floor of the tree. "You can't leave me all alone! I'm only six years old!" she huffs, something I am sure she learned from her mama, and her bottom lip pokes out.

I project her words to Aquilian, who cannot understand what she spoke aloud, and he crouches down beside her. *"It is very dangerous, Kareen."*

"But what if you don't come back for me? I could die *and no one would ever find me!"*

"We will come back for you."

"You don't know that. My other mom and dad never came back for me!"

"Ettrian…" Both Aquilian and Kareen stare up at me, eyes pleading.

So this is what it feels like to be a papa. She is right, of course. What if something happens to either of us and we do not make it back for days? There is not enough food here to sustain her for very long. I sigh. *"Fine."* A snort from the front of the tree has me narrowing my eyes on Yssig, who watches us with a smirk on his face. "You will show us the way, Lightborn."

"I said I would." Yssig rolls his shoulders and then jerks his head toward the forest. *"We should get moving."*

Hours later, I find myself walking behind a male I know I cannot trust, my brother at my side, a rammit, and a sassy kit who knows exactly how to get her way. *We are coming for you, Xia.*

CHAPTER 20

*I*noxia

"Step inside," the fly man who brought us into the interior of the building says, pushing me forward. His translator has obviously caught up because his speech is no longer just buzzes and gurgles.

I take a few hesitant steps, not exactly sure what he means by "inside." There are no outer walls, just the one at the back. Doxal moves past me, stopping near the stark white wall, and then motions for me to follow him. As I move, there's a soft *whoosh*, and I spin around to see that something similar to the outside of the dome they trapped us in has come down between the fly aliens and us. As the alien taps away at the pad in his hands, I take a moment to look around the space behind him. They called this a lab, but it isn't at all what I was expecting. It looks more like a clinic with the metal tables and lights that remind me of operating rooms. My stomach drops a little as I ponder what they use those for.

On the far side of the room are other cells like the one we are in. Aliens I've never seen before pace within them, yelling and throwing around small cots, but I can't hear any of the noise they're making. I step close to the barrier and the fly alien eyes me. "What do you want with us?"

Lowering the tablet, the Tachin turns his head like he is trying to decide if I'm worth his time. His insect-like hand presses against the barrier and I hear him speak, "I have been given permission to answer your questions, female. This tactic has proven successful in gaining cooperation from your species in the past."

"In the past? You have other humans?"

He makes a sound I take as a derisive snort, "Of course there are. You may be harder to obtain now that the Grutex have been destroyed, but you are neither the first nor the last human to come through this facility. You are not special."

Well, jeez, thanks. "If I'm not special, why go through so much trouble to get me?"

"I am part of the last generation of the Tachin born the natural way—the *right* way." If flies could sneer, I'm pretty sure that's what this guy is doing. "Our species is facing a crisis that threatens to wipe us out. Males and females alike are becoming infertile at an alarming rate. It was one of the reasons we aided the Grutex in their quest to obtain your kind. We worked diligently to merge our DNA so that we may save ourselves."

"How will humans save you?" I ask, not entirely sure I actually want to know the specifics.

"You are excellent incubators for our larvae."

Yep, wishing I had never asked. "I don't understand. Couldn't you just take our eggs? Why do you need us to carry your... children?"

The alien huffs like I'm the most unintelligent creature he has had the misfortune of meeting. "Our species do not breed the same way. Simply taking your genetic material will not work. A Tachin male will hunt out a female who puts off the proper pheromones and once he has coaxed her to land, he will mount her and perform the mating dance. If she is not enticed, she will shake him off and move on. But if she accepts him, she will place her ovipositor into the opening of the male's genitals and he will release his sperm into her." He shivers like just telling me about this is doing something for him. "The sperm travel through her channel to her eggs and they are, hopefully, fertilized. When they are ready, the female deposits them into a carefully dug-out hole where they develop into larvae. She will care for them until they mature. Taking your eggs won't do since they must be incubated within a host and our females are incapable of this."

I don't mean to put down another species' breeding habits, but I'm so thankful I'm not a Tachin female. "Hold on—your females are the ones with cocks?"

"They are not cocks! They do not thrust." The Tachin's other hand comes up to slam against the barrier, cracking the tablet he was holding in half.

That one struck a nerve.

"Do not pay her any mind," a second Tachin says as he walks up to our angry fly man. "She will act accordingly or she will be strapped down." He shrugs his shoulders, his wings fluttering behind him. "Either way, she will be inseminated and we will have another chance."

"That will not be necessary," Doxal speaks up from behind me. "One of the males within the dome has already mated her."

I glare at Doxal, wishing I could punch him without injuring myself. He makes what Aquilian and I had sound so cheap. I refuse to believe my alien was with me because these bastards told him he had to be. Maybe this was what Ettrian had been trying to say the day Aquilian had made him leave. Even if they knew about this, Doxal made it sound like he hadn't wanted anything to do with me, and my guys definitely didn't seem to feel that way. I'm not going to let them turn me against the only beings who have helped me.

A light flashes at the station that sits in the center of the open space behind the Tachin, and the one who put us in here rushes away, leaving us alone with the new, scarier alien. "Well, this is good news," he says, placing his hand on the barrier so that we can hear him. "Your vigilance has brought you a reward, Dauur." He motions with his other hand, and we watch as another Tachin flies into the room. Curled in his arms is a small Dauur, a young female not much bigger than Kareen. Her black quills are barely long enough to curve along the back of her head. Like Doxal, her entire body is black. The fly man holding her passes through the barrier as if it doesn't even exist and deposits the girl on the floor before backing out.

Doxal rushes to the girl's side, rattling his quills softly as he runs his hands over her. "Yasi, look at me. Did they hurt you?"

I look up to see the alien I assume is in charge watching us. "What's going to happen to me now?" But he doesn't respond. His hand slips away, and the room is quiet again except for Doxal's soft murmurs. Instead, the fly man turns and joins a small group of Tachin who seem to be poring over tablets and high-tech machines.

"I want Mama!" she fusses, shoving Doxal's hands away. "I want to go home!"

"I know." Doxal sits back, a stricken look on his face.

As mad as I am at him for bringing me here, my heart hurts for them. "Do you want to tell me about your mama?" I ask softly, brushing my hand over her crest. Without quills, I can't rattle to her, but I can try to comfort her in other ways.

Her light blue eyes fall on me and I'm knocked backward when she launches herself into my body, her arms wrapping tightly around my torso. "My mama was the best mama."

"Was?" I turn to Doxal who nods sadly.

"They killed her," the girl, Yasi, tells me.

"The Tachin killed her?"

"No," Doxal says with a shake of his head. "Our village did."

"Your village? Why the hell would they do that?"

"They called our family cursed for producing so many Dark-born kits."

A frown pulls at my mouth. "I don't understand what that means."

Doxal gestures down at himself. "Yasi and I are Darkborn, as is your mate Aquilian. Being this way is... not desired. Yssig is the only Lightborn our parents ever produced. The last kits my mama gave birth to were twins, little males." His jaw clenches before he continues. "Dauur are born a very light gray, like some of the patches on Yasi, but our brothers were born partially colored. Darkborn. The elders heard and claimed that the Sun Father had cursed us for the final time. They ordered the deaths of our parents and brothers."

"Yssig and Doxal took me and we ran away before they could find us," Yasi says, rubbing her face against my chest.

"I'm so sorry," I whisper, running my hands down her back. "What they did was horrible." We sit like that for a while, watching the Tachin as they flutter back and forth, vials in hand. Yasi falls asleep in my arms, and I lean back against the wall, trying to get comfortable.

"We didn't want to do this, but they had Yasi. She has already lost so much. We couldn't leave her alone," Doxal says inside my mind.

"Did they know? My guys?"

Doxal sighs. *"Your mate, Ettrian? They captured him and installed his translator, but something was not right. We were here when they brought him in again, but only briefly. He told them he would not mate with you because you could not understand that you were his, that he did not want to hurt you."*

A broken translator would explain why I could only under-stand a few words. What could they have held over Ettrian to make him even consider doing what the Tachin were asking though? *"Why would he do what they wanted? You and Yssig did it for Yasi, but what did Ettrian do it for?"*

"Your kit."

"My kit? That's a child, right? I don't actually have one of my own."

Doxal huffs quietly. *"Your Kareen. It is my understanding that they threatened to kill her if he did not do as they asked."*

A shiver works through me at the thought of the Tachin anywhere near Kareen. I can't say I wouldn't have done the same in that situation. *"I could be pregnant now and they would take this one... Why would a child that isn't his be enough to make him mate with me?"*

"Dauur—most of them, anyway—believe kits to be the most important things in our lives. Even though he did not know yet that you were his mate, Ettrian would have risked his life for Kareen."

"Why do you keep calling them my mates?"

"What else would I call them?" Doxal glances at me in confusion. *"Their quills changed for you. This is a sign that you are their fated mate. Do humans not have these?"*

"Sort of. We have a deal with the Venium, the aliens who saved us. A bunch of them have found fated mates among humans, but humans as a species don't have fated mates. We pick and choose as we see fit."

The dark male nods. *"A fated mate is a rare find. Dauur may also choose to make a family without the benefit of being fated."* Yasi sits up, and he reaches out a hand to caress her quills. *"You are not pregnant."* The last part is barely a whisper.

"What?"

"You said you could be pregnant. You are not."

A laugh tumbles from my lips. *"I'm sorry, but how would you know that?"*

"You only mated Aquilian, yes?"

"That's hardly any of your business."

"If it was only Aquilian and not his twin as well, then you cannot become pregnant."

I'm sure I look dumbfounded because that's exactly how I feel. *"Wait, I have to be with both of them?"*

"Yes." Doxal looks at me like he can't believe he is having to explain this. *"Dauur mate in trios, two males and a female. That is because it requires the seed of both bondmates to fertilize a female. Since your mates are twins, like Yssig and I, they did not have to seek out a bondmate. Therefore, you cannot be pregnant unless you were also with Ettrian last night."*

"Alien breeding is so strange," I mumble out loud, but I admit I'm relieved to know these bastards won't be getting a baby from me. Not yet, anyway.

Doxal just smiles and closes his eyes as his head falls back against the wall. *"Your mates will come for you."*

CHAPTER 21

*A*quilian

Almost two full days have passed since we set out to find Xia, and we're no closer than we were the day before. Yssig had known exactly where to go and what to do to escape our confinement, but now he seemed to be leading us in the wrong direction. Ettrian and I had not just grown up in the forest; we *lived* in it. We knew these woods better than anyone else in our village, and this male was underestimating us. There was a large fruit tree up ahead of us, its branches curling up and away from the spiral trunk. The purple fruit that grows on it is so heavy that it causes the branches to droop all the way to the ground.

From the notches I carved into the tree this morning when we stopped to pick Kareen something to eat, I know we're going around in circles. I push at the bond, trying to speak to Yssig, but the male has blocked me. The wall he has built in his mind is so strong that sweat beads along my skin as I try to break it. Why would he shut us out?

Bunnyfly hops past me, nearly tripping Ettrian as he bolts between his legs. The little rammit emits an excited vibration, obviously happy to be out of the tree. My twin's lip curls in frus-

151

tration, and he pushes the creature from his path with his foot as he adjusts his hold on a sleeping Kareen. His eyes slide to mine, and I feel him reach out to me along the bond.

"We are going in circles, aren't we?"

"I believe so. I carved notches into that fruit tree earlier, when Yssig wasn't looking."

"We will allow him to believe he has us fooled a little longer. Kareen does not need to see another fight."

"I agree."

A few more hours pass and we find ourselves standing outside the dome. Yssig looks up at the barrier as if he's unsure about how we have returned to the place we left barely a day ago, but there is something in the nervous way he taps his fingers against his thigh that tells me he's trying to figure out what lie to tell us next.

"This is the dome," Ettrian tells him, but Yssig does not acknowledge him until he speaks aloud in the way Xia and Kareen do. Through my bond with Ettrian I can "hear" how frustrated Yssig sounds with my twin's questioning.

"I do not know how we circled around. I must have gotten lost."

"Do not play us for fools. We have allowed you to lead us in circles all day and this is the end." Ettrian rattles his warning, and I can see Yssig preparing for a confrontation. In my arms, Kareen is looking back and forth between the males, her little hands tugging my quills like she can sense the tension.

"We only wish to find our mate, Yssig. Please, help us." His face softens, but before he can answer there is a small disturbance in the trees off to the right. Yssig and Ettrian take up defensive positions, and I step behind my twin as I try to shield our kit from whatever is out there. A bright light pulses from within the brush and I pause, noting the familiar green. *"Lief?"* I reach out toward the alien male's mind, waiting anxiously.

"It is me."

"Calm. We know this male," I say, moving toward the brush. Lief steps out, his skin glowing softly as he eyes my twin and Yssig. I spent many days in this male's shadow, fascinated by his ability to communicate along the bond as if he were one of us and grateful that he did not seem to care that I was Darkborn. He held a special place in my heart and memories.

"Aquilian." He places his fingertips over his chest, a gesture he taught us was to show respect. *"It has been a long time."*

"More aliens?" Yssig asks.

"Lief is a friend." I turn to him with a glare.

"You're Venium." In my arms, Kareen turns, her head tilting to the side as she looks him up and down.

"I am." Lief nods, the ghost of a smile tugging at his lips. *"You are human."* My kit nods her head excitedly. *"You are a long way from home, little one."*

"Aliens took us!"

"Us? There were more with you?"

"Her mama was brought here with her," Ettrian informs him. *"They were placed within the dome and that is where Aquilian found them."*

"If not for our technology picking up the dome, I would not have known to take a closer look. I was on my way to check in with your people when I noticed something was not right."

"She is our mate, Lief. She has disappeared with Yssig's brother." I can feel the panic rising up inside of me, but I beat it back.

"A Darkborn?" Lief asks, turning his gaze on a guilty-looking Yssig, who nods slowly. *"Mmm, I thought so."*

"We have been walking in circles for days because this one does not wish for us to find the aliens that his brother has given our mate to." Ettrian sneers, his quills vibrating with anger.

Yssig's body clenches, his hands curling into fists as he

squares off against my twin. *"That is not what it is. I do wish for you to find your mate."*

"Then why have you been leading them in the wrong direction?" Lief asks casually.

"I took them in the direction I thought it was," the young male insists.

"Ah, then the Darkborn male I saw carrying a human female that way must have just been coincidence." The Venium gestures toward a path going in the opposite direction we traveled in when we left the dome and anger rises up inside of me.

I wanted to believe this male was simply turned around, that he didn't know the forest the way we did, but the look he gives Lief tells me that I was fooling myself. This male knew what he was doing and has given the aliens more than enough time to do unspeakable things to our mate. *"Why would you lie?"* I ask quietly.

Yssig shakes his head, his jaw clenching as he glances around at us. *"They won't hurt your mate, but they would hurt my sister if we didn't do as they commanded. It was the only way..."*

Beside me, Ettrian vibrates in frustration. *"It was not the only way! You could have confided in us."*

"Just like you confided in your brother?"

Ettrian jerks back as if he has been slapped. The accusation confuses me, and I turn to my twin. *"What does he mean, Ettrian?"*

154

CHAPTER 22

*I*noxia

Yasi's quills are pliable and soft beneath my fingers. She reminds me of a kitten—if kittens had flexible rubber spines coming from their heads. The tips of her quills aren't sharp at all and bend easily as I caress them. We've been stuck in here for what I think has been a couple of days now, and honestly if it weren't for Yasi's apparent need of me, I probably would have lost my mind. The little female and Doxal distract me from my worry over Kareen and what's happening with her. I know Aquilian and Ettrian—if he's woken up—would never let anything happen to her, but the anxiety eats away at me. It goes without saying that the sooner we escape this place, the better.

Even without the threat this place poses, with its lab equipment and operating tables, I don't want to be anywhere near these aliens. I definitely don't wish to be away from my family. A sharp pain cuts through my chest when I think about the family we left behind on Earth. My parents and Mina have no idea where I am, and the orphanage would have been alerted to Kareen's absence the day of the festival. Who knows how long we've actually been missing? Even if we never make it back to

Earth, I know that we have at least made our own family here, and I can find comfort in the thought that my family back home would understand and be happy for me. This was moving on from Trent in a big way.

The aliens in the other cells I saw the first day have been disappearing. They leave with a Tachin guard and then never return. It makes me nervous, and I find myself going rigid just at the sight of the aliens anytime they come inside our cell to draw blood or bring us their version of food, which looks like paste that's been hardened into blocks. We haven't been allowed to bathe, and the pretty silk I have wrapped around me is starting to look dingy.

In my arms, Yasi shudders, and a sad whine falls from her lips as she wraps her arms tighter around my left leg. I run my hand over her forehead and crest, cooing to her softly until she calms again.

"You have a natural way with kits, Xia," Doxal notes, his voice slipping into my mind.

"Thank you." A smile plays over my lips as I look up at him. He sits cross-legged against the back wall, his hands resting in his lap, as he watches his sister sleep.

"I am sorry for what I said to you the day I took you."

I manage to giggle a little. *"Which thing are you sorry for?"*

"All of it, but mostly for making you think my twin would do anything to harm your family." There's a drawn-out sigh from the big, dark male. *"Yssig would never have hurt them. I just needed to get you here, to stall them."*

I'm still not happy with them, but the anger I first felt has diminished. After seeing these aliens and the fear they inspire in Yasi and her siblings, I know I would have been just as desperate to do something if it were Kareen's life on the line. Just as I open my mouth to tell him I understand, a flash of green at the edge of my vision catches my attention. The Tachin have returned, but

156

this time it isn't with food or for testing. They don't look particularly happy as they glare at Doxal from the barrier.

"You lied, Dauur." The Tachin I've come to realize is the one in charge of this facility snarls as he walks into the room, two others flanking him and three more waiting outside.

This is not good. Doxal jumps to his feet, a growl rumbling up from his chest. "I did no such thing!"

"Take the female Dauur."

Both of the Tachin on either side step toward me, reaching for Yasi. "No! Get away from her!" I wrap my arms and legs around the girl, not willing to let them take her without a fight. She gasps against my chest and squeezes me tightly as hands clutch at her. There's a scream and a loud thud as Doxal sends one of the Tachin flying across the cell into the back wall. The second soon follows, but the guards who had been outside are on us in a heartbeat. Two of them take Doxal down with high-powered weapons that remind me of the tasers on Earth while one extends a club and begins to use it against the Dauur's back.

"Stop! Do not hurt him!" Yasi screams frantically.

"You told me the female had been bred," the Tachin leader says coldly, flicking his clawed hand to halt the beating. "We have tested her, and every single one has come back negative. Either this female was not bred or you are keeping secrets. Either way, your sister will be removed."

"Wait!" Doxal pants for breath, his arms shaking as he tries to push himself up. "Two males," he mumbles.

"What was that?"

"It takes... two males."

"Doxal, do not—" Yasi begins, but he growls at her, effectively quieting the girl.

"Breeding requires two male Dauur. She was only with one of the males within the dome. This is why she is not pregnant."

My chin trembles, and I know this is not information he's

telling them lightly. My heart sinks as I watch his eyes close in defeat. Blood spills from the wounds the guards opened on his back and he sways on his hands and knees.

"This is false."

Doxal's head snaps up and glares at the leader. "It is the truth."

The lead Tachin sighs and tilts his head, watching the dark male. "We have successfully bred a human with *one* male Dauur not very long ago."

"That is not possible. All Dauur males mate in pairs. I have never heard of what you speak."

"Possible or not, it was done." The Tachin flips his hand nonchalantly as if this is all irrelevant. "We will try it your way." He turns to a smaller Tachin cowering outside the barrier. "Bring me all of the males from within the dome. And you," the guards jerk when he gestures at them, "bring the small female. We will return for the human."

Yasi starts to scream again, clutching at my hands as she's pulled away from me. This time, Doxal doesn't try to fight; he just rattles angrily as he stares down at the floor. With my legs stretched out in front of me, I lean back, pulling with all of my strength. "You can't have her! This isn't right!"

"Remove her!" someone shouts, and I feel myself being lifted from the ground.

I'm suddenly weightless, and I realize at the last second that I am flying through the air. With a grunt, I feel myself crash into something that feels suspiciously like Doxal. Without thinking, I wrap my hand around one of his sharp quills and yank it free. He hisses, and I make a mental note to apologize to him if we are still alive later.

Weapon in hand, I launch myself at the lead Tachin, aiming for the spot where his wings connect to the rest of his body, but I miscalculate. Instead of hitting at the top, the quill in my hand slices through the delicate wings and lodges deep into his side. I yank it out as he screams, spinning on me and swinging his arm out. The clawed hand barely scratches my cheek and I duck down, pushing my shoulder into his abdomen as I bring the quill back down, landing it somewhere near his shoulder. I keep stabbing until I'm pulled away and the quill is knocked from my hand.

"You *vlech*!" the Tachin yells, fury lacing his voice as he trembles on the ground. His guards swarm around him, their wings rubbing together to create a loud, overwhelming vibration.

"Fuck you! You're nothing but an overgrown housefly!" *Okay now, dial it back*, my mind warns, but I'm pretty positive I've lost it at this point. "You all can't figure out how to keep your species going so you abduct innocent people to experiment on instead. You're sick! When my mates find you, they're going to tear you to pieces!"

The head Tachin stands slowly, shoving the others away from him as he stumbles toward me, one hand clutching the wounds I inflicted. "You, little human, are going to regret your actions." A clawed hand grabs my face, squeezing tightly as his eerie gaze bores into mine. "Forget the Dauur. I want this one prepped and on the table. Now!" His command bounces around the room and everyone scrambles to do his bidding. "I will see you soon." With my heart racing in my chest, I watch as he leaves.

"Xia!" Doxal and Yasi call as I'm pushed forward on wobbly legs.

I'm yanked from the cell so quickly that I don't even get a chance to look back at them one last time. *Gods, you've stepped in it this time*, I tell myself. *At least Yasi is safe for now. I bought her some more time.* My Tachin escort drags me out into the open bays that contain the tables and I panic, fighting them. I let my legs collapse and they jerk under my dead weight before another guard grabs my ankles. With a grunt, the aliens hoist me up onto the cold metal. I try to twist away, but there are more on the other side waiting for me. Painful bindings are strapped around my arms and legs, and I start to scream, my throat becoming raw as tears run into my hair.

"Humans have an unsavory habit of leaking fluids when they are scared." The voice near my ear makes my blood turn to ice in my veins and I freeze, my body going rigid. Something sharp pokes my arm, and the Tachin near my head slams his clenched fist on the table I'm strapped to. "No medications! She doesn't deserve them."

My heart is nearly racing out of my chest. I'm not sure what they plan to do, but it sounds like he means for it to be painful. The straps dig into my skin as I struggle, and my tears begin again, leaving hot wet trails on my flesh. A hum fills the air as a blinding white pain resonates through me, a moment before the smell of seared flesh hits my nose. It's so intense that the scream that bursts from my lungs catches in my throat, coming out as a strangled gurgle. Eyes rolling to the back of my head, the pain spreads along my lower abdomen, and it's obvious they're cutting into me.

"Please! Stop!" The scream tears through my mind, and my vision starts fading in and out.

"Check to make sure there is no fetus," a distant voice is saying. "If there is nothing, we will begin the direct injection testing."

The darkness swallows me whole, and I think I must have blacked out because the next time I open them the pain has spread and I can feel pressure inside of me as hands or instruments are moved around. A scream finally makes it past my lips and I begin to shake violently.

"Gag her," someone growls just before something is shoved inside my mouth.

Nausea assaults me as the aliens continue their work. Sickening sounds race around inside my mind, and I want to scream and cry. I want to thrash and tear myself free from these bonds. I want Ettrian and Aquilian to burst through the doors and rip these aliens limb from limb.

"Success, sir," I hear as my vision fades again. The world goes black, and now I'm blissfully numb.

CHAPTER 23

*E*ttrian

Yssig has disappeared. Even with three sets of eyes on him—four if you include little Kareen's—the male managed to escape while Aquilian badgered me about what I kept from him. While the fact that the twins were sent to breed Xia had not seemed like something my brother needed to know at the time, I see now that I should have disclosed this information. I was more worried about finding our mate than taking time to talk to my twin. Although he says he has forgiven me and that he already knew, I feel the disappointment and irritation coming from him along our bond. As much as I wish to go after the runaway male, finding our mate and bringing her home is much more important.

Up ahead of us, Lief raises his hand and we come to a halt. *"The facility is just up ahead."* His eyes fall on Kareen where she stands at Aquilian's side. *"I do not think it is wise to bring the kit until we have neutralized the Tachin."*

The minute my eyes connect with Aquilian's, he seems to know what I am going to suggest and I know I am going to have another fight on my hands. *"I will not stay behind again, Ettrian."*

"Brother, please."

"No! You have kept secrets, left out vital information."

Along the bond, I can feel his anger and I try to soothe him. *"I have, and for that I will apologize every day for the rest of my life if it will help. Let me do this. Allow me the chance to make up for my mistakes."* My hand rests on his shoulder and he rattles softly. *"She cannot stay here alone. Yssig still poses a threat to her safety."*

As he thinks, Aquilian rakes his fingers through his quills before rubbing his hands over his face. Relief rushes through me when he nods, but Kareen is not as pleased as I am. *"Bring her home."*

A small foot stomps the ground, followed quickly by an impressive growl. "Not fair! I want to help. I want to save *my* mama!"

Crouching down in front of our kit, I take her hands in mine, pulling her close. "You are the bravest kit I have ever met, but this is not a task for you. Your Papa Aquilian and I need you to be here when we bring your mama back. She will need your comfort more than anything else." Blunt teeth worry her lip as her shoulders sag, but I can see that she understands. "Xia means the entire world to me as well, and I promise you that I will do everything I can to return her to you."

A sudden fierceness returns to her eyes, her nose scrunches up and her lip pulls back over her teeth in a snarl. "Better not mess this up, Papa." Before I can respond, she launches herself into my arms, squeezing my neck. This little female is the most amazing creature I have ever known. The depth of her love humbles me. "For real," she whispers against the holes in my head. "Don't. Mess. Up."

Pulling away, I stare down at my daughter. A rumble begins in my chest, rolling up my throat before it bursts from my mouth. For the first time in my life, I laugh out loud and not along the bond. While I have seen and heard Xia and Kareen do this, it feels incredibly strange to hear myself make the sound. It feels... good. With a deep breath, I pull my kit back into a quick hug and then force myself to stand. Leaving two of the beings I love most in this world is painful. For the first time, I am thankful that Aquilian and I have grown up as outcasts. Everything we have gone through in our lives led us to this point.

It is obvious that my twin is reading my emotions by the way his face softens. He bends down, pressing his chest to mine. *"Be safe, brother."*

Choking back the uncertainty that threatens to overwhelm me, I pull away from my family and turn to Lief, nodding that I'm ready. From the moment we met this alien, there was an immediate bond. I can remember the disbelief we felt the first time he told us he was from the Sun Father's world. He taught some of us kits that the place we believed the Sun Father came from was actually a planet that his people inhabited. Many in our village believe him to be a liar, but Aquilian had been enamored. This alien male had treated him like an equal.

The world around us is glowing softly, and it helps put me at ease. As I follow closely behind Lief, I try once more to reach out along the bond to my mate but come up empty. There should be something, any little sign that she is alive, but in the place within my mind that she has taken over, I can feel nothing. *"Do you think she is still alive?"*

"If there is one thing I have learned from my brother's human mate, it is that they are a resilient species." Lief's lips curl up, his sharp teeth flashing in the same way Xia and Kareen's often do, and it sends a shiver down my spine. There is something far more daunting when this alien male smiles than when my little humans do it.

"Our human is delicate. Are they not all this way?"

"Perhaps they do not seem capable of great feats, but believe

164

me when I say they have the amazing ability to prevail when you least expect it." He shakes his head and smiles again. *"Any female who has the patience to put up with you, Aquilian, and a kit must certainly be a force to be reckoned with."* We walk on a little farther, coming to a stop near the top of a small incline. *"We are here."*

"Here?" My eyes scan the horizon. I see nothing but trees, ground, and sky above. *"Where?"* Quietly I step up next to Lief and watch as he holds out something that resembles a smooth stone tablet. A series of shapes appear and the male taps at them, his brows drawn in concentration. As if by magic, strange walls begin to emerge from thin air. Where there was once a tree line, there is now a very solid, very alien building. While my village prefers to reside within the trees, there are some Dauur who prefer to construct homes using materials from the world around us, but none of them look anything like what sits before me.

A moment later, the door facing us opens, and I look up to see a satisfied smile on Lief's face. *"We have access."*

That is all I need to hear before I am racing across the ground, sending probes out along the bond to search for her. We do not come across any resistance as we enter. The space within is lit with the same lights I saw before and a wave of anxiety clutches at me. This has to be where I was before.

To our right is a long hallway that branches off from the one we stepped into. The light in this one is dimmed, and there is a sudden sharp noise from somewhere inside that has our heads snapping in that direction. Lief immediately takes off toward the sound, my long stride keeping me right on his heels. The sense of urgency I feel turns to one of shock when a door glides open on its own and a room full of small beds is revealed. These are kits—tiny, newborn kits. They squirm around, hands clenching into small fists that they shove into their mouths. A few of them are curled on their sides as if conserving whatever warmth they have.

As I scan the beds, I spot only one kit out of the eight with features I recognize as those of a Dauur. The skin of the newborn is unlike anything I have seen before, patches of dusky gray mixed in with a color slightly darker than Xia's flesh. The kit's facial features, although mostly Dauur, show signs that they may be human. The small protrusion in the middle is a human nose. My heart aches, and I allow myself to wonder for a moment if this is what my own kit will one day look like.

The little pinpricks of emotions along the bond alert me that the kit is reaching out, seeking comfort. I try my best to calm the little one's sadness, running my finger down their cheek, arm, and little hand softly. On this kit's back is something I have never seen a Dauur born with, and I doubt it is a human trait. Tiny, delicate wings are flattened against the skin.

"Lief?"

"I see them."

I turn my head and see him cradling a tiny Venium kit in his arms. A pained expression paints his face as he runs his finger along the glowing pink fushori. The little wings on their back twitch with apparent irritation as he coos softly. A glance around the room makes it obvious that there are no mamas or papas with these newborns, and my quills rattle with my unease. *"We cannot leave them here alone, Lief."*

By the way he clutches the kit to his chest, I know he does not wish to leave them either. "I know you must make haste and reach your mate, but help me first. I need to make certain these are the only ones here. Check every corner, every door."

I walk between the beds, making sure my initial count is correct. At the very back of the room is a small nook I had not noticed. As I glance within, I am met with a disturbing sight. On a raised platform rests a human female, smaller than my mate. Strange things protrude from the mask covering her nose and mouth. A sick feeling overtakes me, and I know something is wrong with her. *"There is a human female here!"*

Lief comes to my side, the kit still curled in his arms. He runs one finger along her throat gently before shaking his head. "She is struggling. I am not sure what is wrong with her, but she is in critical condition. We will need to be careful when we move her." I hear him sigh and our eyes meet. "Go find your mate. I will stay here and contact my team for immediate rescue."

Without hesitation, I sprint from the room. Almost immediately, I'm aware of Xia's presence, but a moment later sharp pain, absolute agony, shoots through the bond we share. The feeling is so strong that it is like a physical force, making me stumble. Everything inside of me calls out to her, and I practically fly across the smooth floor. My mate is in terrible pain. I have made many mistakes, but I will not make another by waiting any longer.

White-hot fury courses through me at what I see when I enter a large, circular room. Lying on a table, much like the one I woke up on, is my mate, arms and legs bound tight, fabric shoved into her mouth to silence her. Sweat beads all along her pale skin as her chest rises and falls in distress. Her green eyes roll to the back of her head as I watch one of the aliens reach into her open abdomen, ripping a pained moan from her. They are hurting her— killing her.

A red haze falls over my vision, and I feel my body move of its own accord toward the Tachin who works with his back to me. "She. Is. *Mine.*"

CHAPTER 24

*a*quilian

From the large stone I'm sitting atop, I watch Kareen as she plays. Bunnyfly races around her feet, zigzagging so that my kit stumbles over herself multiple times in an effort to catch the small creature. *"You cheater!"* she giggles along the bond. She knows that I am not like her, that I cannot "hear" in the same way she does, and I have noticed that she's made an effort to speak often along the bond so that I may be included in her activities. It warms my entire being. The rammit jumps into the air, its feathered ears carrying it out of Kareen's reach, but she has gone still, her face a mask of anger and her little hands clenched into fits.

"Kareen?" I call to her, but my eyes catch sight of a familiar form dashing through the forest. *Yssig.* The Lightborn male is heading straight for us. My heart races as I jump up, sprinting toward Kareen and pulling her behind me as I rattle out a warning. *"Do not come any closer!"*

"Please, Aquilian! She is in danger!"

"Who?" Kareen asks suspiciously as she peeks around my leg. *"Who's in danger?"*

"My sister. Her name is Yasi. Something is wrong with her." He struggles to catch his breath, and I can feel the worry rolling off of him. *"They are beating her. She cannot defend herself!"*

This concerns me. I have felt nothing along the bond, but that doesn't mean what he says is a lie. Each Dauur has a different sensitivity when it comes to the mental bond we all possess. Familial and mating ties are always the strongest.

"I trusted you before and you lied."

"I am not asking for trust or even help! I am asking you to step aside so that I may reach my family."

Just as I am preparing to respond, a soft brush against my ilo has me spinning around. I catch only a glimpse of wild curls flying in the wind before my kit disappears over the hill that Ettrian and Lief walked only a little while earlier.

"Kareen!" My feet eat up the ground as I take off after her, Yssig right at my side. When I catch up to her, I scoop my daughter up into my arms. I'm shocked when she begins to flail, kicking and vibrating with words I cannot understand. Before I can even consider putting her down, I feel her blunt teeth latch onto my hand. She bit me. This is obviously Bunnyfly's influence.

"Let me go, Quilian! We have to help her!"

"Ettrian and Lief are helping your mama. Calm, little one!"

"Not Mama!" she screams as tears well up in her eyes. *"They hurt me too!"*

"Who hurt you?" I am immediately furious. *"These aliens hurt you? When?"*

Her little body goes limp in my arms like she has given up her fight. The tears flow from her eyes freely now and she uses her fist to swipe them away. *"Nuh-uh. The people at the place I used to live, before we came here. They beat me too, Quilian. We have to save her."*

There have been many moments in my life where I've felt

anger and a sense of unfairness, but always over something that has been done to me. My jaw is clenched so tightly that I am surprised none of my teeth break. That someone who was supposed to care for my daughter could ever do anything to hurt her is appalling. If I ever meet these humans who laid their hands on a defenseless kit, then I will tear them limb from limb and bathe in their blood.

I look up at Yssig, who watches us with sad eyes. We cannot let these Tachin harm anyone else. Although we had never planned on having our kit anywhere near these aliens, I know this is important. My daughter has a past she is wrestling with, and I realize we all have a duty to do what is right. Yssig and I race forward as he follows the call from his sibling. When we finally make it over the last hill, a complex pattern of buildings spreads out before us. The Lightborn male does not falter at the sight like I do. Instead, he rushes forward as if a clan of nolfira are nipping at his heels.

"Sun Father, watch over us," I mumble as I rush to catch up.

The doors are flung open, and it seems as if chaos has taken over. Yssig disappears down another hallway and Kareen points after him. There's an eerie silence along the bond, but it is hard to notice with the emotions of all the beings in close proximity beating at me. Determination, fear, anger, and sadness all assault me, but I push on after the other male. As we come up on an open door, I feel a strange vibration and see Kareen's face pinch in concern.

"Babies!" she says excitedly, but I shake my head.

If Lief and Ettrian have found the kits, then I know help is already on the way. We need to focus on finding Yssig's sister. The rage that slams into me from the bond I share with Ettrian sends me into a panic, but the fact that I still cannot feel our mate scares me even more.

Almost there, I repeat to myself over and over as we make our way to the place I can feel my twin. We cannot lose Xia. The longer I allow my brother's fury to flow through me, the more I can feel my body shaking. In my arms, Kareen is a steadying weight, the only thing keeping me from tearing through this place and killing anyone I come upon.

There is a bright light at the end of the hall, and we suddenly find ourselves in a large open room. This part is brighter than anything I have ever seen, and I squint against the reflection that bounces off of the white walls. Yssig darts off to the right, but I come to a stumbling halt when my eyes fall on Ettrian. Kareen, who hasn't seemed to notice her papa, squirms until I lower her to the ground, running after the other Lightborn male as he searches for his sister.

Too shocked at what I see, I don't try to stop the kit as she leaves. Our mate is laid out on the long table before Ettrian. Her arms and legs are stretched out, and red blood is spilling from the gaping wound in her abdomen. *She is dying.* I feel my knees slam against the hard floor and realize I must have fallen onto them. My heart pounds hard in my chest and my lungs do not seem to be working properly. The entire room begins to spin around me. *Do not panic. She is not gone. She cannot be gone.* As I sit on the floor, I see my twin's mouth moving, but I do not understand him. Someone rushes past me and I am only mildly aware that this is Lief, his green fushori glowing against all of the white around us.

The Venium reaches Xia and begins trying to put her back together. *"Do not hurt her! She needs a pod! Stop!"* I surge forward, stumbling to my feet when Ettrian slams into me, his arms wrapping around my upper body as he tries to hold me back.

"He is helping her! Aquilian, stop! He is trying to save her life." My brother sends soothing thoughts along the bond, and I try desperately to cling to his hope. Just his touch is enough to ground me and bring me back to reality. There are flashing red

lights now, and sharp vibrations race along my ilo. Something is happening, and I have a feeling it's not anything that will help us.

Lief has finished his work on Xia, but she still looks dangerously pale and remains unconscious. *"She will live,"* he tells us, looking up from a monitor at his side.

"Kareen!" I spin away from my brother to look around for our kit. She is within one of the open rooms behind us, cooing softly to a young Darkborn female Dauur as she holds onto her. Yssig is standing over two corpses that I assume belong to whatever guards attempted to stop him. On the ground near the back of the room is an unconscious Doxal. He seems injured, but alive.

"We need to leave. The Tachin have activated the self-destruct sequence for the complex. There is not much time."

Ettrian lifts our mate into his arms, pressing her close to his chest. *"The young?"*

With a quick motion for Yssig to follow, Lief jerks his head in the direction of the hall we came from. *"My team is here. We will grab the young ones and go. No time to search the rest of the facility."*

As quickly as we can, our group races down the hallway back toward the room where Kareen heard the kits. Lief is in the lead, urging us to hurry as the lights flash from points on the walls all around us. As we reach the door, the Venium male stops dead, causing me to crash into him.

Before I can ask what the problem is, I peer inside and see the lone Lightborn Dauur male standing among the beds of wriggling newborns. He's staring down at the tiny kit in front of him, his fingers caressing the patchy skin as a sad rattle fills the room. His hands glide over the nubs on the back of the newborn's head before he lifts him into his arms.

"Place the kit back in the bed and step away," I command, fearing for the newborn's safety.

"He is my son." The male's voice is soft and sad as he brings the kit to his chest, his lips pressing firmly to its head.

"Grab the rest of the newborns and let's move. There is not time to stand here chatting. Move!" Lief shouts.

"Can you stand on your own?" I ask Doxal as he leans against his twin.

"Of course I can," he grunts, bristling at my question.

"Good. Get the human female at the back. She is hurt so be careful. Luz is on his way as we speak. The rest of you who can, grab a kit and move!" Lief orders, and we all jump to action.

CHAPTER 25

*I*noxia

"Do not give up, female. You are still needed here," a gruff voice is whispering in my dreams.

This isn't one of the voices I want to hear, but it's reminding me that I can't fall into this darkness. I need to push forward, but I don't want to go back to the pain. A shiver takes me, even inside of my own dream the thought of that pain makes me feel sick.

Buck up! You can do this!

I want to tell that little inner voice of mine to shove it, but she's also right. I don't want to die—I want to live, to make a life with the people here that I love. I swim through the darkness, kicking and clawing frantically.

Something hurts my ears, a sharp screeching that sends pain shooting through my jumbled mind. A baby's cry? Why isn't anyone helping the poor thing? With all of the strength in my battered body, I lift my heavy eyelids and peer around, trying to find the source of the crying.

The first thing I see is Ettrian's face and I almost begin to cry. *Please don't be a dream.* A grunt is pulled from my throat as I bounce in my male's arms, my head lolling to the side because

174

I'm not strong enough to keep it up. The front of the Tachin lab is behind us, and I know I'll never forget this place. From the corner of my vision, I see a flash of green, but I can't make out who or what it was. Dread settles like a stone in my stomach, and I wonder if it could be one of the Tachin escaping.

"You said you had a team, Lief!" Ettrian yells.

Blackness begins to creep in as the pain in my body becomes worse. Over the buzzing in my ears, I hear a voice that's strangely familiar.

"This is a team!" This is the voice from my dream, the one who helped to pull me out.

"I only see one other Venium. How is this a team?"

"There is also a pilot and Luz is more than capable of aiding us," the dream voice growls.

There's a massive explosion, and a ball of fire erupts from the windows of the lab, sending glass flying outward. Ettrian shields me with his body as he stumbles forward.

"We will never find out the purpose of the dome now," Ettrian mutters darkly. *"We will never know why we were placed within it while the others were tortured in the labs."*

"There wasn't much time to gather all the files while attempting to piece your mate back together," someone is saying, *"but from what I can tell, the mating pairs in the lab were failing. Pregnancies were not taking, and the ones that did gave them unsatisfactory results. Perhaps they thought a more natural setting would be beneficial."*

I want to stay awake, want to watch as this place burns to the ground, but the pain is too much and I feel myself begin to slip under once again. The last thing that floats through my mind before I give in is a plea that everyone taken by the Tachin has gotten out.

∼

*G*ods, my body hurts. People are speaking again, their voices swirling around me as I try to concentrate on what they are saying.

"I cannot fit everyone into the ship. Some will have to travel by foot or wait here for the transport to return," the dream voice says with a frustrated sigh. "I am sorry. We didn't account for this when we set out."

"Of course. Did not bring sufficient backup and did not bring technology big enough for all of us to return on," Ettrian grumbles.

"Give us the young and those that were wounded. We will meet the rest in the village."

All at once, a multitude of rattling quills fills the air, sounding like hail from a summer rain storm on the hood of a car. "We will not be separated from our sister." It's Yssig, I believe. He doesn't sound pleased.

"Nor do we wish to be away from our mate or kit," Ettrian rumbles. "We trust you, Lief, but we have been apart for too long." He sounds different to me, changed somehow. I can't seem to put my finger on why exactly, though. "These females are the most precious beings to us. Take the kits and the human female to the village. They will know what to do to aid them there."

"The Venium pup stays with me," the dream voice growls.

"We would never attempt to keep a male's kit from him, Lief."

Ah, so the dream voice has a name.

"The little female is not mine." He sounds a little nervous, like Ettrian has struck too close to his heart.

"She may as well be."

~

*T*he next thing I remember being conscious for is something I'm not sure I will ever forget. It's a strange yet soothing sensation. How long was I out? *"Kareen?"* I call out, panic making my voice rise.

"Shh, be calm. The kit is asleep. Everything will be okay. Rest." I recognize Aquilian's soft, gentle voice along the bond.

Oh gods, he's going to be so mad at me. Staying inside the tree would have prevented all of this, but I had to know that they wouldn't hurt my family. I needed to know that Ettrian had been left in good hands and helping Doxal get blooms seemed like a good opportunity. Though Ettrian had done wrong, had upset me and pushed me, I still care for him. There's still some force pulling me to him even now. Could it be the bond that Doxal spoke of or something else entirely? It doesn't even matter anymore. The only thing I know for certain is that my family has grown to include a blue-eyed little girl and two big, glowing aliens.

If someone had told me weeks ago that I would have not just one alien male but two as mates, I would have laughed until I cried. Now though? Now these aliens are mine, and I couldn't leave them behind even if I tried.

"Always, Xia. We will always be yours," my sweet dark male whispers.

How Aquilian seems to know exactly what I'm thinking doesn't even surprise me anymore; it's just something I accept. Before coming here, I wouldn't have believed humans capable of a mental bond like this, but now it seems perfectly normal. Whether it's something within the Dauur themselves, or something about this amazingly beautiful planet, there's no way to deny this bond has taken root inside of me and perhaps Kareen as well. I'm no longer scared of what that means for us.

"I shouldn't have left," I breathe as I sink into the sensation that surrounds me.

"I should not have let you," he says quietly. *"Make no mistake, Inoxia: when you are recovered, I am going to spank your bottom until it is the prettiest shade of red for scaring the life out of me."*

"I'm so sorry." Pain pulses through me at the same time desire settles into my lower stomach.

"Do not worry about it now. Just let the seed pod heal you." Somewhere along the bond, I can feel his love and adoration surrounding me as if he's physically touching me. *"We are nothing without you, Xia."*

"Will this work for me?" I wonder mostly to myself.

"I hope so. The trees and seed pods were a gift from the Sun Father himself. The tradition passed down from our ancestors says that he was injured during a battle with a great beast at the dawn of time, and because he could not heal fast enough on his own, he missed the birth of his twin sons, Nebol and Semol. The labor was long and difficult, and he lost his mate before he made it back to her side. With great effort and love, he built the pod, watering the seed each day until it grew large enough to fit even the largest Dauur, because he believed neither should a mama lose her kit, no matter what age. It is our hope that he will bless your healing." He goes quiet for a moment, and I feel his fear and uncertainty, his worry that this may not actually work. *"Our daughter needs you."*

Our daughter, I repeat to myself. He's right. Kareen has always been mine, even when I thought I had lost the opportunity. I'm her mom, and she needs me.

CHAPTER 26

*E*ttrian

"A spanking?" I ask my brother, remembering the conversation Kareen and I had not too long ago when I woke from my time in the pod. *"Was this a punishment?"*

His quills light up, pulsing as his eyes begin to swirl in a rainbow of colors. *"She needed to be punished for leaving the tree when there was danger all about. Doxal and Yssig were in our home when she was defenseless. Our kit was there, Ettrian."* I watch as he rakes his fingers through his quills nervously. *"I disciplined her for it."*

"You... spanked our female?"

"Disciplined. Do not judge me, Ettrian." He huffs when I clench my jaw to keep from smiling. *"You spanked her for merely wiggling on the first day we met her!"*

I quickly avert my gaze, stifling the laughter that threatens to bubble up. *"That was different,"* I mumble.

"Ettrian?"

"Yes, brother?"

"She enjoyed it." My eyes slide slowly back to his face and I can feel the embarrassment and uncertainty rolling off of him. *"A*

lot. We—" His words falter for a moment, and he rubs the length of one quill. *"We mated."*

"You mated our female," I repeat, not quite sure I have understood.

"We did not finish the bond," he rushes. *"I only pleasured her... and myself."*

"This actually makes sense."

"Does it?"

"The bond is far stronger now than it was initially. Even without a translator you are able to understand her." I shrug, tracing the pattern on one of my legs. *"It has happened before when mates are found among other far off tribes. The bond helps with the language barrier."*

"Yes, but I could understand her before we mated. I think it was my anger that pushed it. Are you upset with me?"

His question takes me by surprise. *"Why would I be upset with you, Aquilian?"*

"I mated with her without you. I had not set out to do so, but she drank cinsi tea, which apparently affects humans far differently than it does Dauur." I see anger bloom in his eyes as he recalls a memory. *"I brought you back to the tree, wounded and unconscious, and the first thing I see upon entering our home is Xia on top of Doxal, Yssig's twin, attempting to mate the male."*

"She did what?*"* Shocked, I jump to my feet, preparing myself for a fight.

"They were only trying to help her, brother. Our little female was the aggressor."

"Xia?" My anger deflates, and I fall back into a sitting position. *"I am not the one who should be upset. I attempted to do something unforgivable because I gave into my fear. You showed her the love a male should bestow upon a mate."*

"You felt you had no choice."

The air around us feels thick with the tension I have created.

In the room across from us, I can hear the newborn kit whimpering, and I know we will need to seek the milk of the seed pod for him soon or he will starve. There is no telling what the Tachin fed the poor thing since we found no females aside from the sick human.

Tiny footsteps pad against the floor, signaling to me that our kit has awoken and come to see if her mama is better yet. Pretending not to notice as she slinks into the room, I glance down at my hands where they rest in my lap and grin. She thinks herself quite the hunter. I suspect she has also come looking for Bunnyfly, who is curled up next to Aquilian. Thank the Sun Father the little creature was waiting patiently outside the door of the lab for her or the kit would have been devastated.

A moment before she pounces, Kareen makes a soft noise as if she cannot contain her excitement. I manage to lean forward, tucking my quills close to my skin so that she cannot poke her eyes out on them just before she jumps onto my back with a screech.

"How did you know? That's not fair!" Her laugh is so beautiful that I share it along the bond so that Aquilian can experience it as I reach over my shoulder, flipping her head over foot before dropping her into my lap.

"I will always know where you are, troublemaker." She giggles again when I squeeze her in my arms. *"Why are you out of bed?"*

"Xia—"

"Is still resting. She will be fine now that the pod has her."

"Just like you were?"

"Just like I was." Tucking one of her 'wayward curls,' as Xia calls them, behind her ear, I begin to slowly rock her from side to side. *"If you are not careful, you are going to end up being quilled. No more pouncing."* When I look down to make sure she has heard me, I see that Kareen has fallen fast asleep and I am

certain she did not hear my warning at all. *Kits*. *"What will we do with these males?"*

Aquilian lifts Bunnyfly into the air and rubs his face against the little beast's. *"They have asked to be taken to the village. Kareen and Yasi refuse to be parted. Our daughter claims that they need one another."*

My hand strokes her curls and I feel my heart swell with love. *"Then it is as it should be."*

CHAPTER 27

*I*noxia

My eyes ease open, and I'm immediately confused because there is still only darkness. I blink, hoping to clear my vision, but nothing changes. Reaching my hand out tentatively, I come into contact with something hard and smooth. Whatever this is extends in every direction like I'm encased within it, and I can feel the panic well up inside of me. *Coffin!* I gasp for air, but it would seem that my lungs have forgotten how to work.

I'm not dead! I'm alive! Oh gods, this can't be happening. This has to be a nightmare.

"Help! Please don't leave me! I'm alive!" Fists slamming into the surface in front of me, I scream as loud as I can, managing to draw short panicked breaths. "Please!"

"*Calm, female,*" an unfamiliar voice commands. *"You will injure yourself farther and the pod will keep you inside to heal the new wounds."*

Pod? I'm still in the seed pod? Images flash through my mind of the Tachin, their hands grabbing at me, tools cutting me open. *I was hurt. They* hurt me. The memory of the unimaginable pain makes my heart race, and I fight the panic, willing my breathing to return to normal, counting backward from ten the way I learned in my therapy sessions years ago.

You can do this, Xia. Stay calm. You've got this.

After a few minutes, the pod slowly begins to part, a sliver of light breaking through the darkness. Two large hands tug at the seam, opening it wider before they reach inside and pull me up, lifting me from the giant seed.

"Can you stand on your own?" the huge male in front of me asks.

My legs wobble a little, but they hold steady so I nod. A glance down at my body alerts me to the fact that I'm naked and covered in slime. All of the Dauur I've met aside from Yasi haven't worn any type of clothing. Waking up without a stitch on when you can't remember undressing is odd, but at this point I'm just thankful to be alive and pain free. The male grabs two lengths of the silky material, his eyes never straying from my face as he hands me one.

"Clean off with this one. You can use the other to clothe yourself if you wish."

"Thanks." The slime comes off relatively easy, leaving my skin soft and smooth in its wake. The male holds out the other length and I take it gratefully, wrapping my body as I take a moment to study him. Like Ettrian, this Dauur's colors are light, but he's broader in the shoulders and far more intimidating than my alien. Unlike my males, this one has a length of cloth that crisscrosses over his chest. When he turns his back to me, I see that there is a tiny newborn baby nestled into material that he has around himself. "You've got a baby? I thought I only imagined one crying."

The only response I get is a grunt as he fusses over something on a shelf in front of him.

Not a talker. "What was your name?"

"Ayku."

"Is the little one's mom here somewhere?"

"No."

"Oh." Pursing my lips a little, I frown. "Where is she?"

"Dead."

Well, hell. *Xia, insert your foot into your mouth and leave it there.* "I'm... so sorry." I tie off the makeshift dress and glance around, half-expecting to see Bunnyfly curled up in the corner. "All covered up. Is my family here?"

"They have gone to retrieve food." He turns, looking down at me hesitantly, and I see that his eyes are a pretty blue. This is a color I have seen a couple times over my time spent with Aquilian and Ettrian. "One of the Darkborn males stayed behind."

As if on cue, there's a flurry of loud footsteps before Doxal rushes into the room. "Inoxia!" His gaze sweeps the room, narrowing on Ayku. "What are you doing in here, Lightborn?"

"Your job," Ayku growls. "If you had been paying any attention at all, you would have felt her panicking from across the forest." Doxal huffs in irritation, but the lighter male seems to ignore him. His gaze is on me again as he reaches out to tuck a curly red strand of hair behind my ear. "You have eyes just like my son's mama."

A loud, furious rattle fills the air as Ettrian pushes his way past Doxal to where we stand. *"Keep your hand off of our mate."*

Ayku steps back, his hand falling to his side. *"My apologies. I meant no offense."* A sharp cry from the baby on his back slices through the tension, and he reaches behind himself in a practiced motion, slipping the little one free of the carrier. With his other hand, he attempts to grab something from the pod, but whatever it is seems to be stuck.

"I can take him for you if you want. Just for a moment," I hurry to offer when he narrows his eyes and clutches the infant closer. *"So you can get what you need."*

He takes a moment to consider, eyeing my open arms. *"Thank you, female."* Ayku's eyes flash white before he passes his son over to me, keeping his fingers on the baby for a moment longer as if he's afraid to lose contact.

"My name is Inoxia," I tell him, pulling the baby close. *"And you're welcome."* As I stare down at his little face, I begin to notice things that seem to indicate this baby isn't completely Dauur. In the middle of his face is one of the most adorable human noses I've ever seen, and along his neck and chest I can see a lighter shade of skin, similar to my own. My fingers run over the tiny nubs where I imagine he will one day have quills, trailing down his back until I feel something strange. There are tiny, delicate wings between his shoulders. Neither humans nor Dauur have these. My mind flashes back to something the Tachin said about what they were using the human females for, and I shiver. *"His mother was human?"*

"She was."

Aquilian joins us, and my males stand on either side of me as I cradle the baby against my chest, cooing softly. I feel Aquilian's chest brush my shoulder as he leans down to nuzzle his face against my neck, his warm breath warming my skin. *"How is it possible that you are even more beautiful?"*

There's something in his voice that sends shivers down my spine. *"What happened to his mother?"*

Ayku removes a white liquid from the pod, filling a cup that he has stuck a small length of the silky material into. *"The Tachin killed his mama and my twin—"*

"I knew the Tachin lied when they said they used only one male," Doxal growled.

Eyes flashing red, Ayku glares at the Darkborn male, but his quills remain quiet when he looks down at the baby in my arms. *"They told you no lie. My brother was the only one of us to mate the human female."*

"How is this possible?" Ettrian shakes his head in confusion.

186

"I have never known a Dauur male to produce a kit without a bondmate participating. This does not make any sense."

"Just because you haven't heard of it doesn't mean it isn't possible, Ettrian." I roll my eyes. *"I'm assuming your brother was your twin?"*

"He was. We were indistinguishable, so much alike that our mama had to tie different colored fabric around our ankles to tell us apart as kits." He chuckles sadly, swirling the liquid within the cup.

"It sounds like human identical twins. I remember watching a documentary where they presented research showing that some twins were so similar that they literally shared the same or a very similar DNA code. I'm not anywhere close to being a scientist, but maybe something like that can happen with Dauur too? Maybe your DNA code was so similar that it didn't matter if you both mated with her or not?"

"Akai and I had not anticipated this. We believed that when they had him mate the female, nothing would come of it. Like your male, we had never heard of a lone male fathering a kit." He pauses, holding his hands out for the baby. I gently slip my curl from the firm grasp of the little hand as Ayku lifts him from my arms. *"It is obvious we were wrong and both my brother and the female paid for that with their lives."*

"Why would the Tachin kill them if they were successful?" It doesn't make sense to me at all.

"There is a bond that a child forms with his or her parents, and the Tachin sought to prevent this by killing the mamas and papas after they were born. What they failed to realize is that I am his papa as well. We have always shared a bond." Taking the damp cloth he's soaked in the white liquid, Ayku brings it to the baby's mouth and sighs when he gently begins to suckle.

"What about all of the other aliens that were in the cells?" Doxal asks as if he's reading my mind.

"They are all dead. Once they were sure they had succeeded and a viable kit was born, the Tachin disposed of them."

"I'm sorry you lost your brother and that your son lost two of his parents." The thought that this baby is going to grow up never knowing his human mother or his other father breaks my heart, and I feel the sting of tears at the back of my eyes. A second later, I hear the familiar pitter-patter of my girl's feet as she races down the hall. She flies into the room, blonde curls flying all around her face as she comes to a dead stop. Her pretty blue eyes are locked on me, chest rising and falling quickly. As I watch, her face crumbles, and she lets loose the most pitiful wail I've ever heard before she barrels into me.

"I thought you were gonna die!" Tears stream down her face as she squeezes my leg.

"Oh, baby." My hands run over her tangled hair, tugging out tiny twigs and pieces of grass. Of course my kid has been rolling in nature. The thought that she is mine makes me smile and crouch down, tugging her into my arms for a tight hug. "I'm not going to leave you." She's already lost one mother. I can't imagine how scary that was for her. "I promise I'm not going to leave you." Pressing my lips to her head, I look at Aquilian and Ettrian. I'm not leaving any of them.

"Good!" With a sniffle, she wipes at her wet cheeks as she pulls away to look at me.

"Off to bed with you, Kareen. We need to leave early tomorrow morning and a tired kit is a grumpy one." Ettrian nods to Ayku and begins to herd us from the room.

"Will the other babies be in the village already?" Her face lights up, and she hops around excitedly when he nods.

"Other babies?" My brow arches at Ettrian.

"Later," he replies, bending to scoop Kareen up so that she can press a sweet kiss to his cheek before she goes happily into his brother's arms. "Go with your Papa Quilian for a moment."

As I watch the two of them walk down the hall, Kareen's little hand waving to me, I get a strange feeling. "Hey, I think I should go with her. We always sleep—" But the sudden press of Ettrian's lips against mine effectively cuts me off.

His fingers are immediately buried in my hair, tangling in the mess of untamed curls as we press close together. As if he's my first shot of dark coffee on a Monday morning, I feel my entire body come to life. The sound of my heartbeat pounds out a rhythm in my ears as I part my lips, welcoming his tongue into my mouth. Our breaths mingle as our tongues dance, twisting and exploring. A pained whimper fights its way up my throat, and I moan softly against him.

He pulls back so suddenly that I fall forward, my face smacking into his hard chest. "Ouch!"

"My apologies! I hurt you. I—I did not mean to." His hands brush my face softly like he's checking me over.

"Ettrian." He stops his fussing, but his eyes don't meet mine. "You didn't hurt me. I'm fine." I slide my hands up, tugging on his shoulders in a silent bid for him to come closer so that I can grasp his quills, a shiver running through my body as I pull him down to my level. "Kiss me again." I plead when his breath tickles my lips, moaning when his mouth meets mine gently. The hard outer shell of his quills are cool beneath my fingers, and I trap his bottom lip between my teeth, tugging softly.

He kisses me back with such passion that it feels like I'm going to lose myself within him, and I shudder in anticipation. There has always been a need between the two of us, but our situation was less than ideal. An inferno has been lit inside of me, trying to consume me in its blaze, but before it can, he pulls back. "I am sorry for the things I have done, Xia," he mumbles against my lips.

"For what?"

"For trying… to force you. It is unforgivable."

The shame I see in his eyes breaks my heart, but the reminder is like a bucket of cold water over the head. "I wish you would have just told me."

"I tried, but that is not an excuse."

"I forgive you."

Ettrian goes still, his hands frozen on my face. "I do not deserve it."

I shrug my shoulders, stepping out of his embrace to collect myself. "Maybe you don't, but this is my choice and I'm choosing to forgive you."

"Thank you."

His jaw clenches tightly and I press my hand to his chest for a moment before I take another step back. "I'm going to find Kareen and lie down for a little bit. I missed her, and I'm sure these last couple days have scared her." It occurs to me as I walk away that this is the first time I've ever heard him speak out loud. I know there will be more moments to catch up with Ettrian, to show him that I don't blame him, but right now I just want the comfort of my little girl resting in my arms.

~

*A*s we near the village, I start to realize that this is nothing like I had imagined. Although I've been living in a tree for weeks and Ettrian and Aquilian have told me stories of their people during our journey, I'm still amazed by what I see when we stop within a few yards of the archway.

There's a massive network of huge trees just like the ones I've been living inside of, and I try to get a better view as we wait for the Venium to gather up the babies and the injured who have been on the ship. Lief told us that they waited for us to arrive before approaching. Even though the villagers were familiar with the male, this situation was different.

"Allow Ettrian to do the talking when we greet the tribe. There will be a lot for them all to take in between the kits and the Tachin's deeds," Aquilian tells us quietly as we draw closer.

Before we can even reach the path that leads us to the archway, our group is surrounded by a small band of Dauur males, each one rattles out a warning as if ready to attack at the slightest threat. I pull Kareen close to me and duck behind Aquilian's body when the males part for a small group of older Dauur. Their colors are duller and most of them are bent slightly with age. *"Hey there."* I wave, hoping I don't come off as a threat. *"We, uh, we come in peace?"*

Aquilian shoots me a look over his shoulder that is definitely an 'I told you to let Ettrian do the talking' look and has me pinching my mouth shut. I still haven't received my punishment, and now I'm sure this is going to be tacked onto it.

"Ettrian. Aquilian," the old male speaks along the bond.

"Elder." Ettrian bows as his quills puff at the back of his head. *"We apologize for the sudden arrival, but there are urgent matters we need to discuss with you."*

A soft cry from one of the babies goes up, and though I know they cannot hear it, I've learned from Aquilian that the infants produce an alarming vibration. *"Who have you brought?"*

"There are kits and wounded. They are the survivors of abduction."

"They are aliens," the elder says as if this is something we should be ashamed of.

"These kits were born here. They have nowhere else to go," Ettrian argues.

The elders huddle close and speak together for a moment before turning with a nod. *"The kits may stay. That which is born on Dimosia remains on Dimosia."* She gestures to those of us that are not Dauur. *"The rest of the aliens are free to leave. Gather the kits."* The elder gestures for the Dauur males gathered around us to retrieve the babies, but Lief snarls menacingly.

"You may take the others, but the Venium pup comes with us," Lief growls. While I know for a fact that I would never even attempt to take a Twinkie from this guy, one brave, or perhaps stupid, Dauur male marches forward and attempts to pluck the baby from his arms.

Although Ettrian is translating everything the Venium says along the bond, a translation for what happens next is not needed. Before our eyes, the already large male seems to grow and the Dauur stumbles backward as Luz, Lief's brother and a member of the small rescue team, wraps his arms around his chest and tries to calm him.

"This is his kit. You cannot separate them." Ettrian is trying to remain calm, but I see him starting to lose control. *"I will not allow my mate to be taken either."* A few astonished glances fly our way and I'm pulled forward. *"This is Inoxia. She is mated to my brother and I."*

"And they're my daddies!" Kareen pokes her head out from behind Aquilian, smiling her toothy grin that has even the bravest Dauur taking a step backward.

"By the Sun Father! Move out of the way!" A shout goes out along the bond and the crowd that has gathered begins to part. Whispered words reach me, but "Darkborn Taenov" is all I'm able to make out.

An onyx-colored female finally emerges at the front, her long strides eating up the ground as she walks purposefully toward us. The only color on her are the silver quills rattle in anger. Her eyes are red and swirling as her gaze sweeps across the elders. *"What is the meaning of this?"*

"Safia!"

The relief is evident in Ettrian's voice, and I try and ignore the prickles of jealousy that begin to rise up. *Don't jump to conclusions, Xia. Not everyone is Trent. Female friends aren't a threat.*

Before the elder can speak up, another shout goes up, and this time there's more of a commotion. *"They have been blessed! Let them pass."* A path is created through the crowd and a pearl-colored Dauur female, even whiter than Ettrian, practically glides through. The only other color on her body is the gold-tipped quills atop her head. There is a far more welcoming tone where this female is concerned, but she doesn't seem to feel the same way about the dark female as the others did. She comes to a stop beside Safia, placing her hand on the dark female's shoulder.

"That is Lirseas, a Lightborn Taenov. They have the ability to speak directly to the Sun Father himself," Aquilian tells me.

"The Sun Father has spoken and they are all welcome among us, elder. If the Venium male wishes to depart with his kit, then he may. They are not our captives."

One of the male elders rattles angrily as he glares at Luz and Lief. *"What is born on Dimosia should stay on Dimosia! This is nonsense!"*

"The Sun Father has spoken." Safia snarls, pressing her palm into the elder's chest when he steps toward us. *"You would go against the word of the Lightborn Taenov?"* A murmur goes through the crowd at her words.

The elder male is obviously unhappy, but instead of continuing to argue, he turns on his heel and rushes away with a couple of the other older members close behind. I'm not sure exactly who Safia is, but I think I like her. As the other hybrid babies find comforting arms to nestle into, I reach down for Kareen, thankful that we have one another.

$\sim$

*E*ttrian and Aquilian have been away most of the afternoon making sure the babies are settled into their new homes and the elders have been caught up on all of the recent events that led to a bunch of aliens being stranded on their planet. For the most part, Kareen and I have stayed close to Yasi, Doxal, Yssig, and Ayku since none of us actually have a place in this tribe yet. We're all outsiders here even though we've been welcomed.

Yasi and Kareen are huddled in the corner with Bunnyfly, who is learning that being a pet sometimes means you get dressed up in the pretty silk fabrics and carried around like a baby. My girl leans down and kisses the creature on the nose and tells her new best friend, *"One day, my mom is gonna have a baby and I'll get to hold it just like this!"*

The water I'm sipping comes out of my nose and sprays out of my mouth like I'm some sort of fountain. Where in the world is she getting this from? A gentle breeze flows through the main room as the tree opens up to reveal Lief. In his arms is the injured human he mentioned he was going to retrieve from the ship. The person is so tiny, not just by Venium standards but human ones as well. As he walks by me, I'm shocked to realize I know this human.

"Mina…?" The cup slips from my hand, shattering against the floor, and I rush forward. Taking her hand in mine, I brush the short, matted hair from her face. "Oh gods, is she okay? What the hell happened to her?"

"She is in a coma. I suspect it is medically induced, but we aren't sure why. We did what we could on the ship. Now it is time to see if the seed pod can help her like it did you."

"How the hell is she even here? I know she wasn't in the cells where we were."

Lief shrugs a shoulder and nudges me out of the way. "She

was in the room with the little ones. The Tachin had her sedated and she was being monitored, but for what I am not sure."

"What did the elders have to say about another alien coming into the village?" I ask.

With a snort, Lief shakes his head. "Safia did not give them a choice. That female is a force of nature."

Doxal jumps up when we enter the room where the pod resides and takes Mina from Lief, cradling her against his body, rattling the same way my guys do when they're trying to soothe Kareen or myself. Something about him seems different, but I can't figure it out.

"Why did you not tell me?" Yssig asks from the doorway, his eyes swirling a milky white as he stares at my best friend.

"There was so much going on." His gaze hasn't left Mina's face since he took her, and he runs a finger over her cheek with a sigh. "She may not even make it, Yssig. If something happens... Yasi will need you still."

"She is my mate as well!" The light male growls, his quills rattling in anger.

"Your *mate*?" My head whips around, and I stare at Doxal, noticing for the first that his quills, which have been colorless like Yssig's, are now a beautiful green. "Holy hell."

"Yasi needs at least one of us—"

"You do not get to decide for me!" It's obvious Yssig is upset, and I completely understand why, but Mina is looking far too pale for my liking.

"Guys, can we do this later? Mina is—"

"We cannot risk having both of us mated to her yet, brother."

"Are you going to put her in the seed or are you going to argue until she dies?" the little voice from the doorway silences the room, and we all turn to see Yasi with her hands fisted on her hips, quills flaring out angrily. Definitely something she's learned from Kareen.

With a sigh, Doxal turns and lays Mina in the partially opened seed, gently straightening her legs and folding her arms over her stomach. "Do you think it will take her long to recover?"

"Only the Sun Father can say. It is different for each one of us," Yssig tells me, reaching out to touch her hand.

Before he can make contact, Doxal stops him, blue eyes watching his twin as he shakes his head. "Yasi," he reminds him.

This feels like an incredibly intimate moment, and though Mina is my best friend, this isn't my place right now. I follow Lief, shooing the girls out of the doorway and back into the main room so the twins can have some privacy.

The big Venium warrior looks at me awkwardly and scrubs his hand over the back of his neck. "This is an odd situation."

I can't contain my anxious laughter at the uncertain look on his face. "I guess it is."

"I can take you and your daughter back to Earth if you wish."

Ah, our ticket off of this planet. He's offering us a way back home, but I find the thought of leaving Ettrian and Aquilian behind so heartbreaking that I'm shaking my head before I can even form the words. "I miss my parents so much, and I wish more than anything that they were here, but I can't go back. My family is here—and so is Mina for now. I appreciate the offer though."

"I understand." With a soft smile and a nod, Lief heads for the opening in the tree. "Please pass along my well wishes to your mates. Until we meet again."

CHAPTER 28

*I*noxia

Our temporary tree home in the village is filled to the brim. I haven't had the heart to separate Kareen from Yasi yet, but there isn't any rush at the moment. It's nice to see the two of them having fun, getting to be normal children after everything they've been through.

Ettrian and Aquilian have mentioned bringing us to their tree on the outskirts of the village, but I'm not ready to leave our new friends and the hybrid babies behind. Each one of the infants have been taken in by Dauur females who have offered to wet nurse them along with their own children. All of them are so different and unique, beautiful in their own way.

Besides Ayku's son and the Venium infant, I'm completely unfamiliar with the aliens who fathered the little ones. One of them has gorgeous blue fuzz covering his whole body and a tiny tail that whips back and forth when he's upset. Another little girl sports patches of iridescent scales along her shoulders, arms, and legs. She is one of the quietest babies I've ever met.

Aquilian's fingers stroke through my hair, untangling the long strands as I sit curled up in his lap, watching Ettrian as he dances around the kitchen with Kareen in his arms to a tune he has learned from her. Bunnyfly looks on tiredly from her bed in the corner. Last night, the poor little thing shocked us all and gave birth to her own tiny litter of fluffy babies. Kareen and Yasi fawned over them all morning, begging to keep all three and giving them names. Doxal and Yssig got so tired of listening to the chatter that they took their sister outside to distract her.

They might act big and tough, but those two would give their sister all the stars in the sky if she asked. By the time Bunnyfly's babies are old enough to be on their own, I'm sure all three of them will have found a home with the little dark female. She has them wrapped around her finger, and I can't wait for Mina to wake up and finally meet her. I'm so thankful my best friend is still here, but it makes me anxious that she still hasn't come out of the pod.

One day at a time, I remind myself.

The front of the tree slowly opens and the breeze flows in, drifting over my skin. I turn, expecting to see Yasi bound inside from her little diversion, but instead Safia stops in the doorway. Aquilian stands, pulling me up with him as the female steps inside, waving at Kareen who shouts a greeting along the bond.

"Xia. Aquilian," she greets us. I can't rattle the way my guys do so I just nod to acknowledge her. *"Did you bring me the bloom?"*

Under the hand I have on his arm, I feel him tense, and he shuffles his feet against the floor of the tree. *"Well, no, but—"*

"No? Well," She flips her hands as if she's clearing something from in front of her face. *"No bloom, no mating. Our agreement was obviously off anyway."*

Their agreement? Had there been some sort of plan between the three of them to mate that I ruined when I was dropped into the dome? I know I belong with them, more than I've ever known anything to be true before, but all of those old doubts and insecurities bombard me. They hammer at the fragile wall of self-esteem I'd been carefully creating the last few days. *Ask them*, my mind urges. *Don't assume and risk everything.* While I know I should do just that, have them explain what happened between them and Safia before I even knew them, I can't bring myself to do it right now. I need space, to breathe and clear my head. Jealousy is trying to rear its ugly head, and I won't have it.

"I'm gonna check on Mina real quick. Excuse me." Slipping away, I get to the hall and run to the room where Mina is sleeping quietly. Sinking to my knees in front of the thing that once healed me and that currently fights to save my best friend.

"Mina?" I whisper, leaning my forehead against the firm surface. My heart is pounding frantically, and I'm doing my best not to burst into tears. "I wish you were awake to see the mess I'm making. What if I'm the other woman? What if I've become what I hate? All those times Trent brought those girls home..." A tear slips down my cheek as my breath shudders from between my lips. "What if that's what's happening now?"

I swear I can hear Mina's firm but compassionate voice inside my head. *"Stop asking about what ifs, Xia! Life is about living! If you want an answer, you have to ask the right question."*

"I seriously hate when you're right." I sigh dramatically. "Neither one of them have even tried to get intimate with me since we got here. I know we've been busy with everything, but I just thought—"

A gentle hand comes down on my shoulder, making me jump.

"My apologies." Safia crouches down next to me as she runs her hands over the seed pod in front of us.

"No worries." Liar, my mind mumbles. *You're made almost entirely out of worries.*

When I turn back to her, I see she's watching me intently and I start to squirm. *"Inoxia?"*

"Yes?"

I am caught completely off guard when Safia wraps her arms around me, pulling me into a hug. *"I was never going to mate your males. They were always meant to be with you. I saw this, but I needed to get you away, to speak with you alone. I am sorry for misleading you."*

"You wanted to talk to me about something so you purposely made me jealous?" This woman is something.

With a rattle of her quills she sits back and tilts her head. *"Your mind made you jealous, not me."* I huff, but she cuts me off before I can respond. *"The Sun Father has shown me something that concerns you—something that will be incredibly hard for you and your males to come to terms with. It is best to learn now, before the kit arrives."*

"What kit? Kareen?"

With an amused shake of her head, she lays her hand on my thigh. *"Not Kareen. This kit has not been born yet."*

"Yet?" My eyes widen as my hand comes up, slapping over my mouth. *"Oh gods, I can't be pregnant yet. I was only with Aquilian, and Doxal said it had to be both of them. They aren't even identical!"*

"Calm, Inoxia. You are not with kit, but you will be soon and you will need to heed this warning. Easing into this will make it less difficult."

This woman is talking in circles, and I can feel my agitation begin to mount. *"Ease into what?"*

"I can only tell you what the Sun Father has told me. Your little one will be different in more ways than either of us can imagine. That is his message."

Okay, so she's some sort of psychic who spouts vague warnings about the future. Lovely. The way she looks at me makes me think that she can hear what I'm thinking, and with these aliens, nothing is out of the realm of possibilities. The one thing I can take comfort in from her strange warning is that she never said there would be anything *wrong* with my baby. I can handle different.

"I will be present during your mating ceremony."

Excuse me? *"What mating ceremony?"*

"Have those two not told you anything? A Dauur female, after confirming she has found her males, will go through a ritual trial before she can officially accept the mating bond. Completing the bond before this brings a great risk to the female."

"What sort of risk?" Seems like Aquilian and Ettrian have left out a good bit of information.

"Angering the ancestors."

I want to ask her if she's serious, but I can already see that this isn't some fairy tale to her. Safia believes this wholeheartedly. *"Okay, so what happens during this trial?"*

"You will walk the same path the mate of the cursed twins took when she sought the approval of the Sun Father. At the end of the journey is a temple where our ancestors reside, where the sacred Oya blooms. If you drink of the bloom and the Sun Father does not bless the union, you will join him, but if you survive and make it back to your males, it is said to be the strongest mating bond of all. A fated mating."

"Hold on, hard stop." My hands come up and I shake my head quickly. *"There's no fucking way that is happening. You're asking me to risk literal death."* I'm not drinking the poisoned Kool-Aid, no matter how much I care about these guys.

"You will not die."

Her matter-of-fact tone makes me laugh out loud. *"How do you know this? Did the Sun Father mention that when he told you about my baby?"*

"No." Her eyes light up a dull pink. *"Your mates' quills have*

already changed colors, which means there is no risk. Fated mates are the only ones who participate in the trial."

"So if there's no risk anyway, why continue to drink from the bloom?"

"Tradition," she says with a mischievous look in her eyes.

"Xia?" Ayku peeks his head around the corner cautiously before stepping inside the room. *"I do not mean to interrupt, but I have promised my help and do not wish to bring Akai into the village center with me. Would you mind taking him for a little while?"*

"You know I'd love to." Ayku decided the first night we spent here that he would honor his twin by naming their son after him, and it makes me a little teary every time I think about it. I smile up at him, and he flinches like all the Dauur do.

"I know you said this is an expression of happiness among your kind, but it is unnerving." He steps close, squeezing between Safia and I to lay Akai in my arms. As he pulls away, his hand skims Safia's arm and they both go completely still.

"You?" I can barely hear Safia's whisper along the bond as we both watch Ayku's quills flare with newfound color.

He stumbles backward, shaking his head as his eyes turn a deep, sad blue. *"I cannot..."* is all he says before he rushes from the room.

"What in the world?" I ask aloud.

Akai squirms in my arms, his little body shifting closer to mine. Safia is watching him carefully, her eyes just as blue and sad as Ayku's. *"He is beautiful."*

"I have no idea what happened with Ayku, but he's been through a lot. I don't think he means to be like that."

"I know. He requires time, but I will wait." Her quills rattle softly as she runs a finger lightly over the infant's cheek. *"I am a Darkborn Taenov. Death is something we are all too familiar with. These two... they are mine."*

"Do you want to hold him?"

Akai wraps one tiny hand around Safia's finger as he stares up at her as if he knows who she is to him, but she pulls away with a soft rattle of her quills. *"I will go find his papa."* She stops in the doorway, giving me her best smile, which is terrifying. *"You, I will see at the mating ceremony."*

CHAPTER 29

*A*quilian

Ettrian and I plan on doing something I had convinced myself would never happen for us. Today, we will bring Inoxia before our parents and present her as our mate. This is the first time they will meet the family my brother and I have created, and I find that there's a small part of me that is terrified, even though the rest of me is thrilled. Our mama and papas have never been anything but loving and accepting. From the moment we were born, we have been perfect to them, but what if asking them to accept an alien and her kit is too much?

Beside me, Inoxia slips her hand into mine, squeezing it until I turn to look down into her face. There is something in her eyes —a question? Along the bond we share, I can feel a sense of vulnerability, uncertainty, *fear* that I do not love or want her. I wonder what has caused this. If she truly knew how much I wanted her, how many times I revisited the image of her coming apart in the sling the night I brought Ettrian home, how much I loved just being near her, she would never have doubts. The only thing that keeps me from sending my emotions along the bond is the fact that we have not had our ceremony, but soon she will know.

The fact that I mated with her before the ceremony is enough to get me exiled if the elders were to find out. Although the union has been blessed by the Sun Father, we must still participate in the ceremony, although we are not following *every* part of the tradition. The time before the ceremony occurs is normally spent away from one another, but we have decided to forgo this part since we were already forced to spend so many days apart.

We walk through the center of the main village where tribe members gather to socialize and trade their goods. Many have lengths of silk and other fabrics used for blankets and skirts, while others have brought things like baskets. I recognize the smell of sweet treats and roasted meat being handed out and draw in a deep breath, savoring the moment. Lief once told us that on his planet they must pay for goods with 'credits' instead of trading or merely being given the things they need. If a Dauur is in need, they will be helped. My people may have many flaws, but they have never let anyone go without, no matter their status.

Up ahead of us, Yasi and Kareen hold hands as they run from one trader to another. Their happiness is contagious, and they leave each group in better spirits than before. Bringing our family here was something we wrestled with, but they have been holed up for long enough.

"She is happy," Doxal comments as he watches his sister play.

"There have been fewer night terrors since she has started sharing a room with Kareen," says Yssig with a nod.

There is a small commotion going through the center and for once it is not about me being here. *"Aunt Vayzie?"*

Doxal and Yssig stumble to a stop when they see what, or rather who, has caught their sister's attention.

An older Dauur couple are standing near one of the huts that have been set up at the back of a trader's booth, their eyes swirling white in shock as they stare at the little female. In their arms rest two small Darkborn kits. *"It is not possible... They were killed,"* Doxal mumbles as he rushes forward, Yssig right behind him. We watch for a moment as they pull the older couple into their arms and fuss over the kits. This must be their family. I can feel the bond they share from across the center and gesture for Kareen to follow so that they may have privacy.

Just on the outskirts of the main center sits the familial tree Ettrian and I grew up in. The sight of it still sends a warmth through me, and we find our Lightborn parents sitting outside on the ground near the large opening. Our mama is stringing together beautifully colored glass beads, completing one of the necklaces that is traditionally worn during ceremonies, while both of our papas are busy weaving a pair of shoes that will accompany the jewelry.

Even from so far away, our mama senses when we come into view. Her head shoots up, and joy fills her eyes as she sets aside her beading and stands. It has been so long since I have seen her that I stop and just take her in.

"Well, are you two going to introduce your mama or should we just stand here and admire one another a little longer?" Curiosity sneaks along the bond, but she looks at Xia and Kareen the same way she's always looked at her sons. There is no judgment, no disgust, only love and patience. *Acceptance.*

"I'm Kareen!" The kit wastes absolutely no time, pulling out of Ettrian's grip before she races up the little hill and barrels into my mama's legs. *"Hi! You're my grandma. What are you making?"* A second later, she is cross-legged on the ground, lifting the necklace up like she is assessing Mama's skill. *"Can I help you with this? I'm really good at arts and crafts."*

"Kareen, you know you shouldn't just—" Xia starts, stepping

forward like she means to remove the kit, but Mama is already smitten.

"Of course you can help me! Making something is more fun when you do it with others, yes?"

From the look on Kareen's face, my mama has just cemented a place in her heart for the rest of her life. She nods, her face swinging toward Xia. *"Mama! Come on!"*

"I'm coming, I'm coming," she mumbles before sticking her hand out awkwardly. *"I'm Inoxia, but Xia is fine. It's really nice to meet you."*

With a gentle rattle, my mama reaches forward, wrapping our mate in her arms. *"I am Azila, but Mama is fine."* With a tilt of her head, our mama waves us over. *"My little kits. Where have they gone?"*

"We have not been little for a long time, Mama." Ettrian laughs, his quills vibrating as she reaches out to pull him into her arms.

"Definitely not *little."* I am positive Xia doesn't mean to say this along the bond, but she has not quite figured out how to shield her thoughts properly yet.

The joke is not lost on Mama, who rattles humorously and pulls me into a hug. *"Look at these,"* she calls to our papas as she strokes our quills. *"What gorgeous colors!"* There is a tiny stinging sensation as she plucks a quill from my head, and by the way my twin is rubbing his head, I'm sure she got him too.

"Mama!" we both protest, but she has already spun away.

Papa Eldav and Papa Ekaz introduce themselves and Kareen screeches in excitement. *"I have two grandpas? This is the best day ever!"*

~

"*Y*asi told me that you and Papa Quilian and Papa Ettrian are gonna be mated, but I don't really know what that means.*" Kareen is chatting happily as she strings beads on her very own necklace next to her grandmama, her little legs crossed and her brows furrowed as she concentrates on getting the thin thread through the bead.

"Well, a mating is sort of like getting married." Xia explains.

"Oh, I'd like that! Then you can have babies and I can watch them because I'll be an awesome big sister."

"I love kits. I hope they have many," Mama responds with a little rattle as she nudges the kit's shoulder. *"This is for your mama's ceremony."*

"Have you ever been to a mating ceremony?" Xia asks hesitantly.

"My mates and I are not fated so we have never participated. You have worries?" Mama asks and Xia shrugs her shoulders.

She has never mentioned any, but perhaps this was what caused her to be upset early in the village. *"What is worrying you?"* When she does not answer right away, I look to Ettrian, feeling the concern rolling off of him. *"Excuse us for a moment?"* A startled vibration rolls off of her tongue as I lift her into my arms and make my way toward a favorite spot of mine from when I was a young kit. There is a small stream a little ways behind the tree with a large smooth rock I used to lie on when I was feeling upset. Maybe it will soothe her the same way it did me.

Ettrian takes a seat next to us as I lower myself and Xia to the rock. *"There is something bothering you."*

"Yeah…"

"Is it the ceremony? Do you not wish to take part in it?" Ettrian rattles softly and rubs his face against her bare shoulder.

"It's not that I don't want to. It's just that I'm scared of certain

parts. If I'm being honest, I'm scared of what it means to actually be mated."

"What parts?"

"Like drinking from a poisonous flower that's killed people?"

"The bloom will not kill you. The Sun Father has already blessed us. This is just—"

"Tradition?" She quips with a raised brow.

I shake my head at her, running a finger over the tip of her nose. I love her strange features. *"What else is bothering you?"*

With her lip clamped between her teeth, Xia climbs from my lap, wedging herself between me and Ettrian as she pulls our hands into her lap. *"I was almost married once—mated, I mean. I thought I loved him, but he wasn't a good person. I wanted babies, lots of them, but we tried for a little while and nothing ever happened. There was an orphanage, a place where children without families are taken, and I met Kareen there during a community service event."* Her face brightens at the mention of our kit. *"I fell in love with her that day, begged Trent to fill out the paperwork to adopt her, to make her ours, but we didn't even make it halfway through the process before I realized he wasn't someone I wanted to share a child with."*

Something possessive grips at my insides. I cannot imagine the kit ever being this male's daughter. *"She is ours."* The growl rumbles along the bond before I can stop it.

"I know she is—I know I am. There were so many things I had to work through after leaving him and I'm just... scared."

Ettrian catches my eye over her head before nodding. "Inoxia." She glances up at me and I can see the tears that have collected in the corners. *"If you do not wish to complete the ceremony, we will not ask you to."*

"Aquilian, I've already committed to you two. If I really wanted, I could have asked Lief for a ride back to Earth, been gone before you guys even knew I was missing, but that wasn't

what I wanted." Her hand brushes the side of my cheek as she reaches behind my head to bring her lips to mine in a soft kiss, before she turns and does the same to Ettrian. *"I swore I wasn't going to get myself into another relationship again after what happened with Trent and then I woke up here and met the two of you and I've been terrified this whole time of what I've been feeling. I want to do the ceremony because I've finally decided to stop being afraid."*

~

"*S*o, who gets to be there for the ceremony?" Xia has been trying to find out as much as she can from my mama before it is time to begin. They sit together with Kareen snuggled into our mate's lap as she attempts to make her mama a gift.

"If you would like, I can help you prepare, but the Lightborn and Darkborn Taenovs will be the only ones with you on the journey."

"Can me and Bunnyfly stay with you, Grandma?"

"Who is Bunnfly?"

Kareen's mouth drops open dramatically as she blinks her eyes rapidly. *"Who's Bunnyfly? Oh, Grandma."* Wiggling her way off of Xia, our kit hugs Mama and smiles in her strange way. *"Let me tell you a story. It's about Bunnyfly the Great."*

CHAPTER 30

*I*noxia

The ground is soft beneath my feet as I walk across the forest floor. Nerves have my stomach twisted into knots, and I can feel it crawling up my throat, threatening to choke me as I swallow. The fact that I'm naked for this little jaunt through the woods does nothing to calm my anxiety. The Dauur obviously have no issues with nudity seeing as most of them choose not to wear even the simple skirts I've seen on a handful of the women, and while I'm normally not a shy person, I've also never traipsed around in the nude where anyone with eyes can see.

While I might not be wearing clothes, I suppose I can't say I'm completely naked. I'm wearing the shoes Ettrian and Aquilian's papas wove, and around my neck is the pretty necklace Azila was making when we met. Before gifting it to me earlier during my preparation, she added a quill from each of my mates, and I would absolutely be lying if I said it hadn't made me a little teary to get to have something from them with me while I try to navigate. The quills hang just low enough that they brush teasingly over my nipples anytime I move, and I'm slowly working myself into an agonizing state of arousal.

Barely started this whole thing and you're already close to combustion.

Mama, as Azila insists I now call her, told me about the cursed twins' mate while she helped me get ready, but I'm not sure recounting a story of love and then a horrible death was a great way to start out a mating ceremony. Still, having her there for support when I can't have my own mom with me meant more than I could ever tell her.

When the preparations were finished and I was sufficiently naked and afraid, I was brought to the edge of the forest, pointed in the right direction, and then pretty much told to walk until I find the temple. I have no idea if I'm still going the right way or if I've wandered off the path. All around me are the sounds of the creatures that call this place home. I can hear the smaller creatures as they scurry through the underbrush, their little paws snapping twigs and crushing scattered leaves. According to Mama, there's nothing in this part of the forest large enough to want to eat me, but I'm still wary.

My fingers glide over the top of a large fungus type plant as I walk by. A smile tugs at the corners of my lips when the top lights up beneath my touch. Everything around me is beautiful, but none of it looks like the temple I'm supposed to find.

I reach up and rub at one of the quills distractedly. This one is Ettrian's. I grin as I run my fingers over its red tip, remembering the way it feels to have them clutched in my hands while he's kissing me. I shiver in anticipation as I wonder what being with him will be like. Is he just as dominant and demanding as Aquilian? I'm looking forward to finding out once this is all over. The other quill brushes my nipple, and I moan before I bite my lip to quiet myself.

Up ahead of me, a small rammit—as I'm told they are called

—steps out hesitantly from a bush and I stop to watch. The creature and I stare at each other for a moment before it leaps into the air and uses its large feathered ears to glide away. Just as I take a step forward, a massive wolf-like creature lunges across my path, and I hear a commotion break out as it chases after its prey. That's one big furry nope. I swallow a scream as I take off running, my feet flying over the ground as I jump over rocks and branches.

Where the fuck is this temple?

As I burst through a row of smaller trees, I come to a stumbling halt within a large clearing. Sitting in the center is the biggest tree—or a group of them—that I've ever seen in my life. The tree homes in the village and throughout the forest remind me of much larger versions of the giant sequoias back on Earth, but this is something new. It looks like a living building has sprouted from the ground, as if the planet itself gifted it to the Dauur. Tiny, beautiful flowers bloom along every branch, reminding me of cherry blossoms, only these are glowing a soft yellow, lighting up the entire area. There's a massive archway that welcomes me inside, and I trail my fingers along the rough wood as I enter.

The same yellow flowers illuminate the interior, and as my eyes adjust to the dim light, I'm relieved to see Safia waiting for me. She steps forward, wrapping me in a tight hug. *"Welcome, Inoxia."*

As nice as it is to see her and as relieved as I am to know that I have finally made it to my destination, naked hugs between friends are still on my list of things that make me feel awkward. *"Thank you."* I haven't seen her since the day she found out Ayku was her mate. We were all surprised when he agreed to join her at her tree, but it seemed like the best choice for Akai, who took to Safia right away. *"How are you? Did Ayku and Akai get settled?"*

"I am wonderful, and they are both getting used to their new surroundings... and me." She pulls back with a soft rattle. *"I will*

213

tell Ayku you asked after him." I'm ushered away to the spot where Lirseas is waiting patiently.

"Are you ready, Inoxia?" the Lightborn Taenov asks as we approach.

"As ready as I'll ever be."

With a swish of her skirt, Lirseas leads me and Safia to what looks to be a hot spring in the center of the massive chamber. I don't recall anything about this part of the ceremony, but after my hike through the cool, shady forest, I'm not going to argue against taking a warm dip. *I can get down with this tradition.*

Safia nudges me gently. *"Step in and submerge yourself."*

Slipping off the woven shoes, I step up to the edge of the spring and look down. The first touch of my foot into the pinkish water makes me sigh. Heat envelops my legs and lower half as I step down inside the spring. *Gods, this is wonderful.* A sudden rush of bubbles erupts beneath me, running up and between my legs, caressing my hips and belly. *"What the hell?"* I screech as I rush back to the side.

"Calm, Inoxia," Lirseas soothes as she crouches down next to the edge. *"The cleansing pool will not harm you."*

The calming emotions she sends along the bond help to ease my fears, and I sink back down, submerging more and more of my body. As I go, the Taenovs begin a quiet prayer, whispering things along the bond that I can't quite make out as the bubbles reach my ears. I've learned over the last week or so from living in the village that, while the bond has taught those connected through it how to speak my language, it has not taught me that of the Dauur.

Taking a deep breath, I squeeze my eyes shut and duck my head beneath the water. Bubbles rush over my face and into my hair that has been pulled up and wrapped into a bun. It feels as if there are fingers raking over my scalp, pressing into tense muscles, brushing lovingly over every part of me.

This is far lovelier and more intimate than I ever imagined it would be, and I'm so wrapped up in the experience that I don't realize I've been down for too long until my lungs begin to burn. Fresh air rushes into my lungs when I break the surface, gasping.

As I'm wiping the water from my face, I notice something strange. The spring is now longer just pink; it's glowing, pulsing softly as I move through it. Even more startling than the water is the fact that there's a glow coming from me as well. Every tiny freckle on my body is illuminated, making me look like a snapshot of the night sky.

"What in the world?"

Both Lirseas and Safia are looking on in wonder as I run my fingers over my skin, but only the Lightborn speaks to me. *"It seems you have been given a gift. Perhaps the twins felt you needed reassurance that this was your path."*

She nods to Safia, who retrieves a closed bloom. I take it from her hands, cupping it carefully in mine as I stare down at the pretty blue glowing flower. As I watch, it begins to open, revealing the liquid in the center. This bloom looks similar to something we have on Earth. The flower I was named after, funny enough.

There's a saying among the gardening communities that goes, "You'd be madder than a hatter to take a moonflower." Ingesting one can cause all sorts of horrible things including crazy hallucinations, and yet here I am. Most humans would consider me mad already for deciding to stay here and spend the rest of my life raising a kid with two aliens. Ettrian and Aquilian told me they would love me even if I decided not to do this, but I'm ready to find my place here among these people.

"Bottoms up," I whisper to myself as I put my lips to the petals and sip from the nectar that pools in the middle. My body immediately flushes with heat, and everything around me blurs for a moment. I feel like I'm stuck in some kind of dream, my body moving in slow motion as I reach up to allow the females to pull me from the spring. They lead me from the tree and back into the forest, their hands in mine as we go.

Grateful for the company this time around, I sway on unsteady legs and lean my head against Safia's shoulder. A flash of color catches my eye, and I turn my head to the right, but nothing is there. Again, I see a flash, this time to the left, and I stumble when I see that it's another Dauur. Many Dauur, I correct myself as I look closer. They surround us, running through the trees, jumping over the large boulders and logs. They are wispy, like smoke, there one moment and gone the next.

"You see them?" Safia asks, her eyes scanning the forest around us. *"They are our ancestors, protecting you on your journey home. Those who have been fortunate enough to return to their mates say it is a sight they remember all their lives."*

Just before we reach the edge of the trees, the Taenovs come to a stop. Uncorking a clay jar, Lirseas dips her finger inside before she instructs me to open my mouth. Something sweet and thick, similar to honey, is placed on my tongue, and I swallow like she tells me.

"An antidote." Safia winks at me, and I have to stop myself from giggling at the human gesture. *"Come, your mates are waiting for you."*

A moment later, I'm standing in front of the tree we have taken as our temporary home, my head cleared of the fog. As we approach, the bark splits and I'm met with the sight of two incredibly handsome Dauur. The way their eyes are racing over my body makes me shiver in anticipation, and I reach up to touch the necklace that rests against my chest, drawing their gaze to it. They may not have liked having the quills plucked from their heads, but they sure seem to like seeing them on me. With a shuddering breath, I step into the circle of Ettrian's arms and let them sweep me away.

CHAPTER 31

*E*ttrian

She is glowing. Every tiny spot that is scattered across her skin gives off a soft pink light. I had not considered that she could ever be more beautiful than she was when we left her to prepare, but the sight of her standing before us with our quills around her neck takes the breath from my lungs. She steps toward us, and I hold my arms out, pulling her into me, rubbing my face against the top of her head. A tiny hand strokes my chest just before I feel the soft press of her lips on my skin, sending a shiver through my quills.

Turning slowly, I pull Xia into the tree, which is eerily silent since everyone has left us alone for the night, and lead her into our room. Where there was once a sling there is now a large flower. Its smooth petals unfurl with a gentle nudge along the bond, encompassing a good portion of the room.

"Holy hell, that's amazing. Where did it come from?" Xia asks as she leans down to touch the flower.

"The pheromones of mated Dauur cause a tree to bloom. It is a gift so that we may share a resting place."

"This is seriously gorgeous."

"Not nearly as gorgeous as you are, Inoxia." Aquilian runs his finger down the side of her neck before reaching out to uncoil her hair so that it cascades over her shoulders. *"You accepted us."* As if speaking is too much for her, she nods her head yes, moaning softly when Aquilian leans in to capture her lips in a fierce, fiery kiss.

Stepping up behind her, I nestle my face into her hair and nip at her neck, letting my fingers trail over the necklace she wears that tells others she has our hearts forever. Another moan rumbles through her, and she shivers when I circle the tip of her breast before squeezing and tugging the sensitive nipple. Thinking of the way she moaned the first day we met after I spanked her for wiggling in my arms nearly has me extruding against her back, where my hips are pressed against her. I want to watch her cheeks flush in pleasure as she moans for me again. It was the first time she nearly brought me to my knees.

"I love you," I mumble first against her skin and then along the bond.

Aquilian echoes the sentiment, breaking the kiss to nip at her neck. Head tilted back, our mate's eyes find mine as she reaches out her hand to pull me to her lips for a gentle, teasing kiss. *"I love you both so much."* Her tongue sneaks out to swipe over my lip as her hand slides down my stomach, grazing the top of my slit where I am barely holding myself in.

Wrapping the silky length of her hair around my hand, I give it a sharp tug when I feel her fingers brush closer. *"Do not, Xia."* The warning rolls along the bond. I have never lost control before, but I am incredibly close to it at the moment.

"Do not what?" By the time I see the mischievous glint in her eyes, she is already moving her hand over me, rubbing the sensitive outer barrier until my cock extrudes into her palm. *"Holy shit."* She spins around in Aquilian's arms to stare down at my length as it jumps and wiggles, seeking her out.

"Your males on Earth are not the same?"

With a nervous laugh, she shakes her head. *"Not quite. They don't normally have four heads, or wiggle, and they definitely don't come in neon colors."*

I frown down at my cock, wondering exactly how different she is from our females, but I know it must work if Aquilian was successful. As I watch, her hand curls around my length and slides up and down, pumping the shaft in long, languid strokes. My twin reaches around to cup her breast, tugging on her nipple until she is moaning, head thrown back against his chest as she arches against me. Everything inside of me screams to take her, to mate her until none of us can even crawl from the room. The scent of her sex perfumes the air, and I drop to my knees in front of her.

Lifting one of her legs over my shoulder, I run my tongue along her inner thigh, up to the source of her wet heat. Opening the bond with my brother so that he can experience everything I do, I slowly slide my tongue along the folds of her sex, drawing a whimper from her lips as she grasps my quills tightly.

"Oh gods, Ettrian," she whispers and grinds her cunt against my mouth.

Aquilian's fingers continue squeezing and tugging at her nipples as she pants against his cheek. It is the most magnificent sight I have ever seen. I move my tongue into her slit, lapping at the slick that has gathered. As I pull out, I graze the small nub right above it, and her legs nearly give out.

"Again!" she gasps. *"Please."*

With the tip of my tongue, I flick the swollen flesh and watch as she unravels. Her screams echo through the room and she pulls so hard on my quills that I'm shocked none of them are ripped out.

"So beautiful," Aquilian whispers to her as she thrashes against him. *"Good, my light. Good."*

I could stay between her thighs forever if she let me, just watching her in my twin's arms as she takes the pleasure we are giving her. When she presses her lips against his, I move my fingers to her opening, exploring her with soft, shallow strokes. I probe deeper and deeper, slipping in one finger, then two. My tongue curls around the nub before I press my lips against her and draw it into my mouth, sucking hard. Excitement courses through the bond as Xia breaks away from Aquilian, a scream of pleasure bursting from her as her cunt threatens to eject my probing digits.

"Right there! Gods, Ettrian, yes!"

Enough, my body is screaming at me. Take her, make her ours. I slide my fingers from her body and pull back, rattling as she moans in frustration, her hands clutching at me as she tries to press herself into my face. Aquilian lifts Xia up into his arms, carrying her to the flower where he lays her out in the center. When she reaches for him, he shakes his head and moves aside, looking back at me expectantly.

My quills begin to rattle softly as I let my gaze roam over her, taking in the sight of our mate as she writhes atop the flower. *"Tell us that you want us, Xia. Tell us that you accept our bond."* With a frantic nod of her head, she moves a hand up to her breast, cupping it and pinching the nipple.

"Say it, Xia," Aquilian commands, bringing his palm down on the side of her thigh with a sharp crack.

A moan slips from her mouth, and she stares up at my brother in surprise, heat flashing in her eyes. *"I want you, both of you."* She sighs as he smooths his hand over her pink flesh. *"I accept the bond. Please, I can't wait."*

A growl rolls up my chest as I crouch down and crawl up her body, dropping soft kisses along her thighs, hips, and belly. Her legs wrap around my waist, careful to avoid the horns on my calves, as I position myself at her opening. Running the heads of my cock along the wet folds that open to welcome me, I push forward slowly, claiming the female that my brother and I have waited for our whole lives.

Aquilian leans down to capture one of her nipples in his mouth, teasing her into a frenzy as his hand slides down her stomach to rub the tiny nub. With a groan, I pull out then slide back into her hot, tight body, begging the Sun Father for strength. She is ours. I can feel my control begin to fray as she moves against me, thrusting her hips into mine, pulling me into her. My quills rattle loudly, buzzing as I thrust between her legs.

"Fuck, that feels so good." One of Xia's hands snakes down to where we're joined and grasps the base of my cock as it writhes inside of her cunt, searching out her most sensitive places. Pressing my hands to her inner thighs, I spread her legs wide and piston into her. *"Faster! Please!"*

Aquilian's fingers are rubbing her in time with my sporadic thrusts, his tongue flicking over her breast. The hand Xia doesn't have wrapped around me is buried in my brother's quills, clutching the glowing lengths as I feel her cunt flutter. A moment later, she throws her head back, my name tearing from her throat as she goes rigid beneath me. The rippling motion of her cunt as it clutches at my cock sends me barreling over the edge into a release more powerful than I have ever experienced before. As my knot begins to expand, I press forward, allowing it to tie us together. Shudders rack me as I feel her hand trail up my body until she reaches my cheek, pulling me down for a gentle kiss.

CHAPTER 32

*A*quilian

The sight of Inoxia coming undone beneath my brother is nearly too much for me, and I grip my cock hard in my hand as I lean down to mark our mate between her neck and shoulder as Ettrian kisses her. The metallic taste of her blood flows over my tongue, and I moan against her skin, drawing more of the rich liquid into my mouth. Her heart races, and I can feel her renewed need flutter along the bond.

"She wants you," Ettrian tells me quietly as his knot subsides, allowing him to slip free of her body. I run my tongue over the small wound, helping to seal it, and stand as my twin rolls to the side.

Our mate lies before me, her body flushed, hair tangled around her head, and her thighs glistening with seed and liquid heat. She is the most gorgeous thing I have ever seen. *"Are you ready for your punishment?"*

"Punishment?" Her mouth drops open, and she turns to Ettrian, as if he will back her up, but he only rattles softly and turns her face back toward me. *"I thought maybe you—"*

"You thought I had forgotten?" When she bites her lip, her

eyes flitting to the side, I know I am correct. *"Stand up."* She does as she's asked, stepping forward onto one of the large petals. I trail a finger down the side of her face, neck, and the marks I made. *"If you truly do not want the punishment, all you have to do is say so."*

A grin tugs at her lips and she shakes her head. *"I want it, Aquilian."*

"Good." Taking a seat in the center of the flower, I pat my legs in a silent gesture for her to lay down. As she moves into position, the quills on her necklace scrape across my thighs and I lift it, admiring the way it looks on her. *"Tell me why you are being punished, Inoxia."*

"I didn't listen to you."

My fingers glide along the beading. *"Tell me what you did."*

"I left the tree and ended up being hurt."

Thwack! I bring my hand down on one cheek and then the other. Through the bond I share with my twin, I can hear her moan and gasp after each contact, and it thrills me.

"But you said I could go." She pouts, squeezing her thighs together.

While that may be true, I know her statement is not a protest to her punishment.

"What else, Xia? Tell us what else you did to deserve your punishment." Ettrian tells her as he tucks a few strands of hair behind her ear.

"I put myself in danger."

Thwack!

"When Aquilian asked me to let you speak to the elders, I didn't listen."

I can hear Ettrian laugh along the bond. That wasn't something I had told her, but I admit I felt like taking her over my knee at that moment. If she feels like adding it to her punishment, I am happy to oblige.

Thwack!

Running my palm over the pink skin to soothe it, I slide two fingers along the slippery folds of her cunt and delight in the way she squirms. Ettrian kisses her softly as I give her one last swat. *"On your knees facing me."* Her cheeks are flushed, eyes are glazed with pleasure, but she looks up at me with defiance flaring in them. *"Do you have something you want to say, my light?"*

"I'm not sorry I left the tree."

"Excuse me?" Ettrian moves to sit next to me and frowns at her. *"What was that?"*

With a deep breath, Xia looks first at my brother and then to me. *"I'm not sorry I left the tree that day. If I hadn't gone with Doxal, we might not have found Mina or the babies. We might not have known Ayku or Yasi were trapped there. But,"* her tongue slips out to wet her lips and she fidgets with the quills on her necklace, *"I am sorry that what I did caused you to worry, and I'm sorry that you went through so much to come and rescue me."*

"You almost died, Inoxia. You were almost taken away from us, from Kareen."

"But I wasn't. I'm still here, and I refuse to live my life always thinking about what could have happened. I lived, thanks to you both, thanks to Lief, thanks to the seed pod, and the Sun Father." Xia scoots forward until she's seated in my lap and presses her forehead to mine. *"Forgive me?"* She glances sideways at Ettrian and holds out a hand. *"Both of you?"*

I trail my fingers up her sides, delighting in the way she squirms against me. *"I never asked for an apology."* My fingers slide along the swells of her breasts before circling her nipples. *"Look at me."* A tremble works through Xia's body as I touch her, and when I brush across the hard points I have been teasing, her lids begin to slide shut.

Before I can even move to correct her, Ettrian's hand comes down on her bottom with a sharp crack and she jumps, her eyes

224

flying open in surprise. With a gentle nudge, I get to my knees and rub my face along the column of her neck, inhaling the erotic fragrance of sweat and sex that clings to her. *"I anticipate many more punishments for you. In fact,"* I bring my palm down on the fleshy side of her hip, and a rattle works through my quills when she digs her teeth into her bottom lip, *"I think you enjoy them."*

Behind her, Ettrian gathers up the long curly strands of her hair and wraps it around his hand, drawing her head back so that she is looking up into his face. *"Do you like being punished?"*

Her throat works as she swallows. *"Yes."* Pretty green eyes search me out. *"Please, Aquilian."*

"What is it, my light?" With a featherlight touch, I run the tips of two fingers along the inside of one thigh and then down the other, avoiding the place I know she craves to be touched. I feel the vibrations from Ettrian's quills as they rattle and I know he is enjoying this as much as I am. *"Tell us what you want."*

"I want you inside of me." A red flush warms her face and her eyes dart away. *"Both of you."*

My brother's gaze jumps up to mine, and I can feel his excitement course through me. Our quills rattle and a shiver works its way up my spine as I watch Ettrian's free hand slide across her belly, pressing her against his chest. I stroke the hard length of my cock as I move forward to drop soft kisses onto her cheeks. *"Is that right?"*

"Yes, dammit!" She growls in frustration.

I suppress my laughter and pull her hips against mine, slipping my cock between her legs so that it runs along her wet folds. The vibrations of her moan tease my ilo, and I pull back, dragging the tips of my cock along her sensitive nub.

"Fuck! Please, Aquilian! I can't..." Her breath comes out in short huffs. With one hand, she grips the back of my neck and begins to grind herself against me, while her other hand reaches back to hold onto Ettrian. *"Please."*

OCTAVIA KORE

The sweet sound of her whimper undoes me. With a little adjustment, I push up into her and take a moment to relish in the searing heat of her body. Ettrian's hand curls around her throat as his tongue traces the shell of her ear, and I watch her eyelids flutter as her grip on my neck tightens. *Thwack!*

"Open your eyes, Inoxia." They fly open as my palm soothes her skin.

"Are you going to let me in, Xia?" Ettrian asks as his hand flexes around her throat.

She tenses when he presses his hips against her bottom, but a soft press of my fingers against her nub seems to help her relax and a moment later I feel their pleasure slide against me along the bond. *"Gods, yes!"*

One of her legs hooks around my hip while she uses the other to push herself up and down, slowly sliding herself along our cocks, stretching to accommodate us. For a few heartbeats, we simply enjoy the way she takes her own pleasure, using our bodies to bring herself all the way to the edge, but I've been holding out this entire time and my body is begging for release. With a quick motion, I pull her leg higher and slam into her, falling into a rhythm with Ettrian as if it were the most natural thing.

"So close. Please," Xia pleads, her nails digging into my skin.

A moment later, I feel her cunt flutter before it spasms, rhythmically milking me as I thrust up into her. Head held back by Ettrian's hand in her hair, mouth open wide in a scream I experience through my brother's ability to hear, Xia writhes between us. Behind her, Ettrian presses close and goes still, rattling in pleasure. My own quills vibrate violently as my breath catches and my muscles seize. The knot at the base of my cock swells within her as I finally give in to my release.

~

*I*t takes Ettrian three rounds of mating our female before he remembers to mark her himself. The way his teeth sank into the bare flesh of her shoulder next to my mark sent a shiver down my spine. By the way Xia lies sprawled across the flower, her arms stretched above her head, I would say the mating has been successful. She murmurs in her sleep, and I close my eyes as the vibrations of her speech run along my ilo.

My fingers trail along her hip and then around the indentation of her navel. The fact that she will soon carry our kit within her is almost surreal, but I can see her standing in the opening of the tree, her belly swollen as she watches Kareen play with Yasi. I see Kareen's face light up as her new brother or sister is placed in her arms and the way our mama and papas will rattle with pride when they meet the newest member of our family. My cock twitches behind my slit like it is ready to mate her again to ensure all of these visions become a reality.

"Ettrian? Are you still awake?"

"I am. What is it?"

"Did you hear Lief when he said he would make a run back to be sure the Tachin lab was destroyed?"

"I did."

"When he comes back to speak with the elders, I want to make a request."

My brother sits up to stare at me over Xia's sleeping form. *"What sort of request?"*

"Inoxia belongs here, among our family and her friends. Our papas and mama love her, but I see the way she looks at them."

"What do you mean?"

"She has spoken of her own mama and papa, about them still being on her planet. Even Kareen has said how much they both miss her parents. Perhaps we could speak with Lief, see if he would be able to bring them here."

"I think it would mean a lot to her." Ettrian rubs his face against the side of her breast, and she shivers. *"Do you think there will be a kit by the time they arrive?"*

"If the Sun Father is willing." My eyes slide shut, and I feel myself starting to drift off.

"Aquilian?" Ettrian calls hesitantly.

"Yes?"

"I have something I need to confess." The vibration of his quills runs over my ilo and sends a nervous chill through me.

"Well?" I prompt when he says nothing. *"What is it?"*

"I bedded with Safia before you did."

"I know."

"No, I bedded with her so that she would lie with you." He holds up a hand before I can respond and I see that he is struggling with how best to word this. *"I only wanted to help. You were so distant, constantly going off on your own without me, lying to Mama when she asked where you went. I knew you had sought out the company of other females and that they had refused you and I just... I just wanted to help."* Shame flashes in his eyes. *"I was afraid I would wake up one day without you. I have heard the rumors, the ones about Darkborn who take their own lives, and I could not stand the thought of losing you. It is why I followed you when you left the last day we were in the village."*

My first response to his confession is anger and hurt. Both emotions swirl around inside of me, dropping into my stomach like heavy stones as I watch him run his fingers anxiously through his quills. He bribed a female to mate with me. The thought makes me feel pathetic, but just as I'm wallowing in my hurt, Xia murmurs my name along the bond. As if she can sense what I feel, she reaches out for me, her fingers burrowing into my quills as she strokes them softly. The contact is instantly soothing and I take a deep breath before looking back at my twin. *"I forgive you."*

"What?"

"I said I forgive you, Ettrian." I reach out to run my finger over Xia's nose, remembering the day we met when I thought it was so revolting. *"If you had not done that, I would have never asked Safia to be our mate, which means I would have never been so far out in the forest that day. We would have never found our mate, would have never known our family was out there waiting for us. So yes, I forgive you."*

Because of the decisions my brother made, I will never be alone again.

EPILOGUE

*I*noxia

"Okay, seriously guys, can't you just tell me where we're going?" I laugh, trying not to stumble since Ettrian's hand is covering my eyes. With Aquilian's hand in my own, I reach out along the bond to pry only to be rudely closed out. *"Hey!"*

"It's a surprise!" Kareen squeals from her perch atop Aquilian's shoulders. I protested when he set her up there, but she insisted, telling me she knows to be careful around her 'Papa Quilian's' quills. She's far too grown for my liking.

"Patience," Ettrian scolds. *"We are almost there."*

"Pregnant women aren't as patient as you seem to think, and I'm probably going to have to pee soon so we might need to get a move on." Kareen giggles because talking about bodily functions is hilarious to her at the moment.

A tiny but strong foot gives me a good jab, and I press my hand over the spot, feeling the bump the kit within me has made. As if the little one can feel the heat or pressure of my touch, I feel another sharp kick before he or she pushes up into my ribs, knocking the breath from me for a moment.

"Easy, little one." Aquilian chuckles along the bond. *"Your mama is too small for you to bounce around so much."*

According to Safia, it isn't likely our baby can understand the words we speak to them, but this one seems to enjoy the sounds. This little one, boy or girl, has two papas and a big sister who lie against me every night, whispering how much they're loved and how they can't wait for his or her birth. The way Ettrian and Aquilian love this baby as much as they love Kareen makes me feel weepy.

To my left, I can hear Kareen giggling just before Ettrian shushes her. *"Are you ready, Inoxia?"*

"Ugh, yes!" When he removes his hand, I blink to clear my vision and realize we're standing in front of another one of the tree homes on the outskirts of the village. It isn't the one we're in now, the one where Mina is still resting in the seed pod. We haven't left yet because I can't stand the thought of not being near when she finally wakes. *"I don't get it. I thought we were going to wait until Mina was better?"*

"We are. The tree is not the surprise." Aquilian calls out to the tree, and as it begins to open, I see that there are two people inside, two humans. My parents.

"Oh my gods. Mom! Dad!" I race toward them, not letting the fact that I'm heavily pregnant stop me from getting to the two people I've missed more than anything these last few months. "How did you get here?" I ask as I throw my arms around them both. Pent up tears burst free, and I lean into them. "I've missed you guys so freaking much!"

The little one in my belly must not have enjoyed the bumpy ride because I feel a sharp kick where I'm pressed against my mom. "Oh my goodness! Xia, baby, look at you!"

"I'm huge, huh?"

"Well, I'm not gonna be the one to say that, but I certainly wasn't expecting it." The sound of my dad's laughter is musical.

It's something I never thought I'd hear again. "We missed you, baby."

"We were so relieved to hear you were safe. You left the May Day celebration but we couldn't find you anywhere. Police searched for you, Mina, and Kareen for weeks." My mom gets choked up, but her hand runs over the wiggling baby inside me and she smiles. "I'm so glad you found where you belonged."

"We almost didn't believe that Venium when he showed up saying you were out here mated to two aliens." Dad laughs.

"Where's my little Kareen?" my mom asks, looking over my shoulder.

"I'm here! Hi Grandma! Hi Grandpa!" My girl scrambles down from her papa's shoulders and bounds toward us.

"Oh, we missed you so much! The greenhouse wasn't the same without our best little helper."

As I watch my parents hug Kareen and tell her all about the things we've been missing back on Earth, I'm taken by surprise when I feel warm liquid begin to dribble down my leg. "Oh crap." My cheeks heat in embarrassment as I shuffle backward. "I had to pee so bad on the way here—I guess I couldn't hold it anymore." As I turn to tell Aquilian and Ettrian I need to head inside, a sharp pain nearly brings me to my knees. Luckily, my mom is there to catch me as I stumble forward, sucking in a breath as the pain hits me again.

"Oh my goodness!" She gasps when more of the fluid splashes on the ground at my feet. "Honey, this isn't you peeing yourself. I think your water just broke."

Panic rolls through me, even as I'm bombarded with feelings of calm from my mates. I know the Dauur have shorter pregnancies, but I hadn't thought that would affect me too much. A month early? Sure, but I'm only four months along. I surpassed the 'bump' stage relatively quickly, but I chalked that up to the massive size difference between the Dauur and humans, the fact that I'm a bigger girl anyway, or even the possibility of twins.

"What if something's wrong?" I ask Ettrian as he comes up beside me, but he says nothing, looking over me to Aquilian.

"Mama?" Kareen calls, and I feel her little hand run over my stomach as it tightens again.

"It's okay, baby."

"We need to bring her inside to the birthing room. There is no time to take her back to our tree," Ettrian tells my parents.

"Don't you worry about Kareen, hon. Your dad will keep her busy." My mom squeezes my hand as Aquilian scoops me up into his arms.

Tears prick my eyes as my daughter waves at me excitedly. It isn't like I don't trust my dad to look after her, but she's been with me through so much these last few months that it's strange doing this without her on the sidelines to make me laugh. My mom is right behind us, asking Ettrian a million questions he probably has no answers to.

"Is this normal for your species? How big were the two of you as infants? Where are the doctors? Are there no hospitals here?"

"We need to retrieve the Taenovs," Aquilian tells Ettrian as we enter the birthing room.

"Both of them? I thought Safia only handled the darker side? You know, deaths?" I look between their serious faces and make out a hint of blue in their eyes. *"You think something is wrong?"*

"Only a precaution. I will be back as soon as I can." With a soft rattle of quills, Ettrian drops a kiss on my forehead before darting from the room.

"Why is it a precaution—" Another contraction hits me, and I can feel all of my muscles tense. It's so bad that darkness seeps into the edges of my vision and everything around goes blurry. Oh gods, this is nothing like they show you in those labor and

delivery shows. My baby is going to be born on an alien planet, in a plant sling within a goddamn tree.

Hysterical laughter bursts from my trembling lips, and I try to tell myself to remain calm, that this will all be over soon. *Labor doesn't last forever. "What if he doesn't make it? What if whatever Safia meant when she said he'd be different means he can't make it once he's outside of my body?"*

"Stop, Inoxia. Let me help you." He sets me down in a sling just like the one he sat me in the first time he thought I was giving birth. The memory brings a little calm back, and I recline against the smooth plant.

On Dimosia, there's no tech, so we have no idea whether we are having a boy or a girl, but something deep inside me says I'm going to meet my son today. Worry over Safia's cryptic message has been nagging at me for months, and now that the day is here, I'm terrified of what will happen. I moan when Aquilian's impossibly large hands caress my body. His calloused fingers massaging my joints to help ease the pain feel heavenly. Another contraction tinges my vision red with pain, and I pant as I curl in on myself.

"You're doing so well, baby! Really. I'm so proud of you." Mom caresses my face and arms comfortingly, murmuring encouragement.

Just when I think I'll have a chance to breathe, another contraction slams into me and I scream until my throat is raw. Warmth flows through me as the freckles across my skin begin to pulse with a soft glow, and I feel a renewed strength. *I can do this. I'm not alone.* The next contraction is easier to breathe through.

"You are so beautiful, my light, so strong. Almost there, Inoxia," Aquilian whispers along the bond, his voice full of admiration. He slides my skirt over my hips and rubs my legs. *"Let me see how close you are."* I scoot forward some and let my legs fall open as he crouches down to take a look. Whatever he sees

clearly has him in a panic because he jumps back up and looks toward the door.

"What is it? Can you see the baby?" Poor Aquilian looks terrified, and if I weren't in so much pain, I'd probably be laughing.

We both breathe a sigh of relief when Ettrian bursts in with Lirseas and Safia hot on his heels. *"Inoxia!"* the Darkborn female says cheerfully.

Lirseas is all business as she waves Aquilian out of the way, taking up the position between my legs. *"Oh, you are so close. You are doing a wonderful job. A couple strong pushes and we will have him."*

Fortified by the strength and support of those around me, I focus everything I have into my labor. Aquilian and Ettrian are on one side of me, holding my hand and stroking my hair as they whisper how much they love me, how much I mean to them. My mom is on the other, watching everything with wide eyes. Safia stands near Lirseas, chanting softly as she looks on.

With the next contraction, I push with all my might. Pain rips through me, and I completely understand the term "ring of fire" used to describe natural birth. The entire room is silent for a moment before I hear one of the most beautiful sounds in the world.

My baby cries.

"You have a son," Lirseas whispers before I feel her lay him on my chest.

His skin is a pale gray, and he waves around a tiny balled up fist as we stare at one another. Just like his papas, my little boy has black eyes that I know will change with his emotions, but that little nose in the middle of his face is all mine and I run my finger down it before brushing his plump cheeks. As I move my hand to the back of his head past the shells of his ears, I feel the tiny nubs where quills will one day sprout and it makes me smile.

"Oh, look at that. He's got little wings," my mom whispers. "I didn't know the Dauur had wings."

"We do not." Ettrian frowns as he runs a hand along our son's back before meeting my gaze.

"How? He wasn't even conceived until after the lab was destroyed. There was no way for them to—" But a flash of something from that terrible day comes back to me. The lead scientist mentioned something about direct injection. Maybe the wings are a result of this? Is it possible that every child we bring into the world together will bear the evidence of the Tachin's meddling?

I trace the fingers of one hand over the tiny wings and my baby squirms against my chest. When I look up, I see Safia watching me carefully, and I know this must be what the warning was about. My mates and I had engaged in long conversations over the last couple months about what Safia has said to me, but I hadn't even considered that what the Tachin did that day would affect us this way.

"Well, I think he's one of the most beautiful babies I've ever seen—and I'm not just saying that because he's my grandson." My mom winks playfully at me, and I'm so very thankful to have her here.

"He absolutely is, Mom." This is a little life I've created with the two males I love most in this world and nothing, not even the Tachin, can destroy the love we feel for him.

～

"Mama?" I look and see Kareen standing in the doorway to my room. Her big blue eyes are locked on the bundle in my arms who's happily nursing for the second time since his birth.

"Hey, baby. Come here. I have someone for you to meet." Ettrian and Aquilian give her a little nudge, and she hesitantly

steps up onto the flower where I'm sitting. Her little hand is warm in mine and I draw her closer until she is sitting up against my side. *"This is Immir, your little brother."* My normally confident, loud, outgoing daughter says nothing as she watches the baby nurse.

"What do you think of him?" Aquilian asks as he crouches down next to her, but she only shrugs.

"Do you want to hold him?" Ettrian offers, but again Kareen only shrugs her shoulders as she looks on.

"What's the matter, baby?" Handing the baby over to Ettrian, I pull Kareen into my arms and drop a kiss on her temple. *"You were so excited to meet him earlier. Do you want to tell me what's bothering you now?"*

"I don't want you to stop loving me," she whispers sadly against my chest. *"I don't want to leave you guys."*

"Kareen, we could never stop loving you." Her long curly hair has been twisted into a french braid, no doubt by my mom, and I run my hand over it before tilting her chin up. *"You might not have come from us the same way Immir did, but you've been my baby since the day I met you. No matter how many more babies come into our lives, you're always going to be the one who made me a mama."*

Beside us, Aquilian is running his hands through his quills. The nervous habit is something he still fights, but he's been doing so well lately that it surprises me to see. *"Your brother joining us does not mean he replaces you in our hearts. It only means our hearts grow to make room for both of you."* The sound of a quill snapping startles Immir, who begins to cry.

"Oh no!" Kareen snatches the quill from her papa's hand and rushes over to her brother as he fusses in Ettrian's arms. *"Look, Immir, it's like a glow stick. Snap it and shake it,"* she says in a singsong voice, waving the glowing quill in front of his scrunched-up face.

The glow stick reference has me laughing out loud, and I pull her into my lap for a quick hug. *"Want to hold him now?"* With a little nod, she snuggles into me and holds her arms out for the wiggly bundle.

Two sets of big hands support her as she cradles Immir against her chest and drops a kiss onto his crest. *"Don't worry, Immir. I have lots of room in my heart."*

~

"I can't wait for you to meet him, Mina. Ettrian and Aquilian have been insanely supportive and wonderful, and having my parents here has made this all so much easier." Immir squirms against me as he nurses quietly. I rest my head on the seed pod at my back and sigh. *"Wake up, Mina. Please."*

Something vibrates beneath me and I sit forward. I can't tell if it's coming from the floor or the walls. When it happens again, the seed pod behind me cracks just a hair and I can hear Mina scream. *Oh gods. What's happening?*

"Mina?" I scramble to my feet, slamming my hand against the hard surface, trying to ask it to open along the bond, but nothing works and she continues to cry out like she's in pain. "Doxal! Yssig!" Someone is already running toward the room. "Stay calm. Don't fight the pod, Mina. Hang on!"

Yssig is the first to enter the room, and I stumble out of his way, clutching Immir to my chest as I watch him frantically try to coax the pod open. Doxal is next, followed closely by my mates. Everyone is shouting along the bond, and the room is filled with the sounds out of them beating at the pod. Doxal calls her name and Mina lets out a scream that chills my blood.

"Come outside, Xia," Aquilian is saying, but I barely hear him over the shouting. *"Immir is frightened, Inoxia. Bring him to our room."*

Right, Immir. My poor boy is wide-eyed and his little face is wrinkled up as he screams. As I let myself be ushered out, I hear a loud crack, and the room goes silent except for Immir's whimpering.

"This isn't possible," Doxal says as he takes a step back.

"What? What is it?"

Ettrian looks inside as Mina moans and turns back with a frown. *"I think your friend is in labor."*

OTHER WORKS BY OCTAVIA KORE

<u>Venora Mates:</u>

Ecstasy from the Deep

<u>Dauur Mates:</u>

Queen of Twilight

<u>Seyton Mates:</u>

Breaths of Desire (Blooming Desire Anthology)

WORKS COMING SOON BY OCTAVIA KORE

<u>Venora Mates:</u>

Kept from the Deep

Awoken from the Deep

Kidnapped from the Deep

<u>Seyton Mates:</u>

Breaths of Desire (extended edition)

ABOUT THE AUTHOR

Born in the Sunshine State, Hayley Benitez and Amanda Crawford are cousins who have come together to write under the name Octavia Kore. Both women share a love for reading, a passion for writing, and the inclination toward word vomiting when meeting new people. *Ecstasy from the Deep* (*From the Depths* anthology version) was their very first published work. Hayley and Amanda are both stay-at-home moms who squeeze in time to write when they aren't being used as jungle gyms or snack dispensers. They are both inspired by their love for mythology, science fiction, and all things extraordinary. Amanda has an unhealthy obsession with house plants, and Hayley can often be found gaming in her downtime.

FACEBOOK:
https://www.facebook.com/groups/MatesAmongUs/
SIGN UP FOR OUR NEWSLETTER:
https://mailchi.mp/27d09665e243/matesamongusnewsletter
INSTAGRAM:
https://www.instagram.com/octaviakore/?igshid=1bxhtr1snonz4
GOODREADS:
https://www.goodreads.com/octaviakore
BOOKBUB:
https://www.bookbub.com/profile/octavia-kore
AMAZON:
https://www.amazon.com/Octavia-Kore/e/B0845YHRVS

Printed in Great Britain
by Amazon